MASKED JUSTICE

ALEX J FISCHER

For my Family and Friends

1

"Whoever came up with mandatory schooling should be shot." Ashley slammed the door shut behind her. She tossed her backpack beside the nearby sofa and took a seat in it.

Jim kept working from the recliner. He had it reclined with his feet out in front of him and the laptop on his lap. "You say that now. You'll yearn to be back in that classroom when you're my age. Look at me. I do data entry every single day to get us food and shelter. That's far more boring than listening to an old crone yammer on."

"I'll believe that when I see it." Ashley brought her feet up and laid down on the couch. "Thank God for weekends."

"You know," Jim started, a sly smile on his face all the while, "it was always my experience that you should get homework done as soon as possible."

"Fuck that," Ashley said. She closed her eyes. "I deserve a break."

"That is if you were serious about wanting to go with me tonight anyway." Jim looked up from his work. "Personally,

I'd rather you stayed safe here, so feel free to not do the work now."

"To hell with that," Ashley said. "I said I'd go and so I'm going."

"Then you'd best get your work done now. I will not have my hobby affecting your grades. That was the agreement we came to if you remember. You get your schoolwork done before we even consider you accompanying Masked Justice. Mind you, I'm still not sold on the idea of bringing you along anyway. You should be making friends, having sleepovers, and whatever else young people do now."

"You sound like a grandpa." Ashley sat up and reached for her backpack. She unzipped the faded green container and reached inside. She pulled out a book along with a three-ring binder notebook.

"Well," Jim put on his best elderly voice, "if you need any help, this grandfather would be glad to help if he can." His voice returned to normal. "I was never great at geometry, but I can probably help with anything else."

"It's thanks to your tutoring that I even know what the fuck the teacher's talking about anyway. Missing school for years has that effect on people."

Jim placed the laptop on the floor beside his chair. He raised his hands above his head with a yawn. "Beyond the tedium of student life, how are you adapting to school? Have you made many friends yet?"

"Not really." Ashley's attention moved from the pages of the now open book to the paper she was writing on. "The popular bitches are more focused on demeaning everyone else than making friends with the new girl."

"Then make friends with the less popular ones. Those are usually the better friends anyway," Jim said.

"Moving off my abysmal school life," Ashely said, "what is your job tonight?"

Jim scratched his clean-shaven chin with a grunt. "The Republic is sending me to the next state over for some scumbag who got off on a technicality in court."

"What'd he do?" Ashley asked.

"He was a teacher," Jim said, disdain evident in his voice. "He used his position to groom a small boy and have his way with him repeatedly over a two-year period."

"Christ," Ashley looked up, wide eyed. "How'd he get away with that?"

"The prosecution fucked up, and the defense got the case thrown out with a mistrial. The evidence was rock solid. They had his DNA, the kid had cuts in, shall we say, sensitive areas, and the kid's own testimony was damning."

"Our court system is a joke," Ashely said. "Which is ironic because they're teaching us how the whole system works now in social studies."

"Tell them what they want to hear. That's how you get good grades, and that will lead to better opportunities for a career later. Don't be like me." Jim laughed. "You don't want to be doing glorified grunt work for a living. You should be a teacher or something."

"With my sparkling personality? You must be an idiot." Though she had insulted Jim, her smile betrayed her true tone. "The kids would rebel, and I'd be fired within a week."

"It was just an idea. I just would like you to have a goal after graduation is all."

"I appreciate the fatherly concern, but I do have to remind you that you are not in fact my dad."

"I know," Jim said. "I'm just not sure what I am at this point. Am I your landlord then?"

"Let's go with that," Ashley said, turning the page. "Hey,

what's it called when a case is thrown out due to a technicality?"

"A mistrial," Jim said. "It's supposed to defend the innocent, and it has its place. Unfortunately, like any loophole, it is abused by the truly guilty. They're necessary to a working law system."

"Got it," Ashley said. "What about double jeopardy?"

"What? Am I just doing your homework now?" Jim got up and moved to sit beside her. He looked down at the worksheet she was filling out. He pointed at the question. "I believe it's when you prosecute a person for the same crime again. It's forbidden by the fifth amendment."

"Oh yeah, they want us to memorize those too," Ashley said. "What use is there in learning about some old document made by people in the seventeen hundreds anyway?"

"So you know your rights. It's paramount. Frankly, I'm surprised they're still teaching it. I'm glad they are though. You'd be surprised how many young people are completely ignorant of their civil liberties. They even sometimes make up so called rights they don't in fact have. It's good to be informed so you can make a better decision. I'm not going to get into specifics, but trust me when I say you need to pay attention to our founding fathers' document."

"I'll take your word for it."

"Is this all the homework they gave you today?" Jim asked, overlooking the answer sheet and her responses.

"I have math homework and spelling as well. I can get those done on the drive."

"You'll get them done before you get in the car, or you're not going at all. I won't be responsible for my proclivities being your educational downfall."

Ashley finished the worksheet and filed it away in the folder before pulling out another book. This one had a paper sticking out of it, acting as a pseudo bookmark. "You have the strangest rules. I mean, you're going out and killing folks, but homework is where you draw the line?"

"Maybe I don't want you doing what I do. Did you ever think of that? If I ever am caught, you're to deny all involvement. Is that clear? You have your whole life ahead of you. Mine is already on the rails due to my own poor choices." A ring from his pocket interrupted his lecture. He pressed a button and brought it up to his ear. "Hello?"

Charlie's voice greeted him on the other end of the line. "Hello, old friend. Are you ready for tonight?"

"I'm preparing as we speak." Jim reached down with one hand and stopped her writing with a shake of his head. "Look it up if you don't know. Don't guess."

"Excuse me?" Charlie asked.

"Not you. I'm talking to Ashley."

"Ah yes, homework from high school. That brings the nostalgia flowing back," Charlie said. "Look, I'm calling because I got word there's a slight change. I'll fill you in when I get to your place. I'll be there soon."

Before he even had a chance to say goodbye, the line went dead. Jim hung up and pocketed the device. "That was odd. Charlie's on his way."

"Maybe they don't trust you to do it right," Ashley said, flipping pages in the book. She stopped and read for a few seconds before continuing. "Otherwise, why would they send him to oversee you?"

"He said there was a change. Who knows? All I do know is they pay well, the gadgets they've sent should make this a lot easier, and I have some higher ups looking out for me. I am in no position to argue."

"Higher ups? Like what?"

"According to him, this little republic of hunters is

formed by policemen, police commissioners, politicians, lawyers, and all manner of hoity-toity types. They can suppress investigations or outright dismiss them. Rumor is that some members are in congress and even higher up"

"Higher up you say? You don't mean like the President? Either way, you've got a key to the city proverbially speaking." Ashley scribbled another answer on the paper. "That can be more dangerous when you think about it."

"I don't have total immunity. If I'm a dumbass and have my face seen, I'd be screwed. So long as I'm careful, I'll be fine they claim. Which is okay by me. I don't plan on getting sloppy. Anyway," Jim gave a playful push to her shoulder causing her to lean slightly. "This isn't something you should worry about. Worry about making friends and doing your homework. God knows why you want to help Masked Justice anyway." His tone turned somber. "It's nothing but murder when you get down to it."

"Some people deserve it," she simply said. Her tone was even. "Surely you wouldn't argue with that?"

"I argue with your yammering on about nonsensical topics when you're doing algebra homework."

"Then help me, you jackass," she said, a smile on her face.

He leaned closer and pointed at the paper again. "Alright, for this one you use the Pythagorean equation..."

An hour later...

"This is what you call soon?" Jim said, standing in the doorway. He stepped to the side, allowing Charlie to pass through before closing the door. "Why are you even here anyway? I know the job and the target."

Charlie flashed a smile at his old childhood friend. "You got yourself a partner, buddy. I'm your backup."

"He already has backup," Ashley said. She looked up from the couch over to Charlie.

"I mean official backup. It's sweet that you want to help out your rescuer and all, but the group thinks I'd be the perfect partner in crime for him." He turned back to Jim. "You don't have a problem with that, do you?"

"As duplicitous as you've been over the last who knows how long, I can't say no to the man who was caught along with me on almost every instance when we were kids. I know I can trust you, so fine. I just don't appreciate them treating me like a liability. Let's not lie. Say it for what it is."

"They just want to be sure you settle in the right way is all," Charlie said. "We can't have you causing a royal mess, now can we? That would blow back on the republic."

"I guess I have to prove that I'm not some lunatic street vigilante," Jim said. "Fair enough, because that's pretty much what I am when you think about it."

Charlie reached out and slapped Jim on his arm. "Not anymore you're not. You're a hunter for good now. Think of me as your trainer. I'll get you up to speed and polish that raw talent you have. I've already given you some classes with the blade, but that's just the beginning. Besides, someone needs to teach you how to use the variety of goodies I gave you. Those are sophisticated, delicate, and expensive."

"There it is," Jim said. "They're protecting their investment. That I get."

"I'm going with you two," Ashley said, interrupting the older men. "Don't even try and stop me. I got my homework done and everything."

Charlie gave a puzzled look to Jim. "Seriously? Did you

really gate a teenager coming to a hit by trying to use homework?"

"He sure did," Ashley said, standing up. "I don't think he's realized how stubborn I am yet."

"Trust me when I say I know that already," Jim said.

"Hey!" She sent Jim a dirty look. Her hands were planted firmly on her hips with a frown on her face.

"I see you still have a way with the female portion of the population," Charlie said, taking a seat on the now vacant couch. "It's a wonder you almost snagged Cynthia."

"How is she doing nowadays anyway? She never calls and doesn't answer mine. I assume she wants nothing to do with me," Jim said, taking his seat in the recliner. "Not that I blame her."

"She's just studying for the bar exam. She's been busy I'd imagine. Not to mention your whole hobby is kind of her antithesis. She can't be involved with you. You're lucky she's smart enough to keep quiet. That probably has to do with the body you had her help you bury."

Ashley stomped down hard with her foot. "That's still no excuse to ghost someone."

"It's fine," Jim said, keeping a straight face with an even tone. "Charles, I have to ask a few things before we get going."

"Go for it." He leaned back and crossed his legs.

"How are you going to help exactly? I mean no offense by this, but I usually go into places alone."

Charlie clapped his hands together and jumped up. "I'm glad you asked."

"Why are you so excited?" Ashley asked.

"Because, my curious little bottle of sunshine," Charlie said, "besides the training sessions I've been putting our mutual friend through, I'm also to act as overwatch for him."

"I thought that was my job." Ashley looked over to Jim.

"While I am sure you are very committed to it, unfortunately you're not trained in the more advanced arts."

"Flowery prose for such bullshit. What the hell advanced arts is there in guiding someone around a building using a blueprint?" Ashely asked, a smug grin plastered on her face.

"That isn't so much overwatch as a tour guide. I am trained to find any cameras in the building, deactivate them remotely, and even cause distractions."

"You should teach her that," Jim said.

"Really?" Charlie asked.

"You totally should. I could help. I'm great with a computer."

"It's true," Jim said. "She's a fast typist and a quick learner."

"We'll see," Charlie said. "Anyway, that's my official duties. That's beyond the training I've been giving you."

"You never said what you were learning anyway. All I heard was something about a blade." Ashley narrowed her eyes at Jim. "What was it?"

"He didn't tell you?" Charlie asked. "Seriously? This is the one whole time you get to brag about it, and you passed on it? She's the one person you get to tell. I'm disappointed in you, dude." He reached for his belt line and grasped an invisible handle. He drew out his imaginary sword and slashed downwards. "I'm teaching him how to use a short sword."

"A sword?" Ashley asked. She looked over to Jim. "What kind of weapon are we talking about? A katana, a European short sword, or what?"

"Oh please don't get him started," Jim said with a shake of his head.

9

"Too late. Are you familiar with the term Wakizashi?"

"It's a short sword," Jim said.

"It's not just a short sword," Charlie said. "Samurai used to wear these things alongside of their katanas. Don't either of you find that interesting?"

"What I was interested in was not having to be nearly so close to stick some piece of shit," Jim said. "Twenty-two inches of cold steel is a hell of a lot better than six."

"Fine. He may be a simpleton, but it is a refined weapon. It's silent, razor sharp, and can cut through bone like hot butter with the proper technique and power." Charlie sighed. "Fine, I'll educate the both of you some other time on your good fortune. Just know, old buddy, these weapons are only used by the elite of the elite assassins around the world. You have been maintaining it like I showed you, yes?"

"Yes, I have. Don't worry. Remind me to thank our superiors on equipping me so well then," Jim said. He got up out of the seat. "Everyone follow me. We may as well take inventory of everything before we head out." He moved to the nearby stairwell and ascended.

Ashley leapt up and followed closely behind with Charlie trailing behind a few steps.

"I've been waiting to see this shit," Ashley said. "Why wouldn't you let me see this before?"

"Because it'd distract you from your schoolwork. I can see I would have been right about that." Jim reached the top of the stairs and entered his nearby bedroom. He left the door open behind him as he got to a knee and reached under his bed. He pulled out a large suitcase and hefted it atop his bed. He unbuckled it and threw it open.

"Holy hell," Ashley looked down at the collection. "Is that body armor?"

"It's lightweight and durable - the very best," Charlie

said. "It's protection level three according to the National Institute of Justice. That means this baby can protect from even rifle rounds. It's rated for knife protection as well, so long as it's not too large. It's a little heavy with those curved plates in there, but far lighter than the beefiest of armor."

"Was he not good enough for the better stuff then?" Ashley asked.

"That was my decision actually," Jim said. "I elected for the lighter option. I need mobility, not the ability to be hit with bigger guns. I've already fucked up bad if that happens." He pulled it out of the container and set about putting it on

"Is that a bow and arrow? Do not even tell me you're using that from now on," Ashley said.

"Not yet," Jim said. "I'm still dogshit with it, but I can almost hit a stationary target now."

"I wouldn't call what I saw last time as almost." Charlie leaned his head back and released a hearty laugh. "You are getting better though."

"Where would you even get the arrows for such a thing? Can't those be tracked by buying them at stores?" Ashley asked. "I mean it's cool and all, don't get me wrong. It's also quieter than a gun."

"Master Young taught us how to make our own arrows," Charlie said. "So I'm passing that knowledge around."

"Master Young? I know that name from somewhere," Ashley said, her eyes wandering until they snapped onto one spot. "Isn't that the guy in town offering archery lessons?"

"The one and only. The man knows his stuff." Charlie assumed an archery pose as he spoke. "He learned abroad and brought the knowledge back to the states."

"Got it. The dude was a weaboo and came back home," Ashley said with a snap of her finger.

"Pretty much," Charlie said.

"Either way," Jim reached for the sheathed wakizashi and lifted it out, "this is all I'll need for tonight? That's what you said earlier."

"I confirmed the intel myself. It'll be up close and personal," Charlie said. "I've looked over the floor plans already. It's a small one-story house. His proclivities for kids force him to move every few years. I guess you don't spring for luxurious accommodations when you move so often. I'd still carry your piece on you just in case though."

"Already ahead of you." Jim patted the weapon hanging at his side. "Good idea on the shoulder holster. I like its ease of access compared to the old way."

"I thought those were just suspenders," Ashley said.

"Hey now," Jim said. "I'm not that old yet."

"Not to mention your belt line is now for this beauty." Charlie reached down and pulled out the sheathed blade. He handed over the blade with faux exaggerated respect. "Treat it well, my student."

"You are so full of shit." Jim grabbed the weapon. He pulled out a length of heavy wire. "Now if I remember, you do it this way." He looped the wire of the sheath through a loop in his belt and tied it. "Is that right?"

Ashley reached out and grabbed the sheathed blade and pulled. "It seems steady to me." She looked down at the blade hanging at his side. "You look like some failed anime protagonist. Like you wanted to be a sword hero, but you got a sword too small."

"Yes, thank you for that," Jim said, his face reddening. "Can we focus? We're not here to look cool - we're here to do a job. If I look like a jackass to rid the world of the filth, I will do just that." He pushed past the pair, making sure they were both behind him. His right hand moved down to his left belt line and hovered above the sheath. He gripped it and pulled the blade out in one swift motion. "Huh, that finally worked."

"I knew it'd work if you kept training." Charlie walked up beside him and placed a hand on Jim's shoulder. "Just be sure to maintain an even motion. You can't be jerky, or it'll mess with the effectiveness of the actual slash."

"Training? I remember ripping my stiches because you were so adamant on starting training while I was still injured."

"I put new stitches in, didn't I? You're fine. Don't be a baby. It is no way for a student of the blade to act. You should be dignified and quiet."

"You've watched too much anime in your damned life," Ashley said. "That would never be useful."

"It's a real technique," Charlie said. "I doubt he performed it at a master's level, but it's the basics of a discipline known as iaido. If he ever gets into an actual sword fight, he'll be glad he knows it."

"Yeah, because people are getting into sword fights all the time nowadays," Ashley snickered. "You should probably focus more on swift killing strokes, not flashy movie moves. Still, I bet the authorities will shit themselves when they analyze the bodies and see they were cut apart with a sword. Hey, wait a minute." She reached in and pulled out a small multi colored eye mask. Half of it was white and the other half black, split down the middle. "What is this thing? It only covers the area around the eyes?"

"I convinced the supply division that our friend needed something better than his ghetto ass ski mask." Charlie took it from Ashley and held it to his eyes. "See?" He looked through the holes on either side. "You can't tell who I am if you didn't know before."

"Then why the hell is this in here?" Ashley pointed down at a similarly colored neck gaiter. "It looks like what old timey highwaymen used to wear."

"I think it's called a scarf mask," Jim said, picking up the cloth. He put it on and pulled it up over his nose. The intricate skull design's left side matched with his domino mask's white side. Its right side was darkened to match, creating a brilliant half and half motif.

"So why black and white exactly? Wouldn't black be stealthier?" Ashley asked.

"Symbolism is a powerful thing," Charlie said, puffing his chest out. "It was my idea of course. This guy wouldn't know meaning if it slapped him in the face. The color for justice is black and white. He dubbed himself Masked Justice, so I figured have his masks color coordinated to convey just that. Besides," he lightly elbowed Ashley in the side, "you can't tell me he doesn't look awesome like that."

"You're sure those will stay in place?" Ashley reached up and tugged at the eye coverings first, only to have them stay in place.

"As far as this goes," Jim reached up and pointed to the cloth covering his mouth. "I've ran miles with this, exercised, and did all manner of things with it. It doesn't come off. It's good. I might scare some folks with this getup though."

"You scared people with your little ski mask, but at least this looks better," Ashley said.

"That should be it for your equipment," Charlie said. "My stuff's already in my car. Take that crap off for now and keep it on you. It's time to go to work..."

2

Jim had his blade resting in his lap in the front passenger seat. His right hand gripped the handle as he watched the passing cityscape. He looked over to his left toward Charlie driving. "I hope you know where the cameras are near this place. We don't want your plates getting caught on camera. That'd be just what we need."

"I've taken precautions." Charlie passed a car before switching lanes to the right. "I've got an extra license plate on."

"I assume you mean a false plate?"

"Obviously. A spare plate of my legitimate one would be stupid. Besides, it's a tertiary plan. We won't be caught on camera."

"How are you so sure?" Ashley said, leaning forward between the seats of the small car.

"Because I've researched where the cameras are located. I know where they oversee, and plan on going a different, slower route." Charlie turned the wheel right and pulled onto a new road. "See this ghetto we're going through?"

"Your idea of a detour needs some work," Jim said. He

watched groups of men sitting on their porches watching them go by. "We'll be lucky if we get there alive."

"Don't be paranoid. They don't want us to be here, and we're not going to be here. We're just passing through is all. They don't want police being called here anyway. This is gang territory."

"It gets better and better," Jim said.

"They're just crack dealers, not violent felons. Pay them no mind."

"I'll pay them plenty of fucking mind," Ashley said, lowering down until she was between the men's elbows. "You have no street sense, do you?"

"I'm doing what we need to." Charlie turned off the road and into a noticeably nicer neighborhood. "We're almost there. We'll go over it one last time when we get there. We don't want any mistakes."

"Seriously, again?" Ashley asked. "You're worse than my history teacher, and she's known as the sleep aid of the school."

"Operations are ninety percent preparation and ten percent execution. You'd do well to learn that," Charlie said. "Now, buddy, when you get in there you need to focus and remember what I told you. You want a slicing motion, not a hacking one. They'll both get the job done, but it's good practice. You pull the blade through him, not just brute force it. It extends the cutting edge, and that's where the real damage comes into play. Smooth motions - remember that. You're not a lumberjack with that thing. Just because you managed to chop that pig carcass in half doesn't mean it was done right."

"I'm still working on it, but we'll see what happens."

"You are improved, but you still have years of training before I'd call you competent."

"When the hell did you learn this anyway?" Jim asked.

"Remember when we were in junior year of high school when I said I was learning Judo?"

"You lied," Ashley said.

"In so many words. That was when I was recruited. I learned the blade then."

"It's a regular league of killers I've joined, isn't it?" Jim asked. "They're fucking teaching people to use swords, bows, and God knows what else you're going to have me try."

"That's about it. Swords and bows are quiet, quick, and efficient. There are those in the republic that prefer weirder weapons, but those are rare." Charlie stopped the car in the middle of a nice suburban neighborhood on the side of the road. All the lights were off in the nearby houses, seeing as it was almost two in the morning. "Here we are."

Jim put on his mask and scarf. "How do I look?"

"Like a crazy person cosplaying as a superhero," Ashley said.

"I see we're on message then," Jim said.

"Now first thing's first," Charlie said. He reached for the glove compartment and pulled out two small boxes. He opened one, took out the ear bud, and put it in. He initiated a call. "Can you hear me?"

Jim did the same and fiddled with the device for a moment. "Loud and clear," Jim said, tapping his ear. "These are even clearer than Bluetooth."

"They should be. They cost ten times more," Charlie said. "Let's see what we're dealing with in there tonight. Are there any visitors for Mr. Vivendi? Can you hand me my laptop, kid?" Charlie pointed toward the device sitting beside her in the back.

"Fine," Ashley did as she was asked. "This thing looks expensive."

Charlie placed it above the steering wheel and opened it as far as he was able. The contents were still visible in the dark interior of the car. He squinted his eyes at the piercing white light coming from the screen. "Not really compared to other models." He navigated to and double clicked on a green icon. A new window popped up. Dots showed for a few seconds until a list of IP addresses appeared, replacing them.

"That's not a program I believe I've ever seen for sale," Jim said. "That can't be legal."

"When have you ever been worried about legal?" Charlie asked. "It's not a program that can be bought. We have our own tech people. Before you ask, I don't know them, and I don't want to. All I know is this thing works. I've used it on my own jobs."

"Jobs? Were they like my work?" Jim asked.

"Not your day job. This though?" Charlie pointed to Jim's disguised self. "Yeah. We all have bodies on our conscience here." His voice turned serious, but soft. "Does that answer your question?"

"Sure."

"Good, then let's stop fucking around and get this done. For all we know he has a kid in there right now. If that's the case, I want you to call for me. I'll be in there quick. I brought my kit with me."

"I assumed that's why you're wearing your urban camo outfit," Ashley said. "I can take over in that case. Don't worry. I'm a quick learner."

"You touch nothing of mine, including the laptop." Charlie pointed at Ashley in the backseat.

"Kids!" Jim said louder than before, jolting them both

into silence. "Focus up. I'm about to go murder a guy, and you're both accessories. Are we ready to rid the world of this filth or not?" He reached his hands into the empty space between the group.

Ashley reached forward and placed her hand on top of his. "I'm ready."

"What? Are we coming out of a huddle?" A small, almost imperceptible smile graced his features. "Yes, I'm in." He reached out to place his hands on top of Ashley's but was stopped.

Ashley shook her head. Her free hand reached out and guided Charlie's hand underneath Jim's before she took it back.

"Alright then," Jim said, breaking the impromptu huddle. "Now is there anything before I go in there? I studied the floor plans. I know where his bedroom is. I can take him out easily. Correct me if I'm wrong."

Charlie leaned forward. "I see no other phones, no cameras beside his porch camera, and everything's quiet. You're good to go. Oh, and make sure you're locked and loaded." Charlie said with a shrug. "Swords are cool and all, but it's better to be safe."

Jim pulled out the pistol from his shoulder holster, ejected the magazine. A shine caught it in the dim light as he tilted it to the side checking. "I'm loaded."

"Be careful in there," Ashley said. Her voice for once not her usual sarcastic self, but a sincere one.

"I'll be fine." He looked back to Charlie. "Then I'm going. Keep her safe, would you?"

Charlie looked back at Ashley and nodded. "If I have to."

"Hey," Ashley punched Charlie in the arm as Jim left the car. He shut the door gently, stifling any response. He quickly tied the sheathe to his belt line.

Jim immediately jogged toward the one-story home's front door. The rooftop covered patio cloaked the porch in shade. He got to a knee and placed a finger to his ear. He kept his voice low. "I'm going in." He reached for the doorknob and tried twisting, only to find it locked in place. "Shit," he said under his breath.

"It's locked I take it?" Charlie's voice was in his ear.

"Correct," Jim said, staying low to the ground. "I could pick it, but I'd rather just look for the key."

"Tell him to pick the lock." He could hear Ashley's voice faintly.

"No," Charlie's voice said. "Just look under the welcome mat, under any potted plants nearby, or above the door. Odds are a spare key is somewhere. You have plenty of time. Look around. Just don't make a spectacle of yourself. It's the middle of the night. You'll be fine."

Jim reached down and pulled the welcome mat up. He tossed it to the side and felt around on the wooden deck. He had no luck and placed the mat back to its original position in front of the door.

He could hear Ashley. "Hey, look under the gnome I see in the yard. My money's on that."

Jim shook his head with a loud exhale. He stood up with a grunt and reached up above the door. He felt a ledge above. He ran his hand across until he felt something brush his fingers. He heard the clink of the key as it landed on the floor below.

"Jackpot," Jim said. He quickly found the key and stood up. He placed the key in the lock and twisted.

"Above the door?" Charlie asked. "Not original, but good work."

"I bet you're just proud of me," Jim said. "Now be quiet." He took a deep breath. His right hand reached down to his wakizashi at his side and gripped the handle of the blade. His left turned the door and pulled it open. He rushed inside and shut the door behind him as a loud beep blared in his ears. "Fuck, shit, oh God dammit!" Jim said. He took off into a sprint toward his target's room. He clenched the sword in his hand as the door a few feet ahead swung open.

The large form of a man appeared from within. Jim could make out something in his hand as it seemingly reached for him.

He unsheathed his weapon and swung with all his might as a deafening crack echoed in the enclosed space. The silence was temporary however, as an inhumane screaming and grunting of pain soon replaced it along with the ringing in his ears.

"My hand!"

At the same time Jim fell backward, feeling like someone just clubbed him full force with a sledgehammer in his torso. "Christ!" he wheezed out from his back. He thrust the blade up toward his target who was frantically searching the floor for his recently used firearm. The blade struck true.

It pierced him through the chest cavity, causing his moans to gurgle.

Jim pulled the blade out and rolled to the side. Nothing but the sound of the loud alarm and gurgling of blood filled his sense of hearing.

His target coughed out a little blood onto the carpet below. He fell forward further and cradled his recent wounds, trying in vain to stifle the bleeding.

Jim stumbled to his feet, raised the blade, and hacked downward with a feral scream, ending any further moaning of pain. He vaguely noted the detached hand sitting a few feet away, its finger still wrapped around the trigger. He sheathed the blade, untied it, and took off as fast as he could back to the front door, the loud beeping was now replaced by a robotic voice screaming.

"Burglar alert!" the voice screamed.

Jim threw the door open and sprinted as fast as was possible back into the car. The severe aching in his chest throbbed with every step. The engine started and the back door flew open. He could see Ashley beckoning him over with a look of worry on her face. He vaguely noted how out of breath he was as he fell into the back seat and pulled the door shut. He quickly placed the sheathed blade on his lap. He slumped back in his seat with a cough.

"It's about time." Charlie wasted no time in putting the car into drive. A few lights started coming on as they drove by. "Stay calm."

"Oh my God," Ashley said.

"I'm fine," Jim said with an audible groan of pain. His right hand covered the sight where the bullet had impacted his armor. "At least I think I am. I don't feel any blood. He hit me though."

"You'll have a hell of a bruise." Charlie turned off the street with a laugh. "You're probably out of breath too. I can't believe you just went for it. I'd have bolted once the alarm went off." He laughed again.

"I'm glad you find this so amusing." Ashley sent a dirty look toward the front seat and quickly looked back at the still mask clad Jim. "What happened in there? We thought we heard a gunshot. Did you both shoot at the same time or something?"

"Not quite," Jim said.

"What does that mean?"

"It means I need to clean this thing when we get back and maintain it."

"You actually won when he had a gun?" Charlie looked

up into the rear-view mirror with his eyes wide. "Did you charge him or something?"

"Nothing quite so picturesque." Jim removed his hand.

Ashley immediately leaned forward and inspected the newfound wound site. "You're going to need a new vest."

"He has spares," Charlie said. "Now explain further."

"I was charging his bedroom door. It was dark. I saw something in his hand as he raised his arm toward me. So, I slashed it. He just so happened to have been quick enough to aim and hit me that quick. It was a lucky break is all."

"He slept with a gun," Charlie said. "I never said he wasn't smart. That would be why I said take your piece just in case, dumbass."

"I got the job done, didn't I?" Jim asked, raising his voice.

"This time," Charlie said. "Who knows how long that will last taking shots like that."

Silence filled the cabin as the car continued unabated on the mostly abandoned streets. Ashley reached over toward the scarf mask and pulled it down.

"You're sure you're alright?" she asked.

"Don't worry about me," Jim said in a much calmer voice. "I'm fine."

Charlie spoke up again. "Did you really go full samurai and lop his hand off in a dead sprint? Tell me you're making that up. A novice like you pulling that off? It's unbelievable quite frankly."

"I did, in fact. Believe that or not. That's what happened," Jim said.

"I'll believe it when I see proof," Charlie said. He finally pulled off onto an exit and onto the highway they drove there on.

"Proof? I suppose you'll have it when the news breaks," Jim said with a smug grin.

"You're bluffing." Charlie glanced up into the rear-view mirror at Jim. He looked back to the road. "Aren't you?"

"I bet you a grand I did."

"You're on," Charlie said.

"It always was easy money with you." Jim laughed and stopped with a sharp exhale.

"You're both bloody idiots." Ashley looked at Jim who was now laughing and back toward Charlie in the front, sharing in the laugh. She looked at him with sad eyes and down to where Jim's hand rested.

3

"I can't believe it." Charlie sat on the sofa beside Jim. "There really was a hand that was cut off left over at the crime scene."

Jim held an ice pack to his bruised chest. "Yeah, and I paid for that hand. Just like you. Pay up," he hissed in pain. "Are the higher ups happy?"

Charlie kept reading as he talked. "They sure are. The lopped off body part adds to the fear that kiddie touchers will have when they realize they're being systematically hunted and slaughtered. Management loves that sort of thing. It gets us what they consider good press."

"I'd have thought they'd hate such a thing," Jim said. "Making the news isn't keeping quiet."

"If you can't be quiet, make it as flashy as you can. It's the next best thing," Charlie said. "We want these scumbags scared. When they're scared, they're preoccupied with their own safety and not picking up more kids." Charlie got up and placed the laptop down where he'd been sitting. He held out his hand and took the ice pack that Jim handed him.

Jim watched him leave the living room and disappear into the kitchen. "How long until the next job do you figure?"

"They'll send the money to you tonight. It's up to you to cash out said cryptocurrency. As far as the next job - who knows? It could be tonight, but more likely we'll have to wait a week or so." He walked back into the room with a noticeably larger ice pack and handed it back to Jim. "We'll be lucky if we don't have to fly if I'm honest."

"Surely there's some more targets in the southwest U.S.," Jim said.

"Sure." Charlie picked up his laptop and took his seat. "Word on the grapevine is that there's a big contract coming. A little birdie also told me he was in our very own state. I wouldn't be surprised if you got that job. It's just a matter of when they make it official."

"At least I won't be short of work. How much was our cut of the last job anyway?"

Charlie navigated to another web browser. "According to the current Catcoin website. It looks like you made around thirty thousand dollars."

"Thirty's it?" Jim asked. "I expected more."

"It was your first job. The harder the kill, the more they pay. That was considered easy, despite your best efforts to make it harder. Next time don't go full Shiroyama. Charging a guy with a gun while wielding a short blade isn't smart - as countless dead samurai would tell you."

"What the hell is Shiroyama?" Jim asked.

"If you'd paid attention in history class, you'd know it was where the samurai loyal to Saigō Takamori were outnumbered fifty to one by imperial forces. You don't remember the battle of Shiroyama? My point being they were using swords against guns in open warfare. Don't be that brave, even with body armor. That shit isn't bulletproof, just resistant."

Ashley opened the front door with a loud voice. "We're home!"

"We?" Jim looked over and saw another girl following her in. He removed his hand from his torso. "Hello there,"

"Hey," the teenage girl said. She looked away. The girl had heavy black mascara on. The upside-down cross hanging from her neck jingled as she shifted to look away from the two men and toward the pictures on the nearby wall.

"We're just here to do a school project. I met her halfway and guided her here. We'll be up in my room working."

"I'll bring the pair of you some snacks in a little bit then." Jim smiled at the two girls. "What was your name?

"I'm Skye," she said. She looked back at Jim and Charlie. Her face remained stoic.

Ashley grabbed the young girl's hand and dragged her up the stairs. "Come on already. I want this shit done."

Once the pair was gone, Jim got up and paced.

"What's wrong with you?"

"She lied about all her homework being done," Jim said.

Charlie looked at him blankly for a second. "If I didn't know better, I'd think you were a father the way you're acting. I know for a fact you lied to your parents about homework. I know because I was right there with you in the lies when we'd spent all day playing video games instead of working. I wonder if they're actually doing any work."

"We may never know," Jim said.

A loud chirping erupted.

"That's mine." Jim dug in his pocket and answered. "Hello?"

"Is this you, Jim?" an elderly man's voice asked.

Jim couldn't stop a smile from appearing. "Hey, Ray. How's it going?"

"A lot better, Jim old pal. Thanks for letting me know what businesses allow phone charging. This thing makes everything easier. I especially love the cute videos online."

"That's great," Jim said.

"Oh, that reminds me." The sound of a car horn permeated the call. "I need to see you today."

"Is something wrong?" Jim got up. He looked to the staircase, walking over to the window overlooking the street.

"I know something you want to know. That's all I'll say. Do you know the soccer field by the high school in town?"

"Yes, I know it. Is there a reason you want to meet there?"

"You'll see." Ray hung up.

"Well, that's cryptic," Jim said. "Come with me outside real quick." He beckoned Charlie over as he moved to the front door. He threw it open and held it open for Charlie behind him. The door shut and they went around the back of the house.

"Was it that bad?" Charlie asked.

"They're in the house, you idiot." Jim looked over his wooden fence and saw no one out and about. "That was Ray. He has something that sounds like a job."

"We don't do random jobs from homeless men," Charlie said, shaking his head. "He can give us a tip, and we can investigate the voracity."

"I'm not taking his word at face value, but this old man has done a lot for me. He's helped save my life if you didn't know."

"I'm perfectly aware," Charlie said. "I monitored you during that whole time."

"Then you know he's a good man." Jim kept his voice low.

"He could be a patron saint. That doesn't mean he has all the facts. Gossip can be dangerous for the innocent. We have protocols for a good reason," Charlie said. "Now sure, we can go find out what he has to say. The only problem is upstairs," Charlie looked up at the house and crossed his arms. "What do you want to do - leave the two girls home alone?"

"That's not an option." Jim placed a hand on his house and leaned. "I'll go."

"Are you sure? You don't look too good."

"It's just a little pain. I'm fine." Jim stood up straight, removing his hand from the support. "You just make sure the girls are alright."

"Alright, fine by me," Charlie said. "We need to talk tonight when she goes to bed."

"Why?"

"How long is she staying with you, dude? The longer this goes on, the higher the chance someone at the Republic finds out. I understand the situation, but there are fanatics among us too. All it takes is one slip up. I've kept it secret until now, but who knows how long that'll last. Then it'll be both your and my asses on the line."

"Fine. We'll talk about that tonight." Jim turned and started walking back around to the driveway. "I'm going to see what the news is."

"We can't avoid it forever," Charlie said, watching Jim climb into his car.

He watched it back out and drive away. He reached a hand up and scratched an ear. "Why me?"

Fifteen minutes later across town...

29

Jim got out in the moderately full parking lot. He shut his door and looked around. The soccer field was nearby with some bleachers on the nearer side. He walked toward the group when he heard a familiar voice from beside him.

"There you are," the scraggly old man said. "It took you long enough. The game's almost over."

"Hey, Ray," Jim said. He followed Ray as he walked away from the crowd and toward a path leading away from the game going on. "Why are we here?"

"Just be patient," Ray said with a hacking cough into his fist. "I'm sorry. I just like soccer is all. After my phone's charged I come here to watch a game and maybe get a hot dog."

"I'm glad you like my gift so much," Jim said. "I was worried you'd be disappointed with a phone."

"Nonsense." Ray waved in dismissal. He snuck a peak toward Jim. "I see you're still getting yourself hurt out there."

"For good reasons," Jim said, looking over his shoulder to see no one within earshot. He saw the crowd start clapping. He could hear the cheers still faintly. He looked back to the shorter man.

"Anyway," Ray said, "I've heard some entertaining rumors." He stopped and poked Jim in the chest. "Mind you that's all this is. The story is that there's a teacher in the local high school."

"Can you be more specific?" Jim asked.

"I'm trying to be subtle here, young buck," Ray said. "The story from the local soccer moms is that one of their kids was touched here last year. She went by the name Skye I think it was."

"How the hell does that come up? Wait, did you say Skye?"

"Gossiping housewives hold nothing sacred, young man,

and yes I did," Ray said. He sat down on a nearby bench. "The point is, he was never caught. Have you ever heard of that story? Not many hear about it. It's been kept pretty hush hush by her parents."

"It's the first I'm hearing of it. I mostly looked for scumbags online who tried to go after kids. I didn't keep up with the local scene as well as I'd like. Do you have a name I can investigate?"

"Mr. Kensington was his name. I don't know his first name. It should be easy enough to find."

"He's still a teacher?" Jim asked. He looked at Ray, his eyes full of focus. "How? When they took him to court he'd have been fired."

"That's the thing," Ray said, turning the pair back to face the game a few hundred feet away. He clapped when one of the players made a goal. "They never went to court. It's all rumors. Some say the girl never talks. Others say she went to therapy. It's not my business frankly. The one name that did come up was his though. Some of their daughters had complained about his being a little too friendly. Who knows what that wholly entails?" Ray planted his hands on his hips. "I just thought you might want to know. If it is that teacher, I couldn't live with myself if I let it go on."

Jim patted Ray's shoulder. "I pray you're wrong, but I'll see what he's all about. Rest assured."

"Feel free to not answer, but what happened there anyhow?" Ray asked. "Don't say nothing. I see how you're moving stiffly."

"What would you say if I told you I got shot?" Jim asked, a coy grin on his face.

"I'd say you're lying." Ray paused. A wide smile appeared. "Unless you were wearing a vest."

"I'll leave it to your imagination. Who doesn't love a good mystery?"

"Does it hurt?" Ray asked.

"Like a sledgehammer wound." Jim visibly winced when his hand contacted the impact site. "I'm fine though - no cracked or broken ribs we think."

"You should pay a visit to our doctor friend," Ray said. "It's better safe than sorry. I'd hate to see you die, kid. You're a force for good in this world. It'd be a damned shame to lose you."

"He's not cheap you know," Jim said. He led the pair back toward the parking lot and bleachers area. He saw a hot dog cart ahead of them. "How about I treat you to a hot dog as thanks for this information. Get whatever you want on it, my treat." He pulled out his wallet from his back pocket and handed Ray a ten-dollar bill.

He watched Ray walk up and give his order before looking over toward the field. He saw two adults standing next to the two benches of players. Each one was dressed in their team's colors.

"It's a good game, huh?" Ray came back, taking a bite of his hot dog. He took special care to not let the brown sauce escape.

"You said the guy's name was Kensington?"

"Yep," Ray said.

"I'm going to head out, buddy. You be careful out there," Jim said before turning around and heading back to his car.

4

Jim knocked on the door.

"Come in," Ashley's muffled voice said.

Jim opened the door and leaned to his side on the door frame. "Did your little homework session go well?"

"It wasn't homework. It was a project visit. We had to have it done by Monday, and we forgot in class." She leaned back, planting her hands on her bed. "When ninth period rolled by we were so focused on biology it slipped our mind."

"Let's say I believe you," Jim said. "Did you and Skye get it done?"

"You're so suspicious," Ashley said. She reached under her bed and brought out her backpack. She pulled out the large three ring binder before opening it. She pulled out two pieces of paper and held them out toward him. "Here they are since you don't believe me."

"I just know how teenagers are. It's nothing against you." Jim stepped further into the room and took the papers. He sat down on the end of the bed away from her. He read through the papers. "I'm sorry I doubted you." He handed the papers back and got up. He walked a few paces into the middle of the room and turned back to her.

"You're acting weird. What's going on? Why did you leave earlier?" Ashley asked. "Was that for more training?"

"Not quite," Jim said. "I was out talking to an old friend is all. I figured you were making a friend, so I may as well maintain a relationship."

"It's only more annoying when you tell the truth to hide something." Ashley shifted her position so her legs were under her. She elevated herself using her knees. "Who was it?"

"A homeless guy who saved Masked Justice's life. Does that matter? He's a good man. Tell me, have you heard of a Mr. Kensington?"

"Mr. Kensington?" Ashley stopped for a moment and looked down at the carpeted floor. She looked up at him with a flash in her eyes. "He's the teacher of history and some other classes I think. Why?"

"I'll tell you later. I need to research him. I saw Charlie went home for the night already, so I'll be doing it myself. You can help if you'd like." Jim moved for the door.

"Of course I'm going to help." Ashley jumped off the bed and followed closely behind. "Why did you want to know about him anyway?" She followed Jim down the stairs close behind.

"I'm not investigating him because of my day job." Jim reached down to the coffee table and picked up his laptop. He flipped it open and logged in as he sat down. He felt Ashley sit down beside him as he worked. "Does that answer you?"

"He's a predator?" Ashley asked. Her voice was full of genuine confusion. "The guy looks like if a weasel was given human form. He couldn't hurt a fly. He is kind of creepy, I'll give you that with how quiet he is compared to other teachers." She leaned over to look at the screen.

"The most unassuming can be the most dangerous. I'd have thought you'd have known that by now. Just look at me. I'm perfectly normal looking."

"You have a point, but it's an extreme case and we both know it. How do you have so many catcoins anyway? Was that your payment? Why are you sending it through that service? They take a tax you know. You'd save if you skipped it."

"I'd also lose anonymity," Jim said, tapping the keyboard. "It takes a little while, but it's much safer. I can't have people know of this paper wallet. I need to transfer the funds out of this one and onto a broker site. Then I can cash out. I'll still have to pay taxes on it though as you said," Jim said, giving her a momentary glance. "Money is not an option."

"I hope you're wrong," Ashley said, watching his progress. "It makes my skin crawl to think I could be around another creep like that again. You may as well search for his picture while this is working. I know he'd have his picture on our website."

"Shouldn't you already know if it is?"

"I only log in there when I'm in computer class. That thing sucks. They hired some bottom of the barrel designer to make it. I'm pretty sure if you go to the staff page they have a picture." She pointed at the link at the top of the page.

The page changed upon another click. A photo of each teacher showed up beside a few paragraphs.

"Kensington, where is he?" Jim scrolled down the page until he found his target. "There he is." He stopped the page on a picture of a thin man no more than one hundred twenty pounds. He had glasses on and had a smile on his face. "He's certainly basic looking. If I'm right, he's using his teaching power to influence kids. That's how he would get them, not through physical means."

"What? Like threatening to give them a failing grade if they didn't do what he wanted?" Ashley asked. Her voice grew in volume. She kicked her feet out as she spoke. "It enrages me to think someone could do that to someone. They're just trying to pass the class."

"To the kid, not failing a class is the most important thing in the world." Jim switched the screen back to the background checker site. "To the molester it's all about pleasure, inflicting pain, and their sense of power over an innocent. Ninety five percent of teachers are upstanding members of society, but there's always the underbelly. Those five percent take advantage of their position. I don't know if this guy even did anything yet, but I bet your friend would." Jim glanced over before returning his focus to the screen.

"Skye? What does she have to do with this?"

"Are you two getting along well enough?"

"Don't try and change the subject." She slapped his arm.

Jim gave her an annoyed sideways look. "Just answer my question. How well do you know her?"

"I met her the first day I went to school. So that's like a week now we've been talking. We damn sure aren't besties that tell each other our traumas, if that's what you're asking. She's a goth girl that doesn't talk to many people. She has some folks she hangs out with occasionally during school, but I think she goes straight home most days."

"Have you ever heard Mr. Kensington's name mentioned when you were talking to her?"

"Come to think of it, she always goes quiet when one of her friends mentions homework in his class. I just thought she hated doing homework is all. You really think he could have done that and had the balls to look her in the eyes every day for a year and a half while doing his job?"

"Insects tend to not care for those they hurt," Jim said. His voice was even. "You said she's quiet? It could just be the usual teen angst shit, or it could be something else. This isn't going to get us anywhere guessing like this. Come to think of it," Jim said, staring at the picture of Mr. Kensington, "I saw this guy today." An image of the soccer benches flashed in his mind. "Is he the coach of the soccer team for your school?"

"I think so. I don't pay much attention to sports teams and all that bullshit. I do remember finding it weird such a stick boy was coach of a sports team though."

"Soccer is not known for its ripped participants. If there's a sport for short and fit guys, that's the one." He stared dead ahead. "He's coach of the soccer team, he's a teacher of history, and your friend gets quiet when he's mentioned." He sighed and placed the laptop aside on the floor beside the sofa. "It's not enough to go on. I need more intel before we can act. When I tell Charlie, we'll come up with a plan."

"Do you want me to gather what I can around the school? Highschoolers love some good gossip."

"Don't go asking around. That'll just draw attention. Just listen - be a fly on the wall. Pay attention to Skye's reactions, and tell me how she reacts. Be a friend to her. You said she doesn't have many?"

"Not really. It's me and a few other girls, none of which are very popular. They're a little morbid. People tend to stay away from them. She's quiet, so people leave her alone. The rumor was she used to be trendy like them until last year. Then she completely changed."

"That is interesting," Jim said, rubbing his chin. "Having

said all this, just be friends with the girl regardless of whether it happened or not. From the sounds of it, it'd be best for the both of you to be friends."

"She's nice enough. I'll look out for her," Ashley said.

"Anyway, it's almost time for the both of us to head to bed. It's already ten o'clock." Jim looked at the wall mounted clock across the room.

"Let's just stay up until midnight at least. It is the weekend after all," Ashley said, locking eyes with him. Her bottom lip quivered.

"Don't give me that look." Jim looked away. He sneaked a glance before breaking. "Alright, fine. Midnight. Don't let this interfere with your grades, or it's not happening again."

"So, there's this one movie I've been wanting to see. It comes on momentarily." She reached forward and grabbed the remote.

"Go for it." Jim watched her turn the channel...

Later that night...

"Do you really think she's that dangerous to have around?" Jim asked in a hushed tone.

"Yes, man, I do." Charlie looked toward the stairwell and back to his old friend. "The last thing we want is to be hunted by our own."

"We'd be hunted by police then?"

"Nothing so merciful," Charlie said. "You should know better than that. It depends on who came after us, but it's not going to be pleasant. My best bet would be we'd have our entrails carved out before being force fed them. That's if they send who they usually do when someone betrays the group. It's only happened once in the group's history because of how brutal he is. Everyone calls him Dillon. I don't even know if that's his real name."

"How would they even find out? The only thing coming out of this house to them is what you send," Jim said.

"They have the same skill set I do, dingus," Charlie said, waving his arms around in an animated fashion. "All it would take is her being on a webcam when they're watching, and we're made.

A small creak came from the stairs. Both men looked over. Jim walked over and looked up the stairs to find it empty. He came back over toward Charlie. "It's not happening. She's staying here so long as she wants. She has no one left, dude, except us. If that means I have to take that risk, then so be it. Just tell them you had no idea. That's why you never told them. You're one of their agents. They'd believe you."

"That means betraying you. Do you have the slightest inkling what would happen assuming that worked?" Charlie asked. "I'd be the one tasked with killing you as part of some loyalty test. This isn't just a case of getting fired. You get a nice dirt nap, just like your own victims. I don't want either of us to be in that position."

"It's not happening. Deal with that, and make your peace with it," Jim said, his tone firm and defiant.

"She is not your daughter," Charlie reached out and grabbed Jim by the collar of his shirt. "You don't owe her anything. Just find a place for her to stay. It'd be in everybody's best interest."

"Especially yours," Jim said grabbing Charlie's hand and removing it from his person. "She has nowhere to go, man. It's cruel to even entertain abandoning her like her parents did. I won't do it, and to hell with the consequences!" His voice was raised. "Don't be a fucking coward. We're doing this for people who can't defend themselves. Right? Why is this a special case? Because it's inconvenient for you?"

"I'm just trying to keep all of us alive, alright?"

"We don't need your concern if this is what it looks like," Jim stomped over to the stairs. "You get your head on straight!" He pointed at Charlie and climbed the stairs. Once he reached the top, he looked over to see Ashley eavesdropping. His voice switched back to a gentle tone. "How much did you hear?"

"Enough," Ashley said. "Thanks for that."

"There's no need to thank me. It's what I do. Now get to bed. It's past one in the morning."

"Alright."

5

"Kensington, huh?" Charlie asked, typing away on the mobile device in his lap. "I'll tell you what we'll do." His hands danced across the keyboard with every word. "We'll send this up the line."

"What's that mean?"

"It means, we ask permission since we have reasonable suspicion. You'd be amazed how many resources they can use to ascertain info on this guy."

"How do you mean?" Jim asked from across the room in the recliner. He kicked his feet out toward the coffee table.

"If nothing else, they'd send you to investigate anyway since he's right next to us geographically. It's just good practice to not go rogue and do your own shit. They don't take kindly to that. You may not get paid as much for a wimp like this, but I doubt that makes a difference to either of us."

Charlie pressed the enter key with a dramatic flourish. "There, now we just wait on the answer. Finding actual dirt on the guy, if they agree, won't be too difficult."

"How would we do that?"

"There's only one way to gather information, buddy. It's

not glamorous, but watching him both physically and virtually is the only way. One of us would tail him while the other would be in the seat watching his internet activity. It's not likely we'd see him type in 'How to manipulate a child' or anything of the like, but we're looking for patterns of behavior."

"If we see him doing such things? We'd interrupt and stop it, yes?" Jim asked.

"Of course we'd stop the damned thing from happening. That's the worst-case scenario though. The kid would see everything. Now I'm looking up this Skye girl you mentioned.

"What could you possibly be hoping to find?" Jim asked, standing up from his seat. He wandered over to the kitchen and got himself a glass of water. He spoke, still in the other room. "You don't think he'll go after her again, do you?"

"Why wouldn't he?" Charlie asked. "She didn't squeal on him the first time. He got away with it clean."

"That is true." Jim walked over to the window, glass still in hand, and took a drink.

"How's the gun shot feeling?" Charlie asked.

Jim kept looking out at the suburban landscape. "It still hurts. What a revelation, am I right? I can do a job if I had to, if that's what you're asking."

"Easy," Charlie said. "We have no proof yet. It's Sunday. Do you think the teachers would be in today?"

"I have no idea. I can go check though. I have nothing else to do today." Jim pulled out his phone and looked at it. "Why do you need to know that?"

"What better way to watch him than to physically watch him? It's the perfect way to gather intel while we wait for approval. Just remember, don't do anything rash. We're both on the hook if you do."

"If you're going, I am too." Ashley raced down the stairs. "I know the school better than you do anyway."

"Fine, just know it'll be boring." He turned back to Charlie. "There's got to be more we can do to speed this up," Jim said. "What if he's still active, but the kids aren't coming forward? The longer this takes, the more kids he has access to. He's already been possibly active for at least a year."

"I understand the frustration, but haste leads to waste. Didn't your parents ever teach you that? Can you keep a handle on yourself? Besides, I have something that will help you when you leave."

"Fine," Jim said.

"In brighter news, we got a reply for our mission report. Do you want to hear it?

"Go ahead. I'm waiting with bated breath," Jim said. His voice betraying his disinterest.

Charlie reached up and scratched his head full of hair before beginning to read. "We are pleased that pest is taken care of. It was good work to cut off his hand as a sign. We'd rather it had been quieter, but good job nonetheless. Your pay should already be in your wallet. Be careful out there, hunters."

"We got an 'atta boy'," Jim said. "Yay. Now what was this present that would help?"

"Get a thumb drive and make sure your laptop is charged. You'll need both for this."

Jim jogged up the stairs. "I'll be right back."

"Let's hope he can learn this program fast. Otherwise, this is a waste of time." Charlie prepared the transfer while he waited.

"He'll be fine. You underestimate him."

"Or maybe you overestimate him," Charlie fired back. "Puppy love tends to do that."

"What?" Ashley asked. "I don't -"

She was interrupted by rapid footsteps coming back downstairs. "Here." Jim hurried over and handed him the device.

Charlie plugged it in and started the transfer process. "You need to learn the basics in a hurry, so I'm going to give you the idiot's version."

"What is this thing you're putting on there?"

"The same tech I use to see cell phones on my laptop. You're going to find out Mr. Kensington's phone number and search it yourself. See if you can find any phone numbers and take screenshots of anything you find interesting. The smallest detail could be a breakthrough, so be thorough."

Jim sat beside Charlie and watched as he explained the basics of the program for a solid ten minutes.

"Do you understand?"

"We better hope so." Jim took the thumb drive out of the side of the laptop and put it into his pocket. He stood up, grabbed his laptop from near the sofa on the floor, and headed for the door. "I'm almost out of time."

"Make sure it's the right phone before you do anything!" Charlie called out as the door slammed shut.

At the school a few minutes later in the parking lot...

Jim had his laptop open, and the program was running. He was skimming through the phones, trying to ascertain their owners. "How many teachers come in on a Sunday to school?"

He opened another phone on the app and saw the name Eustace Kensington. "Bingo." Jim selected the phone in the app and hit the button labeled deep dive. "Their software designer would cringe, but the shit works," Jim said, watching the app work as it pulled up various files off the phone and onto his screen. He hit print screen with almost every screen and saved them as screen shots. "That's a phone number." He hit the button again. "That could be useful."

A knock at his window interrupted him. He quickly flipped the laptop lid shut and looked over to see Ashley outside the front passenger window.

She flung the door open once he'd unlocked it. She quickly climbed inside as Jim resumed his work. "Did you find anything yet. Wait." She leaned forward and looked at the laptop. "Kensington? What is this?"

"It's everything on his phone. I'm getting some decent stuff off it." Jim kept at his work, not looking over at his young charge.

"Can you do the same for Skye's phone?" Ashley asked.

"Sure, but why would I invade her privacy?"

"Every so often she says we're going to walk home from school together, but she gets a text on her phone and immediately backs out. There's something going on there."

"It could just be her parents calling her back home. Besides, unless she's in that school, I can't do it right now."

"Then teach me how to use this," Ashley said. "I can use it on my laptop during class."

"There's no way I'm doing that. How about inviting her over to the house? At least that way I'm not entrusting an illegal program to a teenager to take to school."

"You're always so boring. You need to live a little and take risks." Ashley reclined her chair and angled her head to look out the window away from Jim. "Or at least trust me more."

"I trust you with my life," Jim didn't hesitate to answer. "If I didn't -"

"You'd do what Charlie wants and boot me out on my ass?" she asked. "Is he right though?" She rolled her head to look at him.

Jim took his eyes off the screen and looked her dead in the eyes. "I don't know. I'm the new guy. It's immaterial anyway." He returned his attention to his research. "It's not happening."

"It's just I don't want you getting hunted down because of me though."

"Stop it right there," Jim shut the laptop and turned as much as he could in his seat. His voice was firm. "I've made my own decisions. I'll take the full brunt of the responsibility for them. Do not think you've caused anything bad in my life. I'm just trying to take care of you the best I can is all."

"That's more than my parents ever did." She looked away, trying to hide the growing red glow to her face.

"Try not to hold it against Charlie. He's always been jittery. He's usually a nice guy."

"I tend to take it personally when someone wants to toss me out of the closest thing I've had to a home before," she said.

"Fair point," Jim said. He opened the laptop back. "It looks like that's all the intel we can get off his phone alone."

"Let's just go to Skye's place," Ashley said, looking away out the window. "You can check her phone there."

"The only way that would work is if you went inside and I drove you. Otherwise, I'd be a creep."

"You're just driving me over there. You were worried about my safety."

"Sometimes I forgot how witty teenagers think they are." Jim exhaled. "Fine. You might want to call and ask first though. It's rude to show up uninvited."

"Already on it," She pulled her phone out and called Skye. "Hey, are you busy?" She paused and bit her lip. "I just wanted to hang out is all." She looked over with a smile to Jim. "Sure, I don't mind you coming over. What? He's okay with it."

Jim started the motor and pulled out of his parking place. He pulled out onto the street, heading home.

"Do you need a ride? Don't worry about how. We'll be there soon." She hung up with a smug grin. "How was that?"

"Back when I was a kid, I asked my parents if someone could come over, not just assume."

"Is it really a problem though?"

"I never said it was," Jim said. "Now, where does she live?"

"A few minutes away from here." She pointed past Jim. "Take a left here."

Jim activated his turn signal and checked his mirror before taking the turn. "I hope we're wrong about this."

"Then we're just invading people's privacy for no reason."

"Exactly," Jim said. "I'd rather that, then your friend having been molested - or any high schooler for that matter. I don't know if you've noticed, but I kind of don't care about the legal ramifications. As for invading people's privacy - I'm not doing anything malicious with it. Well, except if they screw kids. Then I will."

"The virtuous murderer act only goes so far," Ashley said. She pointed toward the upcoming right turn. "Hang a right here, and she's on this road at the end."

Jim looked over his shoulder and turned on his blinker before changing lanes. A loud horn erupted behind him. He stuck a lone finger out his window before making the turn. "Some people can't drive for shit," he muttered to himself. He looked out over the well-kept lawns and two-story houses. "Her family must be middle class or higher to live in this place."

"I wouldn't know about that," Ashley said, sitting up in her chair. She lowered the window on her side once they got close. "It's right here. The brown brick house is the one."

"I see it," Jim said. He parked the car on the side of the road in front of Skye's house. "Go on and get your friend."

"I'll be right back," Ashley said as she opened the door.

He watched her walk over to the building's front door and press a small button by the door. Within a minute the door opened to reveal Skye clad in all black clothes. He watched the pair of girls approach the vehicle. He gave a small wave along with a smile.

Both girls climbed in the back and buckled in. "Alright, let's go," Ashley said.

Jim didn't wait and got the vehicle back in motion.

A loud male voice could be heard from the still open window yelling. It grew fainter with every foot the car moved.

"Is that your father?" Jim looked back at the now open house door. A tall man shook his fist toward the car before heading back inside.

"Keep going," Skye said, looking down at her lap. "Please," she said.

"Is something wrong?" Jim asked, sparing a momentary glance up into the rear-view mirror. He noticed she had both a lip ring and a visible earring, both pure black.

"He's just a jerk is all. It's not a big deal." Skye refused to look up.

"I see," Jim said. "Did he agree to let you go, or am I about to be wanted for kidnapping?" Jim asked.

"Jesus," Ashley said. "No."

"He wouldn't dare," Skye said. "Trust me."

"Isn't it a little hot out today to be wearing long sleeves?" Jim asked. "You must be burning up."

Skye fiddled with her shirt sleeves and turned to look out at the passing suburban landscape. "I'm fine."

"I'm sorry," Jim said, stopping at a red light. "I'm just trying to fill the silence is all."

"Not grilling her would be a great start," Ashley said. "Sorry about him. He's not too bright."

"Guilty as charged," Jim smirked.

Ashley kicked the back of his chair, eliciting a laugh from Skye. "Don't pay him any mind. Did you get all your homework done?"

"I still have one paper I haven't done, but I was planning on getting it done today," Skye said. She leaned her short dyed black hair back on the seat and looked up at the top of the cabin. "I hate creative writing."

"I think most sane people do," Jim said with a chuckle. "The only people who love writing are complete lunatics."

"Thank you for that insight," Ashley said, her voice dripping with sarcasm. "I'm sorry about him." She kicked the seat again as the vehicle slowed down.

"It's fine," Skye said.

"It is?" Ashley asked. She immediately looked over to find Skye smiling. Her voice lost its usual sharp inflection, now replaced by stupor. "Alright then."

"We're home," Jim said, stopping the car. He placed his right hand on the front passenger seat and turned around to look behind him as he backed in.

Ashley was quiet, instead watching Skye.

Skye looked away and cleared her throat. Her hands clenched into fists, and her legs shook.

Jim was the first to unbuckle himself and get out. "Come on in."

The two girls followed closely behind.

Skye watched her feet as she followed the pair to the front door. She tripped and fell to a knee. She recovered quickly.

"Are you good?" Ashley asked.

"I'm fine," she said in quick response.

"You should get that disinfected inside." He unlocked the front door, pocketed the key, and opened the door. "Come on inside. We'll get that taken care of." He waited until the girls were inside and followed. He closed the door and locked it.

"I see we have visitors," Charlie came down the stairs. "Well, technically I'm a visitor. Anyway, I believe we met before. I'm Charlie."

"Skye," was all the girl said.

"Don't let me stop you," He got to the bottom and moved past the group. He sat down on the couch.

The girls climbed the stairs in haste.

"Now go get my laptop," Jim said, tossing Charlie his key ring. "Remember to lock it back when you're done."

"Is someone sore?" Charlie asked. His voice changed to one you'd talk to a newborn with. "Do you need another ice pack?"

"Shut the fuck up and go get it," Jim said.

"Fine, but only because I'm interested in what you did." Charlie got to his feet and exited the house.

Jim took the opportunity to fall into his favorite recliner. "There we go."

The front door opened again. Charlie had the laptop stashed under his arm at his side. "Here it is," he said as he took a seat on the couch.

"Bring it over here please," Jim said.

"Fine, but only because you said please." Charlie got up, leaned across the coffee table, and stretched to hand it over.

"I have a bad feeling," Jim said. "I really hope I'm wrong."

"Is it something we can't talk about right now?"

"Yes," Jim said, clicking.

"I understand," Charlie looked toward the top of the stairwell. "Are you working on something?"

"You could say that." Jim's eyes were glued to the screen. He kept his voice calm and even. "I don't like what I'm seeing," he said.

"Don't be too specific now." Charlie turned on the television with the nearby remote. "Oh look." The screen showed a large desk. A news ticker crawled across the bottom of the screen. "It looks like some nutcase is running around called Masked Justice."

Jim's eyes lifted and looked at the news. "What the hell?"

"Who hasn't heard of Masked Justice? The news of him busting those kids out of a locked container was big news around here." Charlie had a wide-open mouthed smile.

"Some would say he killed an innocent in the process," Jim said.

"Those people wouldn't be wrong..."

Meanwhile upstairs...

Skye sat in a blue beanbag in the corner of the room near the foot of Ashley's bed. She looked over and up toward Ashley on the bed. "Is that guy your dad? I never asked before."

"No, he's not my dad. Not my real one anyway," Ashley said.

"Sorry."

"Don't be," Ashley said. She smiled. "Life is so much better here than my real parents' house."

"That's good to hear," Skye said. She returned her gaze to the television across the room. "You have questions about me - I can tell. Let's just get this over with. I know you saw and heard my dad back there."

"I'd be lying if I said I didn't have some questions."

"Good. I like honesty. Go ahead. I'll answer if I can," Skye said.

"What was that about? He looked angry."

"That was just the latest freakout he's had," Skye scoffed. "I didn't want to mow the grass. We have one of those old push mowers. Have you ever pushed one of those? They're fucking heavy."

"No, I haven't. Jim does the lawn work."

"Anyway, I told him it was for school. I'm going to get grounded when I get back probably, but that's no big deal."

Ashley fell back on the bed, her hair sprawling out behind her head on the mattress. "You don't sound worried about that at all."

"My room has a tree just outside. It makes getting out easy. The only problem is the alarm. "Even that has its own solution."

"You know the code."

"I know the code. Unfortunately, it's a guessing game as to when both my parents are asleep. Most of the time they fall asleep fast. My dad's a heavy sleeper, but not Mom," Skye said. "Do you not get grounded often?"

"Who do you take me for?" Ashley asked, an obvious sarcastic edge to her voice. She laughed and it went back to normal. "It's usually only when I truly deserve it."

"You're lucky. Is the other guy down there his, you

know?" Skye blushed and looked away.

"What, Charlie? No!" She cleared her throat. "No," she said calmer. "They're friends is all."

"I was just wondering is all," Skye said. She looked up at Ashley.

"Changing the subject off of that," Ashley coughed, "can I ask you something about the school?"

"What's there to know?" Skye asked. "It's a place where we're supposed to go and learn. What about it?"

"I just had heard some rumors about a teacher is all. I think his name was Mr. Kensington."

"Those stories are always bullshit," Skye said

"Like all of them?"

"All of them."

"Alright then."

"Don't worry about what the vapid girls in our grade say." Skye stood up and stretched. "They're always trying to find something new to talk about is all." She moved to the door. "Where is your bathroom at by the way?" she asked.

"Out the door, to the right and it's the second door on your right."

"Thanks," Skye left the room and saw the narrow hallway. She could see where Ashley directed her to and walked forward. She glanced to her left as she did.

Jim's sheathed wakizashi sat atop a dresser in view. She stopped in her tracks and opened the door. "Whoa," she stepped over to it. "Is this thing real?" She reached forward and touched the outside of the wooden sheathe. "I'm going to go with yes."

Heavy footsteps could be heard from the stairs outside. She scurried outside the room and looked over at the stairs.

Jim turned and saw Skye. "You girls need anything? A glass of soda?"

"No, sir."

"You can call me Jim," he said. "Excuse me." He scooted past her in the confined space and entered his room.

"Can I ask you something?" she asked.

"Go ahead."

"Is that thing real?" She pointed at the sheathed weapon.

Jim looked to where she was pointing. "That thing? It's just a display blade. That thing wouldn't hurt anybody."

"Oh, if you say so."

"Excuse me. Don't let me keep you." Jim closed the door without further words, leaving her in the corridor.

She quickly went to the bathroom and returned to Ashley's room. "Sorry about that." She closed the door behind her. She sat a few feet away from Ashley on her bed. "I noticed something a little odd."

"I told you he was an idiot, a well-meaning one, but a moron all the same. A little odd is the perfect description of him."

"No not that," Skye said. "I saw a sword in his room."

"Surely you noticed his physique on the way in here," Ashley said. "He trains. Guys who train in that kind of stuff usually like swords and the like. What about it? He's a nerd who likes his movie sword fights. It's cringy, but not that weird."

"It was just out of the ordinary I guess. It's the first time I've seen someone with a sword before."

"Get your mind off that fool." Ashley got up from the bed and walked to the television. The cabinet to the side had a game console and two controllers perched atop it. She picked both wireless devices up and tossed one under-handed to Skye. "What do you say?"

"If you want to lose, sure."

"Bring it on."

6

"What were you hinting at earlier?" Charlie asked. He was doing pushups in the middle of the room. Sweat dripped down his nose and onto the hardwood floor below. "It sounded bad."

"I guess I can say now that Skye's back at her house." He cupped his hands around his mouth and raised his voice. "Ashley, you might want to get down here."

"What is it?" Rapid footsteps accompanied the female voice. She rushed down the stairs. She looked down at Charlie's shirtless form and crinkled her nose. "Ew, warn me next time he's shirtless."

"I'm working out, kid," Charlie said. "That thing your caregiver will be doing when his little bruise goes away. Hell, he should be doing it now, but he's too damned lazy."

"That is not the point of this meeting," Jim said. "I looked at the files on both Mr. Kensington's phone and your friend's."

"You must have found something, or I wouldn't be down here," Ashley said.

"I found a few concerning texts. Did she ever say anything about Kensington?"

"She immediately shut me down. I asked if the rumors I heard about him being creepy were true. She said they were all bullshit without pause."

"She's probably trying to suppress it, especially to her new friend," Charlie said, still exercising. "No one wants that to get out at her age."

"Which adds more suspicion," Jim said. He's been sending her texts. You said she'd suddenly bail on plans with you?" He locked eyes with Ashley. "Do you remember what day that was? Be specific if you can. This could tie it all together."

"I believe it was Wednesday."

"That lines up," Jim said. His voice was tainted with disgust. "On Wednesday she received a text from that scumbag."

Charlie stopped doing pushups. He got up to a sitting position on his knees. He pushed a strand of hair out of his face with a loud exhale. "Don't leave us in suspense now."

"The message reads, 'I need to see you after school'." He looked up at the pair. "That's not too damning, but according to the history of the gps, she didn't go to his class-room or anything. She went to a residential house. His house according to the records we've dug up. What the fuck kind of teacher brings his students to his house? None that I know of."

"Christ, I was hoping you were leading us on a wild goose chase with this." Charlie got to his feet. "Let me check our messages. Maybe headquarters has given us the green light. They better have."

"You mean she's going through what I did? You have proof now?" Ashley asked. "I'm taking care of it."

"The hell you are," Jim said.

"I'm doing it whether you like it or not. She's my friend, and I'm going to give that guy a piece of my mind."

"Knowing your temper, you mean the blade of a knife," Charlie said.

"That would work too."

"I'd rather you not get blood on your hands." Jim's voice turned somber. "I can deliver it in your stead."

"I've already killed. I'm doing this. You have a smaller version of his getup, right?"

"Why would we have a smaller version?" Jim asked, looking over at Charlie. "Tell me you didn't get her equipment."

"I figured it'd be better to be safe rather than sorry." Charlie shrugged. "You never know when a bullet resistant vest could be useful in our line of work. I was concerned for her safety is all."

"Oh, I'm sure," Jim said. "Anyway, that's not the only concerning text. There are veiled threats mixed in here dating back to last year."

"Such as?" Ashley asked, sitting down beside Jim and leaning close to look at the screen.

"Stuff like this." Jim showed another message.

"The son of a bitch is threatening to fail her if she doesn't show up to his special tutoring sessions!" Ashley screamed. She growled and balled her hands into fists. "I'll kill him."

"She does take after you," Charlie said. "I don't know if that's a good thing or not though."

"Tell me you got me a sword too," she said, turning to Charlie.

"Sorry, girl. To wield one of those things you need training."

"I know you'd have gotten him spares. Let me have one of those. What if the blade chipped or something? How hard can it be to kill someone with a sharp sword?" She thrust her right hand out in front of her. "One quick stab would do it, yes? How much training does one really need to pull that off?" She looked over to Jim and punched him in the shoulder. "Besides, I've already committed arson for you. I have earned this."

"You are a shitty dad figure," Charlie said. "You know that, yes? You had her burn down a house for you?"

"I was stabbed at the time and needed to eliminate my DNA from the place," Jim said. "Don't try and make this about me. We have enough proof to take him down."

"Hold on a minute, cowboy." Charlie grabbed the shirt hanging down from the bannister by the stairs and threw it on. "Let's go see what the higher-ups say. We can't go rogue and do our own shit."

"The hell we can't," Jim said under his breath.

"That collar they have on you seems stifling," Ashley said. "Is the support worth it?"

Jim decided to not answer her and waited for Charlie to return to the room with his laptop.

It was already flipped open. Charlie held it with his left palm and navigated with his right while still standing. "We did get a message back from them. They've said we're clear to investigate." He looked up at the pair. "That's good considering we already did that." He continued reading. "If your investigation yields definitive proof, you are clear to hunt. That means we're good to go."

"I'm going to go get changed," Ashley raced up the stairs.

Jim looked at Charlie. "Did you really get her her own suit and everything?"

"Kind of. It's just a smaller version of yours. She made it

abundantly clear when I was requisitioning all your gear to get her something that would fit. I did that off the books from the Republic. Meaning you owe me about six hundred dollars."

"You son of a bitch," Jim said. "You knew I didn't want her any more involved in this than she already is."

"I think that went out the window when you involved her with your hobby. She can't be half in and half out. I don't think she'll agree to be out, so I did the next logical thing."

"How do I look?" Ashley walked down the stairs. She had a mask that covered her eyes with the same black and white color scheme as Jim's. She also had a scarf mask in a different pattern. Instead of a skull, it was a flower design that was half black on the one side and white on the other. It matched Jim's battle gear perfectly.

"Like some crazy person cosplaying at a superhero," Jim said. "Are you sure about this? Burning a house with two dead bodies is a whole different ball game than ending a life up close and personal. There is no coming back from this. We may look like comic book rejects, but they don't tell you about the emotional toll it takes on them. I don't want you living with being a murderer at your age."

"I've never been surer of anything," Ashley said. "I'd feel much worse if I just let my best friend suffer while someone else fixes the problem. I'm not weak and helpless. Not anymore. I vowed to never again be that weak."

Jim shook his head. "Just follow my lead. No going cowboy in there. I almost died last job. You stay behind me and fine, you can go."

"Whatever you say, Masked Justice. Ooh, what's my new code name?"

"This isn't a game," Jim said.

"What about Blind Justice?" Charlie asked.

"I like that name," Ashley said. "Blind Justice sounds badass."

"Let's focus on the important parts of this," Jim said. "We know where he lives from these texts. We know he's extorted her for over a year. She's not told anybody about it. We need a better plan than last time."

"Let's get planning. Are we doing this tonight or later?"

"Tonight," Ashley said.

Charlie looked from the young woman to his friend. "What do you think?"

"I don't want her getting called there again." Jim got up and walked over to Ashley. "I didn't know they made vests this small."

"I had it special made. That's why it cost so much," Charlie said. "I know a guy locally who makes them."

"Is it too heavy for you to move around in?" Jim asked.

"I'm good," Ashley said. She accentuated her statement with a jump. "It's not bad."

"Hm," Jim circled around her, inspecting her. "There's no way I can talk you out of this, is there?"

"Not even if we spent all night here."

"Then you'd be tired for school. Not that that matters. You'll be dead on your feet if we do this tonight."

"Justice rarely allows us to serve it under our own schedule," Ashley said.

"Aren't you just a regular wordsmith?" Jim stopped when he was in front of her again. He reached up to the fabric covering her mouth and nose and gave it a good tug. He found it secured before he did the same to the mask covering her eyes only. "Fine. Take that shit off your eyes and mouth before we go outside. We don't need the neighbors gossiping."

"We need to research our battlefield if we're to be

successful," Charlie said. "We'll do that while you go get ready."

"I'm on it," Ashley ran up the stairs.

"I don't like this," Jim said, watching her disappear upstairs. "What is with you? First you want her gone, and now I find out you got her equipment. Which side of the aisle are you on?"

"I figure she'll want nothing to do with you after this job. Who's to say I switched aisles? It'll be just like Cynthia. You watch."

"I don't know about that," Jim said. "She's different than Cyn ever was. Cynthia was hesitant about this whole thing. Ashley's hyped and ready to go. I'm worried she'll never want to stop once we start this whole sidekick gig."

"At least you know me better than I thought you did." She skipped down the stairs, looking relatively normal.

"Our target's place looks unremarkable," Charlie said. "If there was ever a business-as-usual job, this is it. It's the perfect mission for her first."

"There's going to be some happy students at school tomorrow." She pounded a fist into her other open hand with a wicked grin. "Mr. Kensington has taught his last day..."

Outside Mr. Kensington's house at one a.m...

"Suit up," Jim said from the passenger seat. He put on his eye cover and pulled his gaiter up above his nose.

Ashley followed suit and donned her mask. She also pulled up the hoodie she wore over her head.

Jim turned around and reached toward her. He fixed her neck gait until it was secured. "There, you need to make sure it can't be pulled off or it's pointless. Speaking of which," he looked down at her lap at the sword, "do you even know how to swing that thing?"

"I don't think someone with two weeks training gets to ask that," Ashley said. "You put the sharp end inside the bad guy. How hard is that? Unlike you, I can be stealthier. I don't weigh over two hundred pounds. That will offset my small stature."

"She isn't wrong. She has more potential as an assassin than you do. What remains to be seen is if she has the balls to end a life," Charlie said, "or if she'll do exactly what your ex did. Speaking of which, she asked about you earlier today."

"Did she now?" Jim asked. "It's good to know she hasn't completely excised me from her life."

"I didn't say that. She asked if you'd gone to prison or died yet. That's all."

"Boys, can we focus up?" Ashley asked. "We're going in there and ending him. This isn't a time for gossip."

Jim looked past Charlie at the double story house. "Alright. Looking at the place, we can guess his bedroom is on the second floor."

"There's no need to guess. I can check his phone and see where it's at," Charlie said, typing on the laptop above the dashboard. "It's downstairs."

"He could just be charging it," Jim said. "It's not often someone has a bedroom on the lower floor.

"It's not unheard of," Ashley said.

"Well then it's a good thing there's two of you." Charlie chuckled. "One of you can go upstairs, and the other can check downstairs."

"Not a chance," Jim said. "We're sticking together on this one."

"Fine, I was just trying to be efficient."

"I'm trying to keep all of us breathing," Jim said.

"Other than that, it's standard. I made sure it doesn't have an alarm."

"How could you know that?" Ashley asked. "You didn't know last time."

He's never bought an alarm system. I dug deeper this time into his purchase history. You two should get going. You are just sitting in the middle of this cul-de-sac in masks. The longer we sit here, the higher the chance someone calls the police in. Get out and get it done already."

"Let's do this. Stay with me," Jim said. He grabbed the door handle and got out of the car. He ran toward the house they came there for. He could hear a car door from behind him along with footsteps. He led her around to the side of the house.

A tall fence cloaked them in shade under the full moon above. The pair stopped, and Jim felt her bump into him from behind. "Be careful," his quiet voice said. "Follow me and be as quiet as you can." Without further words he led the two of them around to the back of the house. Its modest fenced off yard housed a large shed out back. "Do you remember the technique I showed you back at the house?"

"I do," Ashley said. "The thrust is easy enough to remember." She had a hand hovering above the sheathe already.

He reached out and slapped her hand away from the weapon. "Don't be so wound up. You'll get me killed that way. We're not going to get ambushed. We're the assassins here. Do not panic." His voice was calming. "Follow my lead, and we'll be fine." He reached the back door and twisted the doorknob. "Bingo," he said in a quiet voice. No sirens met their intrusion into the dark space.

Jim creeped through the crowded kitchen at a snail's pace. He brought a gloved hand up to his face and wiped away a bead of sweat. He pulled down the hoodie off his head. "Let's find the stairs," he said.

"Right," Ashley said. She followed her caregiver around as they stalked through the place. She held her hands out in front of her. "I can't see a damned thing."

"We're almost to the stairs."

He slinked up the stairs, stopping when a stair creaked. He paused for a few seconds, just listening to the sounds of a sleeping house. He started again, this time skipping a step each stride. He headed toward the bedroom. He held his hand out behind him. He heard nothing, not even footsteps behind him. He turned around to see nothing. There was no sign of Blind Justice in the upstairs corridor. She was nowhere to be seen in the dark. The only thing he heard was a horrified garbled scream coming from below him.

In the downstairs bedroom shortly before...

Ashley was low to the ground as she moved. She mentally ran through the floor plan in her head. "He's going to be pissed." She found the door she was aiming for. She grabbed the handle of the weapon and tried to yank it free. What few words of wisdom she'd gotten earlier echoed in her mind. "Use your thumb to dislodge it, and then pull. It's a lot smoother. Just grip it on the wood and keep the webbing of your hand clear." She could hear Jim's voice. She remembered his stance when he demonstrated the move.

She assumed a similar stance and mimicked the hand position she saw earlier. She felt the blade move. "So that's the trick." She pulled the weapon out with her right hand. She was slow and deliberate with her movements. She could feel her heartbeat picking up the pace. She brought her left hand up to her chest and took a deep breath. "Let's just do it quick." She grabbed the doorknob with her left hand and twisted. The door slid open with a piercing high pitched noise.

She stood perfectly still as she heard the occupant inside rolling around along with the sound of sheets rustling. The sound of soft snoring met her ears. She took this as her cue and moved forward into the spacious room. The television in the room was off. Her target, Eustace Kensington laid below her in his bed on his back, only illuminated by the window on the side of the room. He grumbled in his sleep. She could see his hand underneath his blanket reach up and scratch himself with a contented sigh.

She gripped the blade with both hands, using almost the entire handle and held the blade facing down above his chest. She paused, blade hovering above the man's exposed chest. She looked down at his sleeping face. Her hands shook, her throat got tight, and she was beginning to have second thoughts.

She shook her head and looked down, noticing someone else below the covers. She couldn't help herself. She walked around the bed and inspected the person. "No," she said her voice scarcely above a whisper.

Skye was laying on her side facing away from Eustace. She was curled into the fetal position. She didn't react to the noise in the room.

Ashley walked back around the bed and aimed her blade with great care, making sure her strike wouldn't harm her friend. She heard footsteps above her.

Do it already, she mentally told herself. She didn't need further coaxing as the blade fell quick and decisively. The blade penetrated through Eustace's rib cage. A ripping could be heard that sounded like the sword had reached the bed below.

Eustace's eyes flew open. He looked down at the blade, then looked up with a strained breath. He reached over to the table near the bed and picked up a hardcover book. He swung it with as much strength as he could muster toward Ashley's head.

The blow connected, and Ashley turned from the force of the book. She yanked at the sword, only to find it stuck between his ribcage. "Fucking hell," she muttered.

A sound that could only be described as a garbled gurgle came from Eustace's mouth as force was exerted on the blade. He grabbed the blade, trying desperately to hold it in place. His hand as a result was sliced open from handling the blade bare handed. His largely incoherent moans were replaced with an ear-piercing wail.

"Shut up and die, you piece of shit," Ashley said behind gritting teeth.

"Oh, my Christ," a feminine voice said from beside Eustace.

Skye got up from the bed and fell to her knees beside the open window. "Who are you? What is happening?"

Ashley tried to speak in a deeper voice than her normal. "Call me Blind Justice. You don't have to worry about this piece of shit anymore. He won't touch you ever again."

"What? I thought it was Masked Justice?" Her attention snapped to the doorway to find Masked Justice standing in the doorway. "Who the fuck are you?"

"Masked Justice," Jim said, his voice deeper. "Oh fuck," he approached the two locked in a struggle. "If I'd known you'd go on your own, I'd never have let you come. Come on then." He placed his hands on top of Ashley's, planted one foot against the bed, and helped her get it out.

The wakizashi popped out with a sickening squelch. With it, a river of blood flowed out of the wound site and soaked into the bed sheets below. The smell of fecal material flooded the room. Ashley sheathed the weapon and watched Eustace writhe under the now soaked bed sheet.

Jim kept his voice calm. "Who are y-" His voice paused as his eyes widened. "Never mind. You need to get out of here. Call the police and tell them exactly what he's done to you."

"You're not going to kill me too?" Skye asked, her voice shaky.

"Of course not," Jim said. "I'm Masked Justice. We don't hurt the abused, just the abusers." He reached a hand towards her.

She slowly took it and was helped up.

"Why were you even here?" Ashley couldn't help but ask.

"When I got home tonight, he sent me a text threatening to fail me if I didn't show up. It was either fail out of school or sneak out and do this. I have enough shit at home than to add failing to that." Skye couldn't take her eyes off the body of her former abuser as she spoke.

Jim snapped his fingers, drawing her attention. "Don't look at that. Come with us." He extended his hand.

She took it and allowed herself to be led out of the room.

"You said you were Masked Justice and Blind Justice? I've only ever heard of Masked Justice on tv," Skye said. "Why are you two here of all places anyway? I've never told anyone he was doing this to me."

"We track down and kill those who would molest children," Jim said. "Our methods are secret. Nobody deserves what he put you through. You have our apology that it took us this long. Do you have a phone?" he asked.

"Yes," she said, her voice distant. She reached into her pants' pocket and pulled it out.

"Good." Jim led the pair into the living room. "I want you to stay in here and call the police. Tell them how he molested you for over a year. I want you to tell them that Masked Justice did this."

"I can do that," Skye said.

"As for you," Jim grabbed Ashley's ear and pulled her toward the door. "We have a lot to talk about."

"Hey quit it," Ashley said. "I got it done, didn't I? Let go of me. This isn't cool at all." She swatted at his hand as they exited the house.

The pair exited the front door, arguing all the while.

Skye simply sat down on the sofa in the living room and blinked. "Did that really just happen?" She looked down at the phone in her hand. She dialed the emergency services and lifted the phone to her ear...

7

J im looked at the clock across the room to see it strike three pm. He grabbed the remote perched atop the sofa's arm and turned the television on to the local news station.

"Intrigue abounds today, folks," the female newscaster started the segment. "We have reports of another incident regarding Masked Justice. An eyewitness claims he wasn't alone, however. We have Robert with the witness earlier this morning.

The camera cut to just outside the house they'd been to last night. It was still dark outside the front of the house. A man in a business suit held a microphone. The red and blue from the emergency vehicles tainted the scene as he started speaking. "Thank you, Emma. I'm here with the only witness into last night's murder. Please, can you tell us what happened?" He angled the microphone so the other person could speak into it. "Was it really Masked Justice?"

Skye's face was blurred to obscure her identity, along with her voice being modified. "I saw them with my own eyes," Skye said. She looked away from the camera as she spoke.

"Them?" Robert asked. "There was more than one?"

Skye collected herself before answering. "There was Masked Justice and a person called Blind Justice who did the actual killing." Her voice cracked. "It happened right next to me too. Oh God, the noises he made." She brought a pixelated hand up to her face.

The camera shifted back to the interviewer. "You're telling us he has a sidekick now?" Robert asked. "This is news to us. Did they say anything to you? Were you scared for your life?"

"From them?" Skye asked. "No, I never felt like I was in any danger from them. That piece of garbage Kensington is another story." She enunciated him with a voice full of disgust. "I'll admit it scared me when I woke up to see my abuser with a sword ran through him though."

"I imagine so," Robert said. "Did you get a good look at the pair? The public is dying to know. We've heard so much about Masked Justice, but we've never had an eyewitness testimony before." Robert's voice was full of barely contained excitement. "What did they look like? What color was the masks?"

"It was dark but I could make out they had masks on. It looked like it was half white and half black." She brought a hand up to her face. She gestured to her nose. "They had a cloth covering their nose and mouth. One had a design of a skull, split down the middle. The other was a flowery design. Their eyes were covered as well, further obscuring their identity. I remember they were color matched too. Their masks were half white and half black."

"This is exciting to hear," Robert interrupted. "Tell me one last thing before we have to turn it back over to the studio. How do you feel about them? Some believe Masked Justice to be a dangerous wild cannon vigilante. Others believe he's doing the right thing, cleaning up society. What do you believe as someone who saw him face to face?" Robert asked.

Skye paused for a few seconds before answering. "I don't think anyone has the right to murder another human being, but if someone had to, he's picking the right targets."

"I see," Robert said. "Back to you, Emma."

Jim turned the channel and lowered the volume.

"Can you believe this malarkey?" Dennis asked. "The news is acting like a horny teenager over this serial killer."

"Now sweetie, try to keep calm." Jill patted her husband on the shoulder. She leaned her head on his shoulder.

"It annoys me to no end that this kind of crap is getting glorified. Did you see that reporter, Son? He was asking about the color of the masks and carrying on." Dennis had a visible vein pulsing on his forehead. "He looked more like a paparazzi digging for info on a celebrity, not a news reporter. It's shameful, the state of the media."

"Oh, sweetheart," Jill said. "Maybe Ashley should stay with us from now on. With this maniac running around, he might think you're an abuser. Who knows what he'd think if he found you were housing a minor that you're not related to? He's liable to come here and kill you."

"Your mother's right," Dennis said. "He's a loose cannon going around killing people. God knows if he does any research. Even if he did, I guarantee he doesn't have the resources the police do to make an accurate assessment."

"I appreciate the offer, but her father wanted me to watch her," Jim said. "I'll tell you what, we can ask her when she gets home from school. She should be back any time now."

Dennis looked up at the clock and back to the television. "The news said this lunatic had a sidekick now. Was that how they described it? Do you realize what that means to the masses? Terminology matters."

"That he has help now?" Jim asked.

"No, Son," Dennis said. "It means they're portraying him as a hero. The proper term would have been partner in crime, accessory to murder, or something along those lines. Sidekick implies something else entirely. If they're not careful, they're going to create fans for this bastard."

"It's already too late for that," Jill said. She lifted her head off her husband's shoulder. "Some of the girls at the crochet class are already talking about him. I tried to explain it's wrong to go around killing people. Even if they do abhorrent things, no one man is judge, jury, and executioner."

"What'd they say?" Dennis asked.

"That at least he's taking out the perverts of society who prey on children. That's all that mattered to them. I tried to explain that some of his victims could be innocent, but they were adamant."

"That's God damn dangerous thinking right there. It's how law and order break down. We can't have people running around pretending to be heroes. It's how society collapses. Before you know it, we're going to have civilians running around in masks killing each other for righteous causes, and all order will be out the window."

"For what it's worth, Dad," Jim said, "I haven't heard of any fans of the man. According to Ashley it's the teenagers who gossip about him mostly. Usually the edgy ones who want to be different is all."

"Kids will be kids," Jill said. "They don't know how the world works. Let them talk. Nobody takes them seriously."

"It seems Masked Justice is getting bolder," Jim said. "Surely the police have found something, right Dad?"

"I wish it was so, Son," Dennis said. "All they know is it was done with a longer blade. When I say longer, I mean it wasn't a knife. It was a damned sword. Who the fuck uses a sword nowadays? It was clumsy my contacts say. Clumsy, but brutal. Whoever this Blind Justice that the girl mentioned is, she was cruel."

"If it was clumsy, it could just look malevolent," Jim said. "I'm just playing devil's advocate here."

"The fact someone even wants to apprentice under this serial killer says more than anything." Dennis got up from the couch and paced across the room as he spoke. "What has the world come to?"

The front door opened. Ashley slipped inside. It was obvious she was wearing makeup, and that she wasn't the best at applying it. A part of the black eye she earned last night peaked through the makeup. "Oh, hello everybody," she said in greeting.

"Hello, dear," Jill said. "Can I ask you something? What is that spot of purple there?"

"I was trying to learn how to apply makeup is all."

"Hello," Dennis said, still pacing. "She looks fine, maybe a little heavy, but good for a first attempt."

"Is something wrong?" Ashley watched the older gentleman walk back and forth. "Did something happen?"

"You didn't hear?" Dennis asked. "About Masked Justice?"

"Uh," Ashley scratched her cheek as she looked up at the ceiling before redirecting her attention to Jim's father. "A few kids were talking about some murder last night, I think. Why?"

"Apparently he has a quote 'sidekick' now," Jim said.

"Partner in murder is better fitting," Dennis said.

"I see," Ashley dumped her backpack on the floor next to the door and went to sit down on the remaining empty spot on the couch.

"Sweetheart, we have an important question we need to ask you," Jill said. "We were just thinking. With this crazy person going around killing people, well, did you want to come live with us? That wouldn't draw his attention like this current arrangement might."

"What?" Ashley said, looking across the room to Jim. "Dad told me I was staying here so I could finish school. I don't want to move again. I just got settled in here."

"I know, sweetie, but it's dangerous with him running around out there," Jill said.

"If she doesn't want to, she doesn't have to," Dennis said. "Her father wanted our son to watch her, and we need to respect that." He turned to face his son in the recliner. "All I ask is that you be ready for anything. You have your firearm at the ready, yes?"

Jim patted the shoulder holster on his person. "Yeah, Dad, I'm ready for anything. Though I'd rather not use it if I don't have to."

"That's the right attitude to have. I just want you able to defend yourself from the crazies."

"Have you heard from Cynthia?" Jill asked.

"No, Mom. I haven't."

"Have you still not apologized yet?" she asked. "I know I taught my boy better than that."

"Thanks, Mom," Jim said. "She's busy studying to take the bar exam. I assume she hasn't had the time."

"You should pay her a visit sometime," Jill said. "You two need to make up already. You've been friends your whole life. It'd be a shame if you're too stubborn to say you're sorry and throw away one of the best women you've ever known thanks to pride."

"Can we please move off of my personal life?" Jim asked. "How was school today?"

"Me? Oh," Ashley cleared her throat, "it was boring as usual. Skye wasn't there today. That's the only thing that comes to mind. I had to find somewhere else to sit at lunch is all. I also have a bit of homework I need to get done tonight, but that's normal for a Monday."

"Did you say Skye?" Dennis asked.

"Yeah," Ashley said. "Why?"

"No reason," Dennis said. "I'm sure she'll be back in school before you know it. Be nice to her, would you? She's gone through a lot."

"What's that mean?"

"Nothing," Dennis said. "Forget I said anything."

"I think that's our cue to leave so you two can focus on what you need to." Jill got up from the sofa and moved to her husband's side. She grabbed his hand and guided him over to the door. "Come on, darling. Let's let them get to work on her homework. Maybe our son will one day realize what he's going to lose if he keeps being prideful."

"Yeah, Mom, I'm sure that's the problem," Jim said. "It's not like there's nuance in every relationship or anything."

"Sometimes you have to say you're sorry, Son, even if you're not," Dennis said. "Even if you didn't do anything wrong, sometimes you have to swallow your pride."

Jim got up and escorted the pair to the door. "I'll take that under advisement." He opened the door for them. "Drive safe now."

"You stay safe, Son." Dennis led the pair back to the car. "If anything happens you call me, and I'll be right over with a squad car." Dennis threw open the driver's side door and climbed inside.

Jim and Ashley watched the car pull out with waves of their hands as the car honked at them.

"We're lucky they bought the makeup bit," Jim said through his smile as his parents backed out of his driveway. "Did anyone at school say anything?"

"I got made fun of for it, but who gives a shit?" Ashley said as the car was put into drive and went down the street.

Jim closed the door and leaned back on it. "Christ, last night was a mess."

"Where is Charlie anyway?"

"I haven't seen him since last night. He's probably sending a report of last night if I had to guess." Jim walked into the kitchen. "Come in here for a minute before we start your homework."

Ashley followed his lead and entered the tiled kitchen. "Remove your makeup so we can see how that mark is looking."

"How do I do that?" Ashley asked. "I've never worn makeup before."

"You're asking me?" Jim asked, placing a hand to his chest. "I don't know. I don't wear makeup. Uh," he pointed at the sink. "Wash your face I guess."

"Alright, fine." Ashley turned the faucet handles until a stream of water poured out of it. She bent over the sink and set about cleansing her face.

"You should get some makeup advice from Skye."

"Why would you think she knows shit about makeup?" Ashley asked, still rubbing the water off her face.

"If she was getting abused for over a year, she'd know how to hide it. Add to that the fact that I remember she wore black eyeliner the last time I saw her. She knows more than either of us. Just do what girls do and ask your friend for help. Surely girls ask each other for stuff like that."

Ashley reached for the nearby paper towel roll and tore a piece off. She dried her face off and looked at Jim, the black eye in full effect. "How does it look?"

"Bad." Jim walked over to the freezer. He opened it and took out an ice pack. He grabbed a nearby towel and wrapped it in the fabric before handing it over. "Here." He handed her the pack. "Place this on it. It'll help the swelling."

"I have to visit her today anyway,"

"The hell you do," Jim said. "Not with that shiner you aren't."

"Why not?" Ashley asked.

"Because, genius," Jim said, "she saw Blind Justice get hit in the face you said, right?"

"Yeah."

"So she could put it together. The very next day her best friend has a shiner on her eye. She'd have to be slow to not put it together."

"Then we have a problem," Ashley said. "The teachers asked me to deliver her homework to her."

"They still do that? I thought they just give them to her when she comes back."

"Teachers do tend to notice when a quiet girl like her has a friend. They asked me if I knew where she lived."

Jim shook his head. "You said yes."

"So, it's decided. I'm delivering her homework to her."

"Christ, I wish you'd told me that before I had you take off the makeup." He gave a light kick to the refrigerator.

"It just means more practice for me then."

"Go get yourself ready," Jim said. "I'll drive you after you're done..."

Outside Skye's house a little while later...

"How long will this be do you think?" Jim asked.

"There's no way of knowing," Ashley said, grabbing the door handle. "I have my phone. I'll call you when I need picked up."

"Alright then. Good luck in there."

Ashley opened the door and crossed the street. She could hear Jim head off behind her by the sound of the engine. She marched up to the front door and rang the doorbell.

A tall man opened the door. "We're not doing anymore damned interviews." He looked down to see Ashley. "Oh, I'm sorry. We've had news agencies and every self-proclaimed journalist bothering us all day. You're Skye's friend. Ashley, was it?"

"Yes, sir," Ashley said. She held up the folder. "I'm here to deliver her homework since she missed school today. Is she sick?"

"Not quite," he said. "Come on in." He stepped to the side, allowing her entrance.

She stepped inside and heard the door close behind her. She saw numerous deer heads mounted inside along with a few wild boars hanging all around. "Oh wow."

"She's up in her room."

"Thank you," Ashley took the nearby stairs and retraced the steps she'd come to know quite well over the past week. She knocked on Skye's door.

"Go away," Skye's muffled voice could be heard.

"It's me," Ashley said through the door. "Can you open the door please?"

"Ashley?" Thuds inside indicated she had gotten up and walked to the door. The door flung open to reveal Skye. Her usual dark makeup was running down her face. Her eyes were red and puffy. "I'm sorry. I'm a mess right now."

"Are you alright?" Ashley asked, her voice full of genuine concern. "You didn't show up to school today. I was worried."

"I don't want to talk about it." Skye welcomed her into the room. She shut the door behind Ashley. "What's that?"

"This?" Ashley held up the folder. "This is what you missed today."

Skye took the folder and took out the papers before handing the folder back. She placed them on her desk near the bed. "Thanks, I guess."

"Are you that sick you can't tell me?" Ashley asked.

"No, it's nothing like that," Skye said. She sat down on the swivel chair in front of her desk and rotated it around to face Ashley.

"Your dad said you all had media coming here or something?"

"If you call them media. They're more like paparazzi. They're trying to make a quick buck is all. God knows how they figured it out." She went silent. "Fuck. Forget what I just said."

"You don't have to tell me if you don't want."

"I'm more interested in that," she pointed to Ashley's face. "What's that about? You never wear makeup."

"Huh?" Ashley instinctively reached up to her eyes. "What are you talking about?"

"I'm not stupid." Skye got up and walked over to her. She leaned in close. "That's not eyeliner, is it?"

"I don't know what you're talking about."

"Don't lie to me," Skye said. "What happened? Was it your caretaker?"

"What the fuck? Hell no it wasn't," Ashley said. "Look, if

I tell you this, you can't tell anybody at school, or I might get suspended."

"I won't tell anyone."

Ashley's mind was running a mile a minute. *Come on, who had a shiner today? What was his name?* She asked herself mentally. "I had a fight with Vick today. I gave him a black eye - he did the same to me."

"Vick?" Skye asked. "Why the hell did you two fight?"

"He claimed you were skipping. He then said some unflattering things about you and Mr. Kensington. I decided to punch him in the face following said statements."

"Of course he did," Skye said. She guided Ashley toward the large mirror sitting beside her closet. "He was always the one who believed those rumors the most. The guy's a regular jackass. I can't believe he'd hit a girl though."

"You never know what a person will do."

"I'm beginning to put that together," Skye looked at Ashley with a dead serious look. "You have bags under your eyes. Did you not sleep well last night? Or is that your failed makeup application making it look like that? You know what? It doesn't matter. I'm going to show you the proper way to do this." She picked up a blue pack from the table below the mirror and ripped it open. She pulled out a cloth. "Take this."

Ashley took it. "What do I do with it?"

"Slowly run it over your face where you applied it."

Ashley did as directed with a wince when she touched the bruised area. "Is this right?"

"Oh wow," Skye said. "He really did give you a black eye. Yes, you're doing fine. I'm going to have to teach you how to properly conceal that."

"How would you know how to conceal a bruise?"

"I'll tell you another time. Now it looks like you've gotten most of it. Toss that wipe in the trash and go wash your face. I'll then teach you how to apply makeup and not look like a clown."

"Was I a pretty clown?" Ashley tossed the cloth in the nearby trash can.

"Not really."

"You're no fun." Ashley walked over to the door. "I'll be right back." She left the room, closing the door behind her.

Skye looked down at the floor. She spoke barely above a whisper. "Something's not right." Images of last night flooded her mind. She saw Blind Justice towering above her from the floor. She saw the hardcover book smacking them in the face. "Was that the same eye?" She reached up to her face. "I think it was. No, that's too crazy." Another image came to mind. The wakizashi she saw in Jim's room was next. She remembered the blade looking remarkably similar. "It can't be. It's too crazy."

"What's too crazy?" The door opened and Ashley entered. "Your dad's animal head collection down there?"

"No, that's just his hunting trophies. He takes me out every time he goes. It's a real drag. What I was referring to was that you'd fight Vick. Now get over here and let me teach you a thing or two." She stood up and went to the mirror again. "Are you good with art?"

"Not really. I suck at that stuff."

"Then this will take a while. Let's get started..."

8

"There you are. Where were you?" Charlie stood in the doorway. "Get in here. We have something to talk about that's important."

"How did you even get in?" Jim asked. "I locked up before I left."

"I have my ways," Charlie said, slamming the door shut behind his friend. "The higher ups are happy and pissed at the same time about last night."

"Why exactly?"

"They're happy that Masked Justice is getting some good publicity, but they're pissed because they have no idea who this Blind Justice is. I've been trying to put out that fire all day."

"What did you tell them?"

"That it was me," Charlie said, his voice gaining volume. "What was I going to say? That their agent has a teenage girl as a sidekick that he lives with? They'd kill us both."

"Did they buy it?"

"I don't know. We'll be lucky if they don't send another

representative here. If they do, we're fucked. I bet I know who it'd be too."

"The same guy you talked about before?"

"Probably. The guy's as zealous as they come, with an appetite for brutality to match. You remember I told you about Dillon? He's who they'd send to check in on us I bet. The rumors say he's almost seven feet tall. He's built like a fucking tank, and he's not someone you want to piss off. He's supposed to be an ex-bodyguard for one of our highest-ranking members. The only reason he replaced him is so he could keep peons like us in line."

"How high ranking are we talking?"

"My bet would be a senator or something of the ilk."

"You don't know?"

"You think they introduce us to the higher ups? Do you know who they are? We're the same rank here, buddy," Charlie said. "I've just been here longer and pay attention."

"What are the options?" Jim asked. "I'm not kicking Ashley out before you even suggest it. I'm the closest thing she has to a father figure in her life. I'm not abandoning her like hers did when they sold her."

"There's always the truth, but that's risky," Charlie said. "I doubt Dillon would give a flying fuck for your reasons though. All he'd see is a man living with a sixteen-year-old that's not related."

"I assume hiding this is off the table?"

"That depends if they bought that I was Blind Justice. If they don't, then he'll be here before we know it. God help us if that happens."

"You don't think the two of us could take him?"

"Your plan is to kill the Republic's enforcer? Mr. Benning, have you lost what's left of your marbles? Do you know what kind of hell would rain down on us without their protection?"

"It can't be as bad as abandoning Ashley."

"All that good press we've been getting?" Charlie asked. "It'd be gone. You'd be public enemy number one."

"Do you think they'd have us arrested?"

"No, if only it'd be that easy. They'd hunt us down personally and end us. They don't want us going anywhere near the police. There's a good reason the higher ups are anonymous. They take care of their problems themselves. It would involve moving to a whole new town, never having contact with your family again, and starting a new life. That's the only hope you'd have. If they ever found you, you'd have to start all over again and again. Am I making my point yet?"

"What's your suggestion then?" Jim asked, crossing his arms.

"Have her stay with your parents for a few days," Charlie said. "At least until Dillon leaves. I'm betting he's on his way here as we speak. Who knows how long until he gets here."

"Why are you so sure he's coming?"

"Because leadership gets nervous when one of their agents suddenly has an unauthorized sidekick. I forgot you two love getting put on television. It was my mistake thinking you two could keep it quiet."

"How were we supposed to know her friend would be there that night?"

"You should have called it off." Charlie's voice turned stern. "It was stupid to kill someone in front of a civilian!"

"I didn't do it," Jim said, stepping up to Charlie, coming nigh nose to nose. "She snuck off when I was going upstairs."

"Then it's still your fault. You weren't watching her close enough."

"I didn't even want her there to begin with." Jim poked Charlie's chest with his finger. "You're the one who got her the gear and got her all excited about coming along. I didn't want her to ever do what we do!"

"God dammit." Charlie turned around and walked a few feet. He had his hands on the back of his head as he walked. "We are fucked, man. The only way we maybe get out of this unscathed is if you tell her she's staying with your parents for a few days. Then maybe I can sell that I'm Blind Justice and this all goes away. That's not too much to ask of her. Besides, think of it like her learning more about her foster grandma and grandpa."

"Fine," Jim said. "If you think it will help."

"Finally, you see some sense," Charlie said. He moved to the sofa and plopped down. "Where is she anyway? I'd assumed you went out to pick her up from school."

"I had to drive her somewhere, and trust me, I'm not happy about where she went either."

"Oh no. What happened now?"

"Her teacher gave her homework to deliver to Skye."

Charlie's eyes bugged out. "The same girl that you found last night? The one that saw her get hit in the face? That girl?"

"She's apparently the girl's only friend."

"Oh, for shit's sake," Charlie laughed. "I can't believe this. Do you know what this means?" he asked between laughs. "It means she's liable to notice who she is, and by association, you. That girl could be our downfall."

"Skye?"

"Either one of them. Skye if she is smart, or Ashley for

putting us in this position. Did you make sure her makeup was good before she left?"

"As best as I could, man," Jim said. "I don't know makeup or how to apply it. It didn't look like she had a black eye is the best I can say."

"Why is there always something to worry about when I'm near you? Nothing can ever go to plan. Why is that? Why are you two the way you are?"

"Look, we'll be fine. I'll get her to stay with my parents for a couple of days. They were pushing for the same thing. They'll love the idea."

"For real?" Charlie stopped laughing. "Why would they want the kid?"

"They claim Masked Justice is a psychopath going around and killing kid diddlers." He brought a hand up to cover his eyes. "They're afraid I look like one with her in the house."

"From their mouths to God's ears. Even they noticed it before you did. If even they admit it, what do you think Dillon would think?"

"I got it already. It's only for a few days anyway. It's not like I'm leaving her alone. They're far better parents than I could ever be, right?"

"I see you're not as dumb as you look sometimes."

"Fuck you," Jim said with a smile.

"Your pop's retired, yes?" Charlie asked, ignoring the verbal jab. "It could be an opportunity when you think about it."

"It's not like Dad's still on the force, dude. What opportunity do you think you see here?"

"You don't think he has any files on his computer?"

"I don't think they own a pc," Jim said. He placed a hand on his abdomen. "At least this is pretty much gone." He moved over to the nearby window and pulled the blinds shut, making the room considerably darker.

"How nice for you," Charlie said. "Are you serious? No computer at all?"

"He was an old school type. Best she might get is if he rants about Masked Justice. I'd rather avoid getting him riled up about that though. If he snaps, he could call his friends who are still working. I'd rather avoid that."

"Never mind then." Charlie got up and walked toward his friend, stopping a few feet away. "You should go pick her back up. She needs to pack up and get moved. Call your parents and say you changed your mind."

"Right. I'll go deliver the bad news then, shall I?" Jim backpedaled toward the front door with his thumb pointing over his shoulder.

"You'll be fine, you big baby."

Outside Skye's house a little later...

Jim raised the phone to his ear. He waited as he heard the electronic ring. He heard a click. "Hello?"

"Hey," Ashley said. "Why are you calling?"

"Something came up," Jim said, his free hand tapping the steering wheel.

"Is it really that urgent? We're kind of in the middle of something here," Ashley said. "I was learning something very useful."

"Useful?" Jim asked. "Like what?"

"Skye here's very good with makeup. I've already learned a few things."

Jim looked at the clock on his dashboard to find it read four thirty pm. "Fine, you have one more hour. Learn as much as you can. Be prepared. You're probably not going to like what I have to tell you. Have fun."

"Wait, what?" he heard her ask when he hung up. He tossed the phone on the passenger seat and started the engine again. He drove off toward town. "Let's go tell Ray what's happened. He'd be thrilled to hear a kid toucher was taken out by Masked Justice. Hell," he turned right, "he's probably heard already."

He reached down and turned the radio on. A talk show host, the voice deep and masculine, came over the air. "Have you heard about this guy, Nancy?" he asked. "Apparently there's this wannabe superhero running around killing people with knives, swords, and guns."

An undoubtedly female voice responded. "I sure have, Eli. They say he only goes after those guilty of sex crimes involving children though," Nancy said. "I find it hard to sit here and wag my finger too much at that if I'm honest. I'll be clear here for anyone listening. I do not condone murder. I do not want Masked Justice and Blind Justice to go around killing people. What about you, Eli? What do you think?"

"I think he should be arrested," Eli said. "Think about the stories we've talked about here on the show. There was that time he killed that innocent guard when he supposedly saved those kids in the shipping container, was it? Does that not count? This guy is not qualified to be running around out there killing people he thinks are guilty. We have a system in place. It's called civilization. Civilized people don't go around killing someone based on guesses. He should get the same treatment as a serial killer if you ask me."

"You can't deny him helping those kids out was a good thing though, surely? You heard the same details I did. They were being forced to stay in the dark with nothing but buckets and themselves for company. The conditions were inhumane. We don't treat death row prisoners nearly as cruel. He did rescue them from that. Even you must concede that."

"I admit that in his highly illegal murder spree some good things have happened. That does not come close to excusing his body count. God knows how many of them deserved death is the problem. He could be a frothing at the mouth lunatic that escaped the funny farm. I hear he wears a Halloween getup that would give a teen fangirl a wet dream. The dude is not all there. Surely you concede that much, Nancy?"

"That is undeniable. You can't be of sound mind and run around killing people with blades like that. I heard from an expert that stabbings are the most brutal form of killing. You're up close and personal and struggling for dear life. It takes a certain kind of person to go through with it with a blade."

"You probably see the life fade from their eyes," Eli said. "Which brings more validity to my point. The man needs to be in a mental care center at the very least under maximum security."

Jim turned the radio off. He could see the motel where he and Cynthia had hid out. "It hasn't been that long since then now that I think about it." He pulled into the motel's parking lot.

He got out of the car and slammed the door behind him. "Now which way was his place again?" He pulled out his phone and hit the speed dial for Ray's phone.

"Hello?" He heard Ray's voice in his ear. "Who is this?"

"Hey, Ray," Jim said. "I came to visit. Where are you?"

"At my place. There's no game today."

"Can you come to the motel where we met? I'm there now. I just couldn't remember which way your place was."

"I'll be right there, young man." Ray hung up.

Jim hung up and placed the phone in his pocket. He surveyed the area around him when he saw Ray's semi hunched over form coming towards him. "Hey, over here." Jim raised a hand in greeting.

"What a surprise to see you." Ray got closer, now within ten feet. "What brings you around here? Surely you have better things to do than talk with someone like me."

"Don't put yourself down so much, old man. I investigated that story you told me the other day. I figured you may want to know what I found."

"I have a pretty good idea, young fella," Ray said. He looked around to see no passersby. Plenty of cars passed by though, polluting the relative silence. "The news is saying Masked Justice killed Mr. Kensington. Oh, wait now, it was actually Blind Justice, I think it was." Ray had touched his chin in deep thought. "Either way, he's dead. I assume you must have found something to warrant such a harsh penalty."

"He'd been molesting the girl for over a year, using manipulative tactics to get her to do what he wanted. You know, like he'd fail her if she didn't service him. How he'd recorded all of their meetings and was threatening to release them on the internet if she ever went to the authorities. It was dirty shit, old man."

"To think she burdened all of that in her heart." Ray brought a hand up to his torn jacket and clutched his chest. He grimaced and looked down at the ground. "It's enough to make an old man cry. To think she'd been under that strain. Did you see that the cursed news boys wouldn't even let the girl leave the scene? They swarmed her like hyenas the moment they could. It was despicable to watch."

"I agree," Jim said. He leaned back against his car. "Stations love bad news."

"I'm glad old rumors were able to stop such evil from wandering this Earth, young man. How are you holding up? I know doing what you do," he looked around before continuing, "it must take a toll on you emotionally."

"I'm not so concerned about my head, pops. I'm more concerned for my ward. She's wild."

"Everyone is wild in their youth." Ray chuckled. "Just look at you."

"I'm the one in charge of her safety," Jim said. "Look at me. I'm a failure. She ignored me on the job and did it on her own. Now I've come to a situation where I need to trust her to live with my parents for a few days. How am I to do that?"

"I'm not going to ask why you need her to move out, but I think you just need an honest talk with the girl." Ray moved over toward Jim until he was standing side by side. He slapped Jim on the back, a beaming grin on his face. "In my experience, that works better than any subterfuge. Just ask her to follow your orders. That's treating her like an adult. It's what all teenagers want. It's plain as day she wants your approval."

"How do you figure?"

"Dumbbell," Ray slapped Jim lightly upside his head, "she dressed up just like you and is following in your footsteps while staying in your house. You don't see that? You are dense, son. Did anyone ever tell you that?"

"Cynthia always loved telling me as much," Jim said. He rubbed the back of his head and leaned away from the old man. "I never wanted this for her. She's hell bent on doing this. I try to keep her away, but she is stubborn as a mule."

"I'd keep my eye on the girl then," Ray said. He spit on

the blacktop below before continuing. "You need to keep her in check. With her history, it'd be easy for a young kid to lose it. Especially when she's just taken a life. Do you remember how you felt when you took your first life? Be honest with yourself. That's what she's going through. Your first thought is to dump her at your parents'? That might work, but if I were you, I'd be spending a lot of time there with her; or at the very least allow her to continue in this work you both are doing. I'm sure she can sneak out of your parents' place."

Jim looked up at the overcast sky. The gray clouds above allowed a few beams of light through, causing him to squint. "I could keep her costume and such in my car to allow that without my parents finding it."

"I knew you were a good man. Just remember what I said." Ray reached up and tapped Jim's nose. "Be there for her. You are all she has left in this world if what you told me before was correct. Her parents are gone, Jim. You, Charlie, your mom and dad are it. It wouldn't kill her to spend some time with them anyway, if that helps."

"You always know how to help, don't you, old man?" Jim said. "Here, consider it a finder's fee." Jim took out his wallet and pulled out three one-hundred-dollar bills. He held them out to Ray. "Take it."

The old man swiped the bills before stuffing them in his pants pocket. "Thanks, young man. You keep that good heart, and you'll be fine raising that girl." Ray backed up a few feet as he spoke. "I'm going to go and get some necessities with this cash. Thank you kindly."

"Spend it wisely." Jim raised a hand and waved to the retreating Ray.

"You be careful now."

Jim turned around and threw the door open before

climbing inside. He started the engine and pulled out into traffic. "It's for her own good. She could use a grandma and grandpa figure in her life, right? It's only for a few days." He looked up in the mirror at himself before looking away. "I'm not abandoning her. She'll understand. The question is what am I going to do to pass the time before she's ready?"

9

"Why were you in such a hurry for me to come back?" She climbed in the passenger seat. "I was learning a lot."

"We, meaning I, am in trouble with the Republic possibly."

"What the fuck?" Ashley asked. "What did you do?"

"Do you want the honest answer?"

"Of course."

Jim started the car and pulled out onto the road. "We have reason to believe they are sending their enforcer of sorts to my house. Our only hope is to have Charlie pretend to be Blind Justice. To sell this, you get a trip to grandma and grandpa for a few days if you catch my drift. Mind you, if I have any jobs, I'll come get you so you aren't excluded from that. "

"Did you say an enforcer was coming down for us?" Ashley asked.

"For me. They want to know who Blind Justice is. Our options for them to think is you or Charlie. If they know you live with me, they're going to kill me and Charlie. Do you get me? You'll be back in the house before you know it."

"You are really worried about this, I can tell," Ashley said. "I don't give a flying fuck about staying at your parents' house for a few days. They live closer to school anyway. If this helps you not be in trouble with your sugar-daddies, I'm cool with it."

"Now answer me a question," Jim said. "How did you two get on the makeup bender?"

"Initially she asked me if it was you," Ashley said, her tone casual. "I told her I got in a fight at school. I picked a real piece of work. He's the type to gossip about everybody and make fun of others. It helps that he's been known to pick her as his target."

"You think she bought that?" Jim asked. "Did you at least disguise your voice when you talked to her at the house that night?"

"Obviously I did. I'm not an idiot," Ashley said, reclining her seat back. "Anyway, I learned how to better hide any marks I get in our night life."

"Don't say it like that," Jim said. "It makes my skin crawl."

"Surely I'm not that ugly."

"You're not as witty as you think you are," Jim said. "You'll learn that as I have."

"I take it that when I'm gone, he's going to show up. You are just going to invite him in and have coffee then?" Ashley asked.

"I doubt it will be so pleasant," Jim said. "He's going to dig through my life even after we tell him it was Charlie I bet."

"Maybe I could help." Ashley leaned forward in her seat and turned to look at him with an impish grin.

"How pray tell would that be? You won't be there to influence anything."

"I wouldn't be helping with that issue, dumbass," Ashley said. "I could keep tabs on your dad. You know, just in case he hears anything. It's nice to know what we've let slip through."

"He's not on the job anymore. At most all you'd hear is his side of a conversation."

"I think I can manage with that software of yours. Let me have a copy, and I go peacefully. I'll be helpful, I promise."

"You know they don't even have a computer, right?"

She audibly gulped. "Do they have a basic internet plan?"

"Sure they have internet," Jim said. "I think it's like maybe 1 megabit per second download, and God knows what upload. Have fun with that experience. You should count yourself lucky. When I grew up with them, they didn't even have internet - period."

"Why the hell do they have an internet plan with no pc?"

"I introduced them to handheld devices months ago. They've discovered the joys of the app stores. You can work with a basic connection. It's not like you need blazing quick speed like we have."

"Your dad used a cellphone, right?"

"When he calls his work buddies he sure does," Jim said, slowing the car down and pulling into his driveway. "I'll see if I can get Charlie to part with the program. No promises. It's not even mine to promise."

"Let's get this over with," Ashley got out first.

Jim strived to catch up to her, resorting to jogging up to his door. "We're back," he said, entering his front door. He closed it behind him. "Hey, you know that cell phone program you put on my laptop?"

"What about it?" Charlie didn't look up from his work.

Jim looked down at his laptop and motioned to Ashley. "Did you need that back?"

Ashley bent down and grabbed the laptop as the two men chatted.

"No. Go ahead and keep it. Just don't copy it needlessly. The more this shit gets around, the quicker it gets found out. When it gets found out, it's useless; or worse, a security liability."

Ashley was already halfway up the stairs by this point.

"Alright then. I'm going to go help Ashley pack. We'll be out of here before you know it."

"The quicker the better. I don't like sitting with the hot potato in my lap if I can help it. Also, remember if one of them gets in the house, we should consider this place bugged. Choose your words carefully then."

"I'll miss you too!" Ashley's voice wafted down the stairs.

"I'll be back," Jim tromped up the stairs and into her room.

"Why are you in here? I can pack my own bags."

"I just thought you might want some help. That just means less work for me then," Jim leaned to the side against the door frame. "I trust you'll behave yourself at my folk's place?"

"No promises. You said I could come along with any jobs while I'm there. I doubt they're going to allow me out at all hours of the night."

"I suppose you'll have to learn the art of sneaking out as I did at that age." Jim gave a toothy grin. "Consider it training in your stealth skills. You also need to do ten push-ups a day along with twenty sit-ups, and that's bare minimum. Those numbers will increase as the weeks go by. Let's not go too high too quick."

"Why do I have to?"

"For going rogue on your first job," Jim said. "You could have gotten yourself killed, and it'd have been all my fault. I am going to drill discipline into you by training if it's the last thing I do. That way I won't have to worry about you getting yourself killed doing something stupid. Consider this your official warning. You are to work out every single day. Gym class does not count, though sports teams would. I would suggest cheerleading for the acrobatics training, but that's just me."

"Do I have to?"

"Do you think people who compete in the Olympics want to train every day for hours? The feats of strength, agility, and endurance that we have to have are inhuman. Training is the only way to form such traits. It isn't fun doing this. You knew that going in." His voice turned steely. "Your fitness will determine if you live or die, along with training. Treat this with the respect it deserves."

"Fine," she said. "I'll work out every day. I am not joining a damned cheerleading squad though," She turned around from packing and pointed at him for a moment. "That's a hill I die on. I am not becoming one of those types of girls."

"It would be valuable training for Blind Justice is all I'm saying."

"Fine," she growled. "I'll think about it," she said through clenched teeth. "I make no promises. Skye would never let me live that down."

"She would be fine with it. That girl doesn't strike me as quite that shallow. You should know that. You're her friend. Do you think she'd mock you for your interest?"

"No." She turned back with a soft voice. She resumed jamming as many outfits, articles of clothing, underwear, and socks into the bag in front of her on the bed. "She wouldn't."

"Then give it some thought. Are you almost done?"

"Just packing some essentials if you know what I mean."

"I get it," Jim stood up straight. "You don't have any pictures in here or anything, do you? We can't let him see any hint of you whatsoever." He inspected the bookshelf, windowsill, and closet.

"The only pictures in here are of you. It's just as it was when I moved in. Don't worry so much."

"I'll be sure to help you redecorate when you get back," Jim said. "It is your room after all. You should have posters of bands, movies, or something. Hell, get a band poster. I'll pay for it."

"I'll hold you to that," She zipped up the bag and slung it over her shoulder. She picked up her school bag. "I'm ready."

"Alright then. Let me call my parents, and we'll be off."

"You didn't even ask them yet?"

"They were the ones who offered. I doubt they'd take it back." He dug the phone out of his back pocket and called.

"Hello, Son," Dennis said.

"Hi, Dad," Jim said. "Is your offer from before still on the table?"

"Obviously," Dennis said. "How long are we expecting to host her?"

"Just a few days. I'd say two to five days. She wants to get to know you."

"I understand. We've already prepared a guest room for her to stay in. Well, it's your old room. We removed all your old posters years ago. We're ready whenever you are."

"We'll be there soon, Dad. Goodbye."

"Bye." Both sides hung up. Jim stuffed the phone in his

pocket and turned around, heading toward the stairs. He led her down the staircase. "He's fine with it. You're getting my old room. I apologize now. It was a small room."

"At least it's only temporary. Does it have a desk so I can do homework?"

Jim pushed the front door open. "Not a big one, but yes."

She closed the front door behind them. "That's all that matters. I just need a place to work."

The pair got into Jim's car. Ashley kept the pack on her lap and buckled up.

Jim secured himself before starting the car's engine. "I hope you don't mind snoring."

"Do not say it," Ashley said. "I cannot stand snoring. Tell me the door to the room is thick."

Jim tried to hide his look of amusement. "I'm going to go with no. Don't worry." Jim reached in front of her and opened the glove compartment. "Here." He reached inside and pulled out a box. "I always keep a pair of earplugs in there. For now, they're yours. Dad's snores are legendary. That should help you sleep."

"I wish you were this nice all the time." She took the box and closed the glove compartment. "Thank you."

"You're welcome. I envy you, getting to eat Mom's cooking. It'll give you enough energy for that exercise regimen I ordered you to follow. In life there's a cost to everything."

"Just shut up and get me there..."

10

"Finally. It's good to be home again." Jim closed the front door.

"Hello, Mr. Benning," a colossal man said, sitting on his couch. He got up with a hefty grunt. "Do you know who I am?"

"I have a good guess," Jim said. "I'm guessing you're Dillon?" he said with a smirk. "I bet you have a ton of questions for me."

"I see you do your homework, or at least pay attention to the email we sent you. I like to show up early. It's professional you see." He straightened his tie, a fake smile adorning his face. He looked down his nose at Jim. "Your partner - Charles was it? He has already been escorted to another site for his questioning. I prefer man-to-man. I find people in general tend to be more honest then."

"I can guess why," Jim looked at the unusually tall gentlemen head to toe. "Let's talk."

"I took the liberty of checking your house while you were out," Dillon said. "Now tell me. Who was that girl you drove to your parent's house earlier? I am mighty interested in that. I do not want to believe our newest and most capable agent could become that which he hates."

"She's the daughter of a friend of the family. She's staying with my parents. She just comes over here for tutoring."

"For your sake, I hope you're telling the truth. I will be asking your parents the same questions to confirm your story. Your friend already told us he's this Blind Justice character. Do you have anything to add to that?"

"It is true. We thought it prudent to work together in the field on that operation. He happened to guess the bottom bedroom. We had a bet going you see. I bet him he was asleep on the top floor and well, it turned out I lost some money."

"Be quiet," Dillon raised a hand and placed his enormous finger against Jim's lips. He took his finger away and rested his hand on Jim's shoulder. He kept his voice even and amiable. "See, I have reason to believe the two of you are lying. You're probably wondering what reason I have. See, Mr. Kensington had a personal computer in his room."

Jim looked down at the massive hand resting on his shoulder when he felt it squeeze hard.

"That personal computer had a webcam. Now the police may not check such things in this Podunk town, but we do. Especially when we have questions. Now unless Charlie got a lot shorter, he was not the one who stabbed that trash bag. The voice was also nothing like his. What do you have to say to that, Mr. Benning?"

"A cheap twenty-dollar camera isn't the most reliable piece of hardware. The camera lens of many webcams obscure the picture to such a degree it'd be hard to reliably pin down who someone was in a dark room."

"I'll give you two one thing - you stick up for each other."

Dillon removed his hand from Jim's shoulder. He instead gripped Jim by the collar of his shirt and lifted him off the ground, choking him. "Do not try to mislead me. I have an inkling that girl is involved."

"Inklings are not proof," Jim said. He barely managed to get the words out before shooting his leg out, striking Dillon between the legs. He dropped to the floor as Dillon backed away, holding his privates. "Also, do not touch me again without permission. Didn't your mother teach you it's bad manners, big boy? Now do we want to have a civilized conversation, or are we dancing for real? I'd rather just talk."

"I'm sure you would." Dillon managed to stand up straight. He swung a monstrous hook toward Jim, causing him to duck.

Jim circled around the large man and backed up a few steps. "Can we at least take it outside? I don't want to break all my shit as I beat the fuck out of you."

"You are a fucking worm," Dillon charged ahead full speed. His shoulder impacted with Jim's chest and picked him up. He charged full bore toward the wall and squished him between himself and the wall. He tossed Jim down on the floor and looked down at him. "You talk a big game, but look at you. You can't beat me."

"Nonsense," Jim scrambled to his feet, getting himself out of the corner. "I just don't want to hurt the big guy from the Republic is all. I'm that good of a little soldier. I don't want to hurt anybody on the same righteous path."

"That remains to be seen. Technically your story checks out, but I am not convinced." Dillon bared his teeth. "Do not treat me as a fool. I'm not leaving this shitty state until I find out the truth. I'll leave this house for now, since I've proven my point. I'll see you around, Mr. Benning. Pray I do not find out you've been lying to me."

"Where the hell's Charlie, and when is he coming back?" Jim asked.

"That depends entirely on your friend. If he's playing ball, he'll be back by tonight. If he insists on lying and being difficult, you might never see him again. Your life hangs on what he says too. He may not be quite so cool under pressure as you." Dillon opened the front door and looked back at Jim. "I have my own theory about what's going on here, and it's not the story you're telling us. Would you like to change it before it's too late? Do you want to admit you're using the girl as your sidekick now, or are you committed to this deception?"

"I'm just her tutor is all."

"The best lies are cloaked in truth. You are quite the skilled liar I see," Dillon snarled. "I'd watch your back and be careful if I were you. If you'll excuse me, I'm going to go see how the questioning of your partner is going." He walked through the open doorway and slammed it shut behind him.

Jim looked around the room at the nigh spotless state of the room. "At least we didn't break anything. That's good news. It's about the only good news I have tonight," he said in a glum voice to himself.

At the same time at another undisclosed location...

"You're still sticking with that story, huh?" the masked female asked.

"It is the truth. It's hard to tell a different version unless I want to lie," Charlie said. His hands were tied behind the chair he was sitting in. He struggled against the binding as he spoke. "Are these necessary? I'm not a wild animal sitting here. It's demeaning."

"It is protocol," the questioner said.

"You know," Charlie said, "I bet if you took that mask off, you're cute."

"Subject is trying to change the subject," she said in a tone more suited to watching paint dry. "That means he's trying to hide something."

"I can't tell you anything else or I'd be lying." He flashed a suave smile. "I decided to accompany our agent in the field on this one operation. Is that so hard to believe?"

"Considering your orders were to not involve yourself directly, it is, to a degree."

"My orders were to make sure the operations succeed at any cost. I did precisely that. I don't see what everyone is so concerned about. The job got done, Masked Justice got some more positive press, and we got away clean."

"There are those who believe that wasn't you in the house that night. That is the issue we are here for," she said. "Some say the figure we saw was too short to be you."

"Figure you saw?" Charlie asked. "What are you on about? There were no cameras in the place. I checked it myself before we went in."

"No standard cctv cameras, no. However, there was a computer in Mr. Kensington's room. That pc had a webcam. Do you deny the allegation that it was someone else claiming to be Blind Justice?"

"Oh, I see." A bead of sweat rolled down the side of Charlie's head. He kept his demeanor calm and collected. "It's hard to tell much from shitty webcams. I'd be surprised if you could even see anything in there to be honest. Did you see the moment the sword got caught in his ribcage? That was my favorite, it was just stuck there. I had to get Jim to help me get it out of him. He deserved nothing less in my opinion. It was an ugly death. I promise you that."

"How riveting," the female interviewer said. "Subject is avoiding direct questions. This is mighty suspicious."

"I'm beginning to wonder if you all are even trying to find out the truth; or if you're just on a hunting mission, and I'm the prey. It sounds like you're out to get me."

"I just want the truth, and there are irregularities. I am here to find out the root cause of these disturbances, along with Mr. Dillon. He should be at your friend's house right about now. I am gentle compared to him. Count yourself lucky you got me as your interviewer." She pushed up the glasses over her eyes. "Now let's try this again. If that was you, why did you appear so short on the camera?"

"That computer was on a small ass desk. It makes determining height near impossible, especially in such low light conditions as that. Surely to goodness you'd even agree with that point. I don't know what you want me to tell you."

"I see this is going nowhere," she said. "What about the girl? Who was the girl your friend was spotted driving from his home to his parent's house? Why was she there? He lives alone, yes?"

"That kid's just a family friend's daughter. She's staying with his mom and pop. He's just a tutor. She's not doing too good in school, so he's just helping her out then driving her back to ensure she gets home safe."

"I see," she scribbled down something on the paper in front of her on the table. "Is there anything else you wish to say before I bring in Mr. Dillon's protégé? Now would be the time. I doubt you'll have the wherewithal to say much during his ministrations."

"If you don't want to believe the truth, I have nothing

else to say," Charlie said. He felt the zip ties dig into his wrists as he twisted in their grip.

"I see." She picked up the phone sitting near the pencil and paper. She pressed a button and brought it to her ear. "Send him in. He's being stubborn."

A few moments later the only door to the room swung open to reveal a physically fit man cracking his knuckles.

"Let me guess, you're the muscle?" Charlie asked.

"I am the one who gets the truth," he said. "You have one last chance before the pain starts."

"Do you think I can change reality just because I'm in pain? I can't tell you anything different considering that's what happened."

"He's all yours." The woman got up and slid past the man in the doorway. She disappeared around the corner, leaving only the two men in the room.

"I am George." He rolled his neck in a circle, eliciting a loud crack. "I am Mr. Dillon's second in command."

"Delighted to meet you, Georgie..."

11

The sound of tires screeching in front of his house got Jim's attention. He got up and ran over to the window. He pulled the shades to the side and peeked outside. He saw a body laying face down on his front yard. "What the fuck?" He hurried outside, barely able to catch a glance of the vehicle. He sprinted over to the body and flipped him so he laid on his back. "Charlie? What happened to you?"

Charlie offered no answers seeing as he was unconscious.

Jim hefted him using a fireman's carry and brought him inside. He carefully lowered him to the couch. "What did they do to you?" Jim asked. "Why would they?"

Words from earlier in the night echoed in his mind. *Your partner Charlie has been escorted to another site for his questioning.* "Questioning? This looks more like a beat down." Evidence of dark bruises were all over Charlie, ranging from his face all the way down to his legs. "You sons of bitches," Jim said with barely restrained rage.

"Mm," Charlie mumbled as he came out of his stupor. "Where am I?"

"You're at my house," Jim said. "You're alright now."

"The hell I am." Charlie closed his eyes. "I hurt all over."

"I imagine so," Jim said. "You're bruised all over. Why did they do this to you?"

"I told them what happened repeatedly. I don't think they believed me. How did it go with Dillon? I assume you two had a chat like mine."

"He didn't work me over anywhere near this bad," Jim got up and jogged to the kitchen. "I'll get you an ice pack." He raised his voice loud enough to be heard from the kitchen. "He did nearly choke me out though. Who did this to you?"

"Dillon's protégé is how he introduced himself. The man didn't seem all that bright, but he knows how to apply pain. I'll give him that." He saw Jim enter the room again.

"I assume you told them the truth?" Jim said, handing over the ice pack.

"Obviously, you don't lie to these guys." Charlie took the pack and pressed it against his ribs. "You know they're going to talk to your parents, right?"

"I assume as much," Jim said. "So long as they don't hurt them, that's perfectly fine. Maybe once they keep hearing the truth, they'll believe us."

The webcam of Jim's open laptop on the coffee table had its light on for this whole conversation. The red light indicated it was active.

"They're just doing their due diligence is all," Charlie said.

"Is that what you call battering your own agents?" Jim said. "Especially when we just got a major win - it's baffling to me."

"For some reason they think we're lying," Charlie said

with a groan. "I guess I shouldn't have gone in there with you after all, buddy."

"They'll get over it." Jim sat down opposite Charlie on his favorite chair. He reached forward and grabbed his laptop on the table between them. "Oh, hello there." He saw the light on the camera on. "Are you enjoying the show, Dillon?"

The light turned off at the mention of his name.

"Alright then," Jim said. "I guess he didn't want to hear anymore."

"We're going to be under watch until they get tired and leave," Charlie said. "We'd best get comfortable with that reality."

"Right," Jim said. "Let me check my email and see if they sent anything else. I do have a message here."

"Share it with the class, would you?"

"You are under investigation. You are to fully cooperate with Mr. Dillon and his second in command, George. Failing to do so will constitute guilt and will be dealt with in accordance with our values."

"That's fancy talk for killing us," Charlie said.

"There is more to it," Jim said. "You may still receive assignments at our discretion."

"They're keeping their options open," Charlie said. "You know why they beat the shit out of me, right? It's obvious."

"They're waiting to see if Blind Justice shows up again right afterward," Jim said. "That's why they're liable to get us a job and see."

"That's my best guess."

"You're staying here tonight," Jim said. "You can take the bed upstairs if you want."

"I'll sleep here," Charlie said. "I don't want to try to get up. Georgie boy was thorough if basic in his methods. Blunt force trauma using a wrench does a number on the human body."

At the same time at Dennis and Jill's...

The doorbell rang. Dennis hefted himself out of his chair. "Who in heaven's name is coming by this late?"

A sinking feeling settled in Ashley's stomach. She glanced over toward the front door from her position at the kitchen table. The papers in front of her were forgotten as soon as she watched Dennis open the door.

A man wearing a police uniform towered over Dennis. "Hello, Mr. Benning," he said. "I am sorry to disturb you on this fine night." He looked over Dennis's shoulder and saw Ashley looking at him.

"What do you want, Mr.?"

"Call me Dillon."

"What do you want, Mr. Dillon? I think you may have the wrong house."

"This is the Benning household, yes?" Dillon asked.

"It sure is. You have yet to explain why you're here though." Dennis eyed the man head to toe. "Do I know you from the force? Were you a new guy when I quit or something?"

"Oh, my apologies, sir," Dillon said. He pulled out a suitably convincing police badge and flashed it before pocketing it again. "We at the station have been dealing with this Masked Justice stupidity recently. We're making rounds around the neighborhood, seeing if anybody has seen anything? We're paying special attention to households with children in it, due to the nature of the case. I see you have a minor in the house."

"We're housing her, yes. She's a friend of the family's kid.

What about it?" Dennis did not back down from the staring war. "You must have gotten the short end of the stick to be driving around knocking on doors at this time of night, sir. My condolences for that, but we were just preparing to settle in for the night if you don't mind."

Ashley tried to look like she was doing homework, occasionally stealing glances at the man in the doorway.

"How long is she staying here, if you don't mind my asking?"

"Until her father comes back and gets her. He wanted her to finish high school here. We're her guardians for the moment."

"He's such a nice man," Jill came up behind her husband, a warm smile on her face. "He's a bit of a softie, but he's a good father."

"I see," Dillon fished into his jeans' pocket and handed Dennis a small card. "Here's my number if you see anything out of the ordinary. Be careful, Mr. Benning. There's a pair of crazies going after people they perceive as criminals. Take care."

"You don't have to tell me twice." Dennis tapped the holster at his side, displaying the semi-automatic pistol on his person. "No vigilante is taking us out."

"You all have a nice night," Dillon said. "I'll take my leave now." He turned around and walked back to the unfamiliar vehicle parked outside.

Dennis shut the door with a grunt. "That was odd."

"What was sweetheart?" Jill asked. "He seemed nice enough - maybe a little odd."

"That is not police procedure in this kind of case, and that badge he flashed me was suspicious."

I know who that was and why he was asking about me, Ashley thought. She kept writing on the worksheet in front of her, adding to the already numerous lines of the essay question answer.

"I'm going to call Frank tomorrow morning and see if he checks out. There was something off about him."

"Surely it's not worth bothering the men, honey."

"Impersonating an officer is a crime, Jill sweety." Dennis turned around and gave her a hug. "I'm just doing my civilian duty in reporting suspicious behavior is all."

Ashley filed away the paper and put the folder into her backpack beside her chair on the floor. "I'm done. I'm going to head upstairs and lay down. Who was that guy anyway? He's here awful late."

"I don't know," Dennis said. "I'll figure that out tomorrow. Now don't worry about him and go get some rest. You have school tomorrow. What time did our son make you go to bed?"

"Eleven."

"I see he's lenient," Dennis said. "While you're here, you'll be in bed by ten. Is that clear?"

"Crystal. It's your house, it's your rules."

"Honey, she's our guest, not our child. We should allow her to go to bed at eleven if that's what she's used to," Jill said, her voice mixed with honey. "Don't you agree?"

"I suppose so," Dennis said. He turned back to the door. "Something is not right here."

"You just need some sleep." Jill patted his back. "Why don't you head on to bed? I'll join you in a few minutes."

"Alright then, just let me set the alarm first," Dennis said.

Ashley watched his movements with rapt attention. Her eyes were glued to the numbers.

He moved to the nearby wall that had a keypad and a few different green lights. He punched in the code with an assortment of beeps accompanying the action. "There, it's set. Now don't go outside. You'll set it off."

"You have an alarm system? Wow, Jim doesn't."

"He's a little absentminded, but don't worry. It'll give us advanced warning if Masked Justice decides to bust in here. You'll be safe," Dennis said. "Alrighty then. Good night, girls." He climbed up the stairs slowly but surely.

"Did you catch the alarm code, dear?" Jill asked.

"I did see it, yes. Sorry."

"I'm not mad. If you're going to be living here, you should know, just in case." She pulled her into a hug. "You are honest. I like that." She took a step back and led Ashley up the stairs. "Now let's show you to Jim's old room. I already made the bed for you. There's an alarm clock if you need it as well. We wouldn't want you to be late to school after all." She showed her to an already open room. "Have a good night now." She continued down the hall and entered a farther door.

Ashley investigated the room and threw her bags on the floor nearby. "I may as well make myself at home."

12

"It was the damnedest thing I'd ever seen, Son," Dennis said. He motioned with his hands. "This was a man that had to be nigh seven feet tall. He gave me the creeps. I know he wasn't a damned policeman. You want to know how I know?"

"How?"

"I called a friend on the force. I asked him. I said, 'Tom, is the department sending unis around asking about Masked Justice?' He said no. They're doing their investigation a different way. I didn't ask any more due to security. I know who that was last night though. It wasn't Dillon or whatever he claimed his name was."

"How could you know that, Dad? Did you have them run a background check on him or something?"

"No one is going to use their real name like that. Think about it. It's an alias. Of course he'd have an alias. You know why? That was Masked Justice last night. I'd bet almost anything. It all makes sense when you analyze it."

"You really think Masked Justice just walked right up to your house?" Jim asked. "Why would he do such a thing?"

"He was looking for kids in suspicious houses. He noticed Ashley behind me in our meeting. He immediately brought her up. He thought maybe we were sickos. Think about it, Son. Your old man knows what he's talking about."

"I hope you're wrong, Dad," Jim said. He sat across the kitchen table from his father. He lifted a mug to his mouth and gulped the contents down. "I don't want you tangling with him. He's dangerous, even trained as you are."

"You should never underestimate another. I'm glad I taught you well. Still, a gun beats a sword any day."

"Unless you let him get close. How quick are you on your feet, old man?"

"He couldn't get the jump on me, boy," Dennis unholstered his weapon, flipped the safety off, and aimed it ahead of him in one swift motion. "I still train every day just in case I have to defend your mother, God forbid."

"Shit," Jim said.

"I like the kid, but you need to find another place to house her. Send her to her father. She'll have to adjust, but she'll be fine. Sometimes you need to be the bad guy if you want to be a good caretaker."

"What about Cynthia?" Jill asked from a nearby recliner.

"What about her?" Jim asked.

"She could maybe stay there," Jill said. "All you'd have to do is call and ask her. Masked Justice isn't going to mess with her when he thinks she's here with us. Even if he does, no one is going to suspect foul play with a young woman and a teenage girl. She'll be safe there."

"Call her, Son," Dennis said. "You're the ones who were making googly eyes at each other just a couple weeks ago. Don't think your mother didn't notice. She talked my ear off about how you two looked at each other. I don't understand what your little fight was about, but you need to move past it. Girls like her only come along once in your life, and right now you're squandering it."

"Mom, Dad, it's a little more complicated than you're giving it credit for. There's a bit more to it than me being immature."

"You've always been like this ever since you were a kid," Dennis said. "You never were good at saying sorry to her, were you? Have you at least apologized?"

"Yes, Dad, I have," Jim said. "I'm telling you she'd be more open to it if someone else asked though. She's petty at times. I know you and Mom never saw it, but she's just as bad as you make me out to be."

"One day you'll emotionally grow up." Dennis sighed, pulling his phone out of his pocket. "I'm not sure what age that will be, but fine. I can't believe you're making your old man call your friend for you." He dialed her number. "Yeah, hello Cynthia. How are you doing?"

"You should be embarrassed," Jill said, quiet enough to not be heard over the line. "Making your father call her is sad."

Jim watched as his father engaged in small talk with his ex-flame with a roll of his eyes.

"Yeah, here's the thing. Do you mind babysitting just for a night or two." There was a pause. "You're sure? Alright then." Dennis looked over at his side with a smile. "I'll send Jim over with her. Thank you so much. I'll see you around. Thanks for helping the kid out. She's a nice girl. She won't be a bother. Okay, he'll be over soon." He hung up and pocketed the device. "She got home an hour or two ago. She should be upstairs in your room. You should go get her. You're welcome by the way."

"Yeah, thanks for arranging a meeting so I can be bitched at. I appreciate that. That's all she'll do."

"Sometimes you have to take it and move on."

Jim moved to the stairwell and looked back to his father. "That doesn't sound right. That just sounds like domestic abuse with more steps."

"It never does, but sometimes it's what has to be done for an adult relationship to function. Just be honest and kind. That's all your mother and I ever taught you," Dennis said, giving his son a thumbs up. "Don't make us look bad. Show her you know how to treat a lady again. She'll be out of this tizzy she's in in a jiffy."

"Whatever you say, Dad." Jim jogged up the stairs and came face to face with his old room's door. He reached up and knocked.

"Come in," Ashley could be heard inside.

Jim opened the door to see Ashley sitting at the desk in the corner of the room. A book was splayed out open on one side. Her hand flicked the pencil all around as her other hand tapped the desk below. She turned around and her face lit up. "Look who it is. Am I coming home already?"

"I wish that were the case." Jim closed the door behind him and lowered his voice. He approached her and sat on the edge of the desk with crossed arms. "That enforcer dude came to this house last night I hear."

"I saw his face," Ashley said, leaning toward him, lowering her voice to match his. "He was a big muscle-bound jerk. He had this fake nice persona you could see right through."

"Anyway, Dad thinks it's safer if you move to Cynthia's place. Personally, I was against it; but he's convinced that Dillon is Masked Justice. He doesn't want you in danger."

"He thinks that big guy's Masked Justice?" Ashley looked confused, her brow furrowing. "I guess I can see how he could think that. It'd make logical sense from his perspective." She looked up at him and spoke in a whiny tone. "Do I have to stay with Cynthia? I don't think she likes me very much."

"Why would you possibly think that?" Jim asked. "You only met her the one time, didn't you?"

"She was snippy."

"I'm just going to stop you there and tell you now, she's very nice. You caught her at quite possibly the lowest point of her life that night. Give her another chance, for me?" Jim asked, reaching his hand out toward her.

Ashley took it and shook. "Fine, only because you asked though."

"I knew you could be nice when you wanted,"

"Fuck off."

"Unfortunately," Jim looked around the cramped space. "You'll have to say goodbye to living in my old room. Her house is much nicer, trust me. You'll have a full-sized room and everything. It probably won't smell like this."

"I don't mind it, but fine. I can stay with her. Just promise me I won't miss anything. You know what I mean." She hopped up, stuffed the school material in it, and grabbed the bag. "I never did unpack, so this is easy."

"We'll talk about your condition in the car over. There're some things you should know," Jim said. "Come on then. God, this will be awkward." He threw open the door and led her down the stairs. "You're sure you got everything?"

"I'm sure," Ashley said.

"We're sorry, dear. We just don't want you to be near that lunatic. That Masked Justice might come back tonight," Jill said, near the bottom of the stairs. "It wouldn't be safe here, or we'd love to have you stay."

"It's better to be safe than sorry," Ashley said. "That guy last night was scary. Something about him was off."

"You're not wrong," Dennis said, standing beside his wife. His arm snuck around his wife's side and pulled her close. "I've been face to face with psychopaths, sociopaths, and every other term the shrinks use. That man was the first time I'd ever truly felt fear in my life while simply talking to someone. There was a deep anger, violence maybe, hidden deep behind his eyes. He was just sizing me up it felt like."

"Do try and make up with Cynthia, dear. I hate to see you two waste this opportunity," Jill said.

"Thanks for the advice, Mom." Jim made for the door in all haste. "We're leaving. Love you."

"Be careful out there." Dennis walked over to the door and watched the pair head toward his son's car. "He's in a hurry to get out of here," he said just loud enough to be heard by his wife.

"Maybe he's in a rush to make up with her," Jill said.

"It might be." Dennis watched them enter the car and back out onto the road. "I think he just wants to keep the girl safe. He doesn't want her near here with that maniac creeping around, and I don't blame him." He closed the door and turned around. "Let me set this alarm," he said as he moved toward the control panel. "Then we'll be good and safe."

Meanwhile in Jim's car...

"I have some bad news," Jim said. He kept his eyes on the road.

"More?"

"Not so much bad news, but you'll just hate it," Jim said.

"Go ahead and say it. I have an inkling as to what it is anyway." Ashley reached forward and turned on the air conditioner. Cold air flooded into the cabin.

"We're going to have a job tonight, but you can't come along with us. They have to think Blind Justice is Charlie. Think of it as a short vacation to focus on your studies."

"If it's just a temporary thing, then I'm fine with it." Ashley puffed out her cheeks. "It doesn't mean I have to like it though. I'd rather just be home if I could."

"I'd rather you be home too," Jim said. "That's not the cards we were dealt this time though. Don't worry, this is just until the Republic isn't curious. They're not going to leave one of their top agents out here for too long."

"Are you sure?"

"Honestly?" Jim gave a momentary look over toward his passenger. "I don't know. Charlie has been in the group longer than I have. What I do know is things will be back to normal soon. Then we can focus more on your training. Hell, I need to get better with the sword myself. We both," he took his right hand off the wheel and gestured toward himself and Ashley, "need to get stronger, both in our personal lives as well as physically."

"Speaking of which," Ashley said, snapping her fingers, "the school does have a cheerleading squad."

"I'm glad you reconsidered joining."

"Oh, I'm not joining them." Ashley let a genuine laugh loose. "I was going to say that there's a volleyball team. I was thinking of trying out for it."

"There's nothing but advantages to balance, agility, and speed," Jim said. "It's not my style, but I can see the appeal. Do you think you could handle such intense physical training? I know they're rigorous."

"I'm always up for a challenge. Especially if you think it'd be useful on future jobs."

"I do," Jim said as the pair settled into a comfortable

silence. "You know, we haven't had a lot of time to talk recently. Are you really okay?"

"What do you mean?"

Jim took a hand off the wheel to rub his stubble laden chin. "I'll be blunt since I was never good at these things."

"Go for it," Ashley said.

"Did I ever tell you about my first kill?" Jim asked.

"I don't think so."

"I had lured a guy over to my house, pretending to be a young girl." Jim slowed the car to a stop at the stop sign. He saw in his side-view mirror that a car had pulled out, turned, and was following them. "I videotaped the encounter, and my legions of social media followers made his life a living hell."

"What did he do?" Ashley asked, visibly interested. Her voice was nonchalant all the while.

"He came back the very next night. Cynthia was there helping me move in and unpack. She received a mysterious text saying get out of there."

"Who sent it?"

"We found out later it was Charlie. Now be quiet. I'd like to finish before we get there. Anyway, he busted down my front door and pulled out a knife. I was armed with my pistol, so when he charged I ended the threat to my life."

"I appreciate you telling me this and all, but why are you recalling this?"

"You killed a man in his bed while he was asleep. Now my first time was self-defense. It broke me inside. I felt like the scum of the Earth. I figured yours might be worse. I don't know. I'm not your dad - hell I'm not even legally your guardian yet. I just wanted you to know you have someone you can talk to. I'm here anytime, alright? Are you okay mentally with having ended a person's life?"

Ashley looked down at her lap for a few moments. "I don't know. It didn't feel like I thought it would. I thought it would be freeing to finally end someone like my abuser. I feel kind of empty I guess? My parents sold me off, I was violated for months by some demon in human skin, and then I'm living with the guy who got me out. I'm still trying to process this whole thing."

"I didn't even consider that," Jim said. "Christ, I should have never had you follow along."

"I'm not saying I'm like depressed or anything," Ashley said. "I have one constant in my life right now. That's me, with all due respect. I make my own choices. You're probably the next closest."

"Then I hope you won't bottle everything up inside. I've done it. The results are not pretty. Now," he looked away and forced a cough, "I think we're done with the overly mushy crap. I have to warn you about what you're about to witness."

"What the hell are you going on about? I've met the woman before. It wasn't that long ago in fact."

"You don't understand," Jim said. "I almost royally screwed her entire life plan up. She's pissed at me. I deserve everything I'm going to get. I hope you enjoy the show."

"Were you two together?"

"Almost," Jim said. "I just screwed it up with an honest mistake."

"What does that mean? What did you do?" Ashley asked. She reached over and gave a punch to his arm. "Fine, be that way."

Jim didn't speak the rest of the car ride as Ashley carried the lion's share of the conversation.

13

"I see you still haven't grown up," Cynthia exited her front door as Jim exited his car along with Ashley. "You had to get daddy to call and ask for a favor. Really?"

"You'd have said no if I'd asked," Jim said.

"You have no way of knowing that."

"I know you." Jim brushed past her and continued to the doorframe before looking over his shoulder. "I'd say better than anyone in fact."

"At one point you did," Cynthia said. She looked back toward his car. "Hey, kid." She motioned toward her house with her head. "Let's get you inside and get you set up. You're still in high school, yeah?"

"Yeah," Ashley said, approaching the young woman.

Cynthia showed her inside. "Come on then. I have some questions before your caretaker vanishes into the ether again." She closed the door and locked it behind her.

"Why did you lock the door?" Jim asked.

"That would probably be because I'm about to lose my shit," Cynthia's voice was sugary sweet, but the dangerous smile betrayed her. "Do you think I'm an idiot?"

Ashley looked over to Jim but stayed silent, awaiting his answer.

"No," Jim said. "I'd never say that about you."

"Then why are you treating me like one? I know you're Masked Justice." She pointed at Jim. "I am betting you're Blind Justice." She moved her finger to point at Ashley. "Do you want to tell me what kind of shit I'm involving myself with here, or should I just kick her out now and take the flak from your parents? I won't be involved with murder again."

"Hey, that's rude," Ashley said. "You have no evid-"

"Shh," Cynthia shushed her. "Be quiet. I remember you. You were the girl he saved that night. I saw that look in your eyes. I saw wander, relief, but above all, you were excited. Are you going to tell me you're not Blind Justice? Are you really going to insult my intelligence? As for you..." She turned her attention back to Jim. "You have a lot of guts for getting me involved again. I assume it was for a good reason, considering I told you to leave me out of your stupid decisions."

"Aren't you a regular ray of sunshine?" Ashley asked.

"You're right. There is a reason we're here," Jim said. "Do you really want to know what it is?"

"If I'm going to house your little murderer here? Yes, I want to know the kind of shit I'm welcoming into my house. Why did you have her staying with your parents and not with you? There's something else at play here."

"You never told me she was so suspicious," Ashley said.

Cynthia held a lone index finger up in Ashley's direction. "Be quiet."

"She's rude too."

"Look," Jim said. "A Republic enforcer of sorts is in town and he's investigating me."

"I think I can put it together from there. You don't want

to be seen housing a sixteen-year-old minor. What? Are you afraid they'll kill you?"

"It's a possibility. Personally, I'd rather just face the music if it was just me; but Charlie's involved too, and I can't risk his life. It'd be like if it was you."

"Do not even try to pull on my heartstrings. It's not going to work. Wait, why would Charlie be involved? Did you get him involved too? God, you just ruin everyone's life, huh? It wasn't enough he got beaten to near death." She turned to Ashley. "You'd best distance yourself from him. He screws everyone else over in his childish little quest. You're just caught up in the heat of youth. When you grow up, if you're not in prison, you'll regret allying with him."

"Look," Jim said. "I never told you because you ignored me ever since, but Charlie's not who you think he is."

"What the hell does that mean? He's been our friend since grade school." Cynthia planted her hands on her hips. "Don't lie to suit yourself."

"Do you remember the night when you went with me to that meeting?"

"The one where the guy tied me up? How could I forget? I thought they were going to kill me."

"That was Charlie that tied you up. He told me himself. He was watching us the whole time that assassin was coming for us. He was the one scouting me to join the Republic. He had orders to harm you that night, but he disobeyed those and just tied you up."

"Bullshit," Cynthia said. "There's no way Charlie's involved in all that nonsense. He's just a partygoer. He gets high, stoned, and lives life chasing the next high. There's no way he's a part of that organization."

"He's not lying," Ashley said, dropping one of the bags. "All he's asking is to let me stay for like a night or two. There will be no death, no murders, or anything of the like. Is that so hard to believe?"

"Nothing is ever so simple with him." Cynthia didn't take her eyes off Jim.

"Look, I already apologized for what happened before. We both thought you might be targeted; I was just trying to keep us all alive."

"Yes, that is the heroic tale you tell yourself. You forgot the part where you go around murdering people at night. Let's not forget that time you accidentally killed an innocent guard."

"I got those kids out of there," Jim pointed at her, his voice firm. "That's what matters."

"A man's life was ended because you wanted to play hero, and you still don't understand how it's your fault. God, he had a wife and kids. Did you know that? You took a kid's father away, and you don't seem to care."

Jim looked down at the ground and away.

"That's not fair," Ashley stomped on the floor. "He also killed the serial killer guard who was the evil guard. When he got there, she was already killing some young man. It was a hell of a spectacle. There was blood everywhere when she was done with him. My point is this. You two knew that there were kids being held like cattle. In some cases, the ends do justify the means. I bet if that man knew what he was guarding, he wouldn't have blamed him."

"That's a lot of assumptions," Cynthia said. "Assuming you're telling the truth, that doesn't excuse it. That's like saying, well I killed the murderer, but I accidentally killed an innocent to do it. It doesn't make it right. It just means you're sloppy and should leave it to the professionals. A fact which, if you'll remember," she approached Jim "I told you to do."

"Will you watch her or not? If not, I'll probably be killed tonight, straight up." He angled his vision up to look her in the eyes. He looked deflated along with his tired voice. "Along with Charlie. That's your choice."

"You can't make me choose to house a murderer or you both die? That's not fair!" Cynthia's voice rose.

"I don't know if you've noticed," Ashley said, "but life isn't fair."

"I don't need to be told that by a bratty teenager," Cynthia said. "I know that all too well. Let me get this horse shit straight." She gestured toward Ashley. "I have to watch your little apprentice, or both you and Charlie will be killed tonight?"

"That's the long and short of it."

"Why on God's blue earth would they kill you? You work for them, yes?"

"That's precisely why," Jim said. "They don't take kindly to their agents living with underage minors they aren't related to. You can imagine why."

"You lay with dogs, you get fleas. Have you never heard that saying before?" Cynthia asked. "You made your bed, now you lie in it."

"Fine," Jim said in a calm voice. "Come on then, Ashley. I don't want to force anything. You're coming back home."

"You can't just send him out to die," Ashley walked over and kicked Cynthia in the shin.

Cynthia hopped on her good leg. "Fucking hell. That hurt."

"You deserve it for acting like this. That man there isn't perfect," Ashley said. "That doesn't mean because you're pissed you get to turn your back on him, unless you never cared for him in the first place."

"I will not aid and abet a murderer again."

"It would be a shame if that connection went public, now wouldn't it?" Ashley asked. "The young aspiring lawyer being caught in bed with the newest vigilante could be bad, couldn't it?"

"Ashley, don't."

"You little cunt," Cynthia said. "I have worked harder than you'll ever know. My bar exam is coming up, and I will not have it ruined by a little groupie like you."

"Groupie?" Ashley stood toe to toe with Cynthia. "You little vindictive bitch. You won't help out your childhood friend, and you're going to stand there and let him die? You're a terrible person."

"That's enough!" Jim yelled. He grabbed Ashley's arms and pulled her away from Cynthia. "Both of you, that's enough. She doesn't have to. I'll find some way to deal with this. I always do. I don't want you two fighting."

Cynthia looked at the pair. She saw Jim smile and almost instantly saw Ashley's demeanor calm down. She brought both hands up and massaged the sides of her head. "You two are insufferable. Not to mention you're idiots."

"Hey," Ashley was cut off as Jim covered her mouth.

"But," Cynthia said, "as stupid as the both of you are, I can tell you are telling the truth. Fine, she can stay. Nothing had better happen though, or I'm holding you responsible." Her eyes drilled into Jim. "I don't want assassins chasing my ass down while I study for the bar exam."

"That won't happen," Ashley said.

"Even if it did, she'd be here for your protection."

Cynthia looked down at the shorter girl and back to Jim. "I don't think she could do much against an assassin. No offense, girl."

Jim eyed Cynthia up and down. "You still work out I see."

"Now is not the time for hitting on me."

"What? No. I just came up with a good idea."

Ashley let a high-pitched whining noise escape. "Oh no, don't do this."

"What are you proposing, and why are you smiling like an evil villain?" She switched her focus from Jim's smirk to Ashley's frown. "Why does my working out matter so much to either one of you?"

"It was a good opportunity to flirt for one," Jim said, eliciting a roll of Cynthia's eyes. "As for the actual reason -." He patted Ashley's shoulder. "I've had her adopt a new workout regimen. I figure you could maybe teach her a few things. You know, make sure she does the workouts."

"That would be my pleasure," Cynthia said. To her credit, she mostly hid the smile on her face. "I'll keep her in shape while she's here."

"That's perfect." Jim patted Ashley's shoulder. "See? She can be nice when she wants to be."

"I object to that," Cynthia said. "I'm always nice to people who deserve it."

"That's fair," Jim said, stepping around Ashley and coming face to face with Cynthia. "God knows that's not me nowadays."

"What are you doing?" Cynthia took a step back.

Jim stopped a few feet away from her, not daring to broach her personal space any more than this. "I just wanted to thank you is all. Can't an old friend do at least that?"

"You can thank me from a distance." She looked away, trying desperately to hide the flush permeating her cheeks.

"Fine," Jim took a few steps back, coming shoulder to shoulder with Ashley. "Thank you for this. I just have one last thing to ask, and I know you're going to love it."

"Here we go," Ashley said, her voice soaked in sarcasm.

"I need you to help me with a deception of sorts."

"I am not lying for you. Not again," Cynthia said, regaining her composure. "Think again, Buster."

"It's nothing quite so dramatic," Jim said. "Okay," he shrugged, "maybe it is."

"Spit it out so I can say no already," Cynthia said. She shifted her weight. "You're lucky I'm even doing this in the first place. I knew you were greedy, but I had no idea apparently."

"I'm being followed right now I bet. I think I saw them on the way over here," Jim said. He pointed toward the door. "I'm betting as soon as I step foot out that door, Dillon will have eyes on me. He just saw me bring a minor, and I've been here a little while now."

"Get to the point already, killer," Cynthia said, tapping her foot on the floor.

"I guess I'll come right out and say it." Jim stepped forward toward her again. "I need you to kiss me goodbye when I step foot out that door."

"Okay, now I know you're fucking around," Cynthia said. "There's no way you think I'd do that."

"What's a little kiss between old friends if it keeps one of us breathing for another day?" Jim asked. "You're free to say no, but it would really help me out here."

Cynthia glanced over to see Ashley's glaring at Jim. She couldn't help as a smirk appeared. "Fine, I'll help you out."

"What?" Ashley asked.

"Seriously?" Jim asked. "I never expected you to say yes."

"You realize this is only a one-time thing," Cynthia said. "I'm still beyond pissed at you. That doesn't mean I want you dead." She strode forward in her shorts and t-shirt toward Jim and grabbed his hand. "Let's see you off then."

"Hey, wait a minute." Ashley tried to separate the two but found their grip iron tight.

Cynthia opened the front door and stepped outside with Jim a few paces. She released his hand. "Come back soon," she said in her best seductive voice. She got on her tip toes and planted a full-on kiss on Jim's lips. She wrapped her arms behind Jim's head. She backed off and winked at him. She turned around before closing the door. She saw Ashley glaring at her. "It was just an act, sweetheart. Besides, you're too young for him."

"The fact you can kiss someone as part of an act speaks more than anything," Ashley said. "Now where is my room?"

"Aren't you pushy?" Cynthia asked. She walked past the young girl. "I'll show you. Follow me..."

Later that night...

"Is studying all you do?" Ashley asked from across the room. "You've been glued to that laptop for three hours now."

"I don't know if you realize, but becoming a lawyer isn't exactly easy," Cynthia said, her face illuminated by the artificial light of the monitor. "It's not like I can just do my homework and call it a day."

"You don't like me very much, do you?" Ashley asked. "Don't lie. I can tell."

"It's not that I dislike you," Cynthia spared a look over to the other couch. "I just don't want to be involved with the craziness that Jim starts. I've lived that life, and I don't wish to go back to it. You're young, so you don't get that yet."

"You know what I do get though?" Ashley asked before answering her own question. "He's trying his best to help the kids like me. The type that can't fight back. The ones who get taken advantage of by evil people. That's what he's doing."

"I'm going to stop your little manifesto in its tracks and offer a rebuttal," Cynthia said, still typing away. "He has no right to kill people as he pleases. Full stop."

"No, not full stop," Ashley said. "Without his efforts, there would be over ten kids that would still be abused. Don't they matter? Doesn't their happiness merit some creative bending of the rules?"

"I can see we're not going to agree, so let's move on."

Ashley lifted her legs and now took up the whole couch. "Why were you even there that night he found me anyway? You seem to hate this whole thing we're doing. I don't remember you being particularly nice."

"That was a culmination of a great many things. It was also after I told him I was through with him. Neither of us were at our best that night." Cynthia looked up into the dim room, only illuminated by the television and the laptop.

"How did you even get involved if you're this strict anyway? I can't see how you ever helped him," Ashley asked.

"You do not know subtlety I see," Cynthia said with a mirthful laugh. "Neither does he. It wasn't like I had much of a choice."

"I don't get it."

"I mean…" Cynthia said with a loud exhale. She moved the laptop to the table in front of her. "He told me some assassin was coming after me. He'd gotten some intel that said that I might be targeted. I didn't want to die, and he was the only person who knew what was happening. So, I clung on."

"An assassin? Who would send an assassin?"

"A local law firm. They were known to hire some, shall we say, less than savory folks. They targeted kids if you get my meaning. Jim had started his descent into madness and killed a few of them. It was feasible such a law firm could hire a hitman, and that they might I thought. I couldn't go to the police seeing as they'd never believe me, and there I'd be."

"I get it so far," Ashley said. "That on top of learning about your best friend being a killer probably had you in a daze."

"That fits it perfectly," Cynthia said. "That's how I got dragged into his blood-filled life full of death. I was hoping I'd be rid of it, but here you are. Maybe I was just fooling myself."

"So, you know of his hobby and don't report it. That's illegal, yes?"

"You better believe it," Cynthia said. "That's not the worst part."

"You can't stop there."

"Before I tell you, tell me something. Were you the one who killed that man and called herself Silent Justice?"

"I am," Ashley said. "That guy you're talking about was touching my friend from school. I wanted to do it myself. He'd been doing it for over a year. You tell me it was a bad thing? I don't believe you. I'm ashamed I didn't do it sooner."

"That's not something to be proud of," Cynthia shook her head. "My point for asking was so I could tell you this. We eventually caught that assassin."

"How could you manage that? They must have been incompetent."

"I was used as a distraction along with some homeless guy. We got him knocked out with a mixture of drugs and dragged him right down in the basement." She pointed below the pair toward the floor. "He was right down there. We took him out to a local forest and dug a grave."

"That's fucking hardcore right there. You went with him to bury a body?"

"I did," Cynthia said. Her voice was glum. "I was such an idiot. I tried to make light of what we were doing in whatever way I could. I didn't want to face the reality of what I was doing. We were killing the man and burying him six feet under on publicly owned property. It was my idea on leaving the sedative-soaked cloth over his face the entire time he was transported. He probably died mid transport if I had to guess. I never bothered to check." Her voice broke. "I wanted to pretend it never happened."

"The guy was there to kill you!" Ashley said. "Why do you feel so bad? He'd ended dozens of lives before. His ticket was due, and you two just happened to be the ones who punched it."

Cynthia leaned forward, her arms on her knees. She looked down into the engulfing darkness of the shadows on the floor. "I killed a man. That's the point."

"You defended your friend and yourself. That's how I see it. Is that why you've been treating him like shit?"

"He's been avoiding me, and I haven't been seeking him out. Truthfully, I hate knowing who and what he is. I'm nearly a lawyer. Do you get it? If I didn't know, at least I'd live in blissful ignorance."

"Talk about a childish world view. Life's not perfect." Ashley got up and walked over to the other couch. She sat down across from the laptop. "Just because there are flaws doesn't mean we can ignore reality. We have to face it and make our decisions. That's what I've learned the past few weeks."

"I am not getting life advice from you," Cynthia said.

"I've also learned to not turn your back on those you love. My parents sold me into slavery," Ashley said. "Don't squander your friendship. That's my honest advice, girl to girl."

"Oh, just friendship is it?" Cynthia asked. She had a playful smirk. "I saw those looks earlier. You're just trying to get me to friendzone him. I know how your mind works." She tapped the side of her head with a finger.

"That's the last time I give you advice. Did anyone ever tell you you're worse than him?"

"Not a one."

"I suppose you do need acting skills as a lawyer. You must have been practicing those since you were a kid with how they talk about you."

"I'm just that good."

14

"Are you good?" Jim asked, already with the masks on. He looked over at Charlie in the passenger seat fumbling with his own wardrobe malfunction. He eventually got it and had the cloth pulled over his nose. The moonlight above was the only light in the cabin.

"It's just bruises. I'm fine." He gripped the blade sitting in his lap. "Pain is only weakness leaving the body."

"Is that what that is?" Jim asked. "We know our target, and we know he's guilty; so the only thing left is to go deal some justice."

"I couldn't have said it better myself. There's just one thing before we go in. We don't know if there's anybody else in the house." Charlie turned himself around in his seat with a grunt and grabbed the laptop in the back seat. He opened it, logged in, and turned the screen so Jim could see. "There are two phone signals in the house. Now, he could have two cell phones. That's smart with his proclivities, but we can't ignore the possibility of something like last job. We need to be smart and thorough."

"Agreed," Jim said. "I'll take lead - you follow. I'd rather you not exert yourself when you're in that much pain. Just back me up if something happens."

"I got your back, man," Charlie said with a thumbs up.

Jim reached a hand over, which Charlie met halfway. They bumped fists before each exiting the car in silence. Once they were out of the car the pair dashed toward the house. The small chain link fence did little to obscure their forms from others. The pair continued around the house, finally emerging into the backyard.

A small doghouse sat in the corner of the yard.

Jim's voice was barely above a whisper. "Oh shit,"

"Ignore the dog. Let's get inside already." Charlie pushed Jim forward.

"Fine." Jim turned the corner and spotted the back door barely a dozen feet away. He hurried over and gripped the knob.

"Hurry it up," Charlie said when an audible growl interrupted him. He looked over his shoulder. "Now, get it open now."

Jim quickly threw the door opened and hurried inside. They closed the door and looked out its glass window. A small dog finished crawling out of the doghouse and yawned before looking at them and barking.

"You were scared of that thing?" Jim asked.

"For all I knew it was a bigger breed," Charlie said.

A sudden and large thump from above them interrupted and silenced the pair.

"Was that our guy?" Charlie asked.

"There's only one way to find out." Jim led the pair through the darkened house. Numerous footsteps were heard upstairs as they creeped around. A quiet inhale was all they heard as they approached the stairs. More footfalls accompanied the rapid retreat they were hearing.

"Someone knows we're here," Jim said. He pushed the blade out and unsheathed it with his right hand. "Back me up. We're going up there." He led the way up the stairwell and into a wide corridor.

One door was conspicuously open on the right along with two closed doors on the left side.

Jim pointed right. "Check the open room."

Charlie pushed past him, unsheathing his own sword. He crouched as he got closer to the open doorway. He peeked around the corner and looked back to Jim. "Our target's dead. He's in there with arrows in him."

"Arrows?" Jim asked under his breath. He raised his voice and talked in a deeper tone. "We're not going to hurt you. Is someone in there?"

To their surprise a female voice answered back from just beyond the door Jim was at. "Yes. Who are you?"

"I am Masked Justice," Jim said. "I'm going to open this door, and we're all going to be calm. Please, we don't want to hurt you."

"Okay."

Jim pushed the door open to see a short girl, obviously in high school, standing in the middle of the room. She had a scarf mask pulled up over her nose. She had a bow pulled and aimed in his direction. She abated and pulled the arrow loose from the string. She stuck the projectile into the quiver on her back, secured by what looked like a belt.

"Holy shit," she said. "It really is you." She took a step back, her hands shaking.

"Calm it down, miss," Jim said, sheathing his blade at his side. "I'm not going to hurt you. Wait a second."

"What?" She looked behind him and saw Charlie's masked form behind him. "Is that Blind Justice?"

Jim looked behind him and back to her. "I've heard your voice before."

"No you haven't," the girl said. "Now are you going to let me leave?"

"We don't have any reason to kill you," Jim said. "Why did you kill that man in the other room? What reason could you have?"

"The dude got away with touching kids." She stuck her arm through her bow and carried it on her shoulder. "I looked it up - it's on the public record. He got off on a technicality. Why are you asking? I figured you knew this better than anybody. That's why you're here, right?"

"Fine, we're on the same side here." Jim reached behind him and pushed Charlie out of the way as he backed up. "We have no desire to harm you. I advise you to stop doing this though, kid." Jim was now out in the hallway. "Trust me when I tell you that this is not what you want to be doing with your life. Just look at me."

"You're the inspiration for me being here." She took a few steps forward, stopping a few feet away. "Well, to be more accurate," she pointed behind Jim toward Charlie. "She's the reason, but you're the boss man in the duo from what I gather. So, I suppose I owe you one."

"Just get home safe. Take your bike or however you got here. Don't draw attention if you want to stay free. I hope for your sake you have a hairnet on under that hoodie."

She slipped past him and headed toward the stair well. "It was nice seeing you again. I'll see you two around. Be safe out there," she said and suddenly took off into a sprint down the stairs.

The pair heard the door downstairs open and close quickly after.

"Why can't a damned job ever go to plan with you around?" Charlie asked.

"I don't know. Don't look at me..."

15

Jim and Charlie both had their laptops out and typed at a furious pace. "Who the fuck was she?" Jim asked himself. "I swear I've heard that voice before. She used a bow and was damned good with it to boot. I don't know anyone that fits that description."

"I'm not finding anything either. It's either a new player on the scene or someone who's damned good at staying away from the media." Charlie set his laptop aside with a shake of his head. "This is pointless. We'll never find out who that was with conjecture." A beep from his side got his attention. "Oh, good news for a change. How refreshing is this?"

"What's it say?" Jim asked.

"It says that Dillon is leaving. He's satisfied with what he's seen and is heading home - wherever the hell that is, who cares?" He looked up at Jim. "It looks like you're in the clear if this is correct."

The doorbell interrupted the pair.

Jim climbed out of the chair and walked over to answer the door. His eyes went wide when he saw the behemoth of a man on the other side. "Mr. Dillon?" he asked.

"I trust you both have seen the email we sent? We are satisfied everything here is on the up and up." He looked over to Charlie. "I trust your wounds are healing well? George has always been a bit too gung ho. I'll have to better educate him in knowing when to apply force and when not to. I apologize for that."

"Apology accepted, Mr. Dillon," Charlie said, standing up as quickly as his battered body would allow. He bent over at the waist to punctuate his sincerity.

"I am sorry to have wasted your time. I pray for what was her name? Ashley, I think it was? I pray that Ashley's high school life goes well at your parent's place. Teach her well, Mr. Benning. Do not stray from the path of righteousness, and your life will be fruitful. With that, I bid you both farewell."

"Goodbye," Jim said, giving a small wave to the giant of a man leaving. He closed the door once he'd gotten inside his car and moved to the window overlooking the front yard. "I think Ashley should stay with Cyn for one more night. You know, just to be sure they left."

"That's wise," Charlie said. "They could have my old partner still watching us."

"Oh yeah," Jim said, turning around. "Who was that guy I talked to?"

"I don't know his name. I think it's a man, but I don't know. He wasn't my friend per say. He was a business associate is all. He still operates around here so it's possible."

Jim's ringing cell phone interrupted the pair's conjecture. "Yeah?" he asked, answering the call.

Ray's tired voice greeted him. "Hey, young man. Did you ever go see Edmund?"

"I hadn't got injured, so I hadn't prioritized it yet. No, why?"

"He's in real trouble, Jim. You need to go talk to him and help him get this settled if you're not too busy."

"Fine, I'll go check on him. It's not like I have any job right now anyway. I need to ask you something anyway, just not over the phone. I'll be heading out momentarily. Bye." Jim hung up before Ray had a chance to say bye himself.

"Who was that? As if we don't have enough on our plates now, you decide to do someone a favor it sounded like," Charlie said. "We have no idea who that arrow bitch was last night. That's kind of mission number one right now. You do realize that?"

"Ray might have a clue. He keeps his ears to the pavement. If anyone has an inkling, I bet it's him. Besides, the guy who kept me alive a few weeks ago is in trouble. You know, the backstreet doctor. I owe him I suppose."

"Didn't you pay him well?"

"I did."

"Then you don't owe him shit," Charlie said.

"What's the alternative?" Jim moved to the door. "I sit here and look for last night's interloper on the internet? At least this way I have a chance at new intel."

"For all you know this doctor is in with a loan shark or in debt. You can't be everyone's savior."

"I can try," Jim said before opening the door and slamming it shut. He marched out to his car and climbed inside. As he backed out onto the road, he could see Charlie at the window staring out at him. "Sorry, buddy," he said. "This is something I've got to do. They saved my ass. Now it's time for me to pay it back."

A bit later in a familiar back alley...

Jim climbed out into the dingy alley and spotted the door from all that time ago. "This is the place alright." He meandered over to the door and knocked on it with force three times. "He could be with a patient I suppose."

Within a minute the door swung open. Edmund's normally calculating eyes were marred with dark bags underneath them. "Yeah?" he asked. "Oh," he said, "it's you. Did you get yourself shot or stabbed again?"

"Nothing quite so extraordinary," Jim said. "Do you mind if I come in? I have something important to talk to you about."

"I bet I know what that is." Edmund stepped to the side, allowing Jim entry before shutting it behind him. He turned around and moved to the desk in the corner of the room. "You don't look injured." He sat down and leaned back. "Did Ray send you then?"

"Something like that. He said you were in big trouble and needed help? What's going on? He seemed worried."

"He shouldn't have told you anything," Edmund said. "It's not your business frankly with all due respect. It's my problem. I got myself into it - I can get myself out of it."

"According to Ray, you're in over your head here. There's nothing wrong with getting a helping hand, especially after you've saved my life a few times. What's wrong with paying it back? Look, I don't know the situation, but I'm betting I could help in some way."

"I am not looking to hire a hitman. No offense."

"I'm not for hire, but I get it. Look, I don't have to kill whoever it is. Scare tactics could work. You'd be amazed how frightened people can get if they wake up to someone pointing a blade at them along with a little creative word play for threats."

"You know this from experience?"

Jim sat down across the desk in the allotted seat. "Not so much honestly, but I'd imagine any sane person would be petrified. Now spill it, what's got Ray all in a tizzy?"

Edmund pulled out a drawer from the desk and dug around inside. "If you really want to stick your nose in my business, fine. Who am I to argue? I don't know if you've noticed, but this place isn't exactly on the up and up. I had one gentleman employ my services. He paid for treatment, and everything went smoothly until it didn't."

"Could you be a little more specific?"

"He was from a local street gang." He pulled out a photo with the name 'Manny' scribbled onto the bottom. "This is him."

"Do you keep photos of all your clients?" Jim looked down at the picture and back up to Edmund. "Do I need to be worried?"

"I delete images as soon as that customer leaves, except in cases like this. It's for my own protection you see. So no, I do not have your photo sitting around. I'll be deleting the footage of you coming in as soon as you leave. Don't worry."

Jim reached over the table and took the photo. "This guy looks like the definition of piss ant. What did he do?"

"You know how those hood rat types are. He threw around the weight of his little gang of misfits."

"What did you do to piss this guy off anyway?" Jim asked. "Rather, what did he think you did?"

"He wanted pain pills for free. He was lucky the knife wound he sustained was able to be treated here in the first place. He got loud, obnoxious, and started making veiled death threats. I told Ray about it while having a laugh, and he called you apparently."

"I don't recognize the gang tattoo he's sporting below his eye. What group is he with?" Jim asked.

"I believe they call themselves the Shooting Stars."

"The Shooting Stars?" Jim asked. "That is a unique street gang name."

"They're a bunch of high school dropout rejects. I'm betting one of the leaders of their little squad is a nerd. I don't want them hurt. I don't think the kid will really do anything, but try to explain that to Ray. He's a regular worry-wart. He probably has blood pressure problems if the truth came out."

"I'm pretty sure you could help with that part. I assume you have meds here other than antibiotics?" Jim looked over his shoulder toward the cabinets housing meds. He pointed over his shoulder with his thumb as he turned back around to face Edmund. "I forgot the pain pills, but regardless, my point stands. Help the guy out. Hell, how much do they cost? I'll pay for them myself."

"I don't have access to the things he'd need. I'm only the local sawbones. Technically, I'm not even certified anymore. The pain pills you bought? Those come from a street contact of mine. I test them by getting them lab tested."

"Do you mind if I temporarily keep this?" Jim asked.

"I don't want it. You keep it and destroy it or something," Edmund said. "Just don't hurt the kid too much, alright? I know the old coot's worried," Edmund said. "I just don't think they're going to do anything. Think of it like you're teaching the kid not to make death threats to people. He'll be in prison soon enough acting a fool like that."

"You want me to teach him not to make death threats by scaring him with death threats?"

"It's the way of the world. You're just keeping him from getting turned out inside the pen." Edmund stood up himself and guided Jim back toward the door. "Think of it as a public service of sorts."

"I'm not sure that's how the law would look at it." Jim stopped a few feet away from the door. "I'll go see him. He'll be fine, unless he tries to kill me. All bets are off then. Deal?"

"I wouldn't blame you defending yourself," Edmund said. "We can't have Masked Justice going and getting himself killed, now can we?"

"Are you accusing me of being that menace?"

"I can do basic reasoning. I do watch the news occasionally in this line of work you know." Edmund pointed toward a small twenty-inch television sitting near his desk. "I can't be housing America's most wanted in here. That's bad for business.

The sound of a car door shutting outside came through the nearby door.

"You however seem to be smart and have decent reasoning in how you work. Now get out. I hear a patient just outside." Edmund opened the door for him only to find a man hobbling over to the door.

"Come in, sir. You do have money, yes? I don't do charity work."

"I got your damned money," the man grunted, pulling out his wallet. He handed him the money before looking over at Jim. "Who the fuck are you?"

"Just a patient. You're in good hands," Jim exited the building through the still open door and shut it behind him...

16

"This is what you're focusing on?" Charlie stood behind Jim's recliner and looked down at the monitor in Jim's lap. "You're looking up some gang banger? I might remind you we're not in the murder for hire business. Okay, maybe that's not true, but he doesn't fit our targets."

"I'm not going to go there and kill him," Jim said. "I'm just going to scare him is all."

"You're going to go scare an excitable, likely armed criminal who has no respect for human life? That's stupid. All just to help some back-alley doctor?" Charlie asked. "We have bigger concerns right now."

"No, we don't," Jim said. "Dillon went home. He told us himself. They're not going to keep someone as important as him in this piss-ant town for long. Still, to be safe, I won't be bringing Ashley along." His phone rang in his pocket. "Hold on a second." He answered the phone. "Hello?"

"A little birdie told me your assassin has gone home today," Ashley said over the line.

"You planted a bug here? How much do those even cost anyway?"

He heard her giggle over the line. "In these days? Not much."

"Son of a bitch!" Charlie said, loud enough to be heard over the ongoing call. "That's where it went? I was wondering where my tertiary bug was. She took it?"

"She learned how to use it apparently. Did you teach her?" Jim asked.

"I didn't teach her that much."

"Yes, fine," Jim said. "He's supposedly gone, but it's better to be safe. It's just one more night over there."

"If he's gone, then what's the harm?"

"Are you serious?" Jim asked.

"Say no," Charlie said quietly.

"I heard that," Ashley said. "Come on, I'm bored over here. All she does is do homework and study."

"Isn't that what you're supposed to be doing? That and your daily regimen. Have you been doing the exercise I told you to?"

"I sure have," Ashley said, her pride radiating even through the call. "Every morning, just like you said."

"Put Cynthia on the phone."

"You don't trust me?" Ashley asked.

"I don't trust teenagers in general to tell the truth. I was one a while back if you'll remember. I know your ways. If you did it, then you have no reason to weasel around like you are right now."

"Fine," Ashley said. Audible footsteps were heard over the line. "Hey, he wants to talk to you."

"Me?" Cynthia's faint voice asked. "Who is it?"

"Who do you think it is?"

The sound of shuffling around met his ears briefly before Cynthia's voice was loud and clear. "Jim?"

"Hello, Cyn," Jim said.

"Why did you want to talk to me anyway? Are you interested in how my studies are going?"

"Yes, but that's not why I wanted to talk to you." Jim walked into the kitchen, leaving Charlie in the living room.

"Oh God, is this about the workout routine?"

"Partially. Is she doing it?"

"I've made sure of it myself. I woke her ass up an hour early and even taught her a spot of yoga. It should help her in the long run. Is that all you wanted with me, or can I return to my studies?"

"That wasn't the main reason I wanted to talk with you, Cynthia," Jim said.

"Get on with it already."

Jim sat down at the table. "Can't a guy just want to hear if his friend's alright?"

"You are full of shit."

"I am in fact being serious."

"Then come over to the house, and we'll talk in person. I have something you might want to know about. Did you watch the news today?" Cynthia asked.

"Can't say I have."

"Then I'll see you in a bit. I don't want to talk over the phone about it."

"See you soon." Jim hung up. He walked back into the living room. "Did the news say something today?"

"They reported on that body with the arrows in it I think." Charlie was at the sofa now. "Why are you asking? That's not going to lead to our mysterious interloper."

"Just curious. Cynthia wants me to head over to her place. She has something to tell me. She wouldn't say over the phone. You want to come along?"

"I'd like to rest if you don't mind. Dillon's apprentice

messed me up. It hurts to get up, it hurts to walk, and it even hurts to breathe with all the chest and back bruises."

"Maybe I should take you to Edmund after I fix his problems. He'll get you fixed up."

"They're just bruises. We'd be paying for peace of mind and that's it. Bruises are not especially dangerous. Besides, just because you trust your little unlicensed doctor, doesn't mean I do. If I was truly afraid, I'd go to a regular doctor. At least I'd know they're qualified."

"Alright then." Jim checked his pockets to find a pleasant jingling. "I'm off then. Feel better, man."

Somewhere nearby in a car...

"He's moving," Dillon said from the back seat. "He may be one of ours, but the dumbass didn't even check his car. It was simple to bug it when I went to his place before. Pull out and follow my directions. I want to know where the hell he's going. It looks like he's heading toward that Cynthia girl's house, but I'm not sure."

"I know the place, sir," the driver said.

"Their mission report last night was strange," Dillon said. "The news backed it up to boot. They're not lying about that."

"Are you talking of the Silent Justice note left on the body, sir?" the driver asked.

"The very same, George," Dillon said. "They told us they found the body already dead with arrows stuck in it. That follows the news verbatim. They never mentioned the note, but it was dark, and they probably didn't see it with the girl still in the house. I can hardly blame them for being preoccupied with such an unknown in the house with them."

"You don't think the girl, Cynthia, is Silent Justice, do you?" George asked.

"He's still heading toward her house," Dillon said. "I don't know my friend. It could make sense. He's Masked Justice after all, and they are best friends since childhood. My only hang-up on that theory is she's about to take her bar exam soon. It's exceedingly rare for a lawyer to be a vigilante. It's like something out of some farfetched comic book."

"You can never rule something out just because it's unlikely, sir. You told me that," George said. He took a hand off the wheel to scratch his bald head. "For all we know, the other girl could be Blind Justice. The sixteen-year-old that's staying with his parents I mean."

"Or she's Silent Justice, and the men were telling the truth about Blind Justice. There are too damned many things we don't know."

"Is that why you told them we left, sir?" George asked, turning the wheel. "So they'd let their guard down?"

"People act differently when they know they're being watched. I want to know how they act when they think the investigation's over. That's how you find out the truth. He's parked at the woman's house. I suppose he could be going over for a social visit. They did look like they were together. Park up the street a ways so we can still see them, but not too close. I want to see if he walks out with anyone."

"Yes, sir." George pulled over to the side of the street and turned the engine off. He looked over his shoulder at his boss. "It could just be a copycat killer, sir. I mean this new Silent Justice. The media has been kind of hyping Masked Justice."

"That is a possibility. If that's the case, our agent's life just got harder. He won't want some random hooligan going around causing bad publicity for him. Our media outreach can only do so much if they start killing non-pedophiles. For now, we need to focus on what we know. What we don't know will come in time."

"Yes, boss." George cleared his throat. "We know that his partner really is Blind Justice. He was telling the truth, boss."

"What do you base that on?"

"The girl never left his girlfriend's house last night. She was there all night. I had a guy watching her just in case. It was a hunch of mine that turned out to be wrong. Charlie, or whatever his name, is Blind Justice."

"I'm not convinced of that yet," Dillon said. "The heights don't match up. My money's on that teenage girl being Blind Justice. I think they're covering up for their lie. It's smart too. Corrupting a minor into killing is not a small offense as you know. The penalty for that is death in this organization. Children are our future, George. Turning them into murderers is unacceptable, even if they're used to further our cause. That is why we are watching. If he takes that girl home tonight, we have our answer."

"His parents might just want a night off, and he's there to transport her. I don't think she has her license yet."

"Then his next stop would be his parents. We will be fair about our Judgement. If he does move her back there, then all is good. Regardless," Dillon said, "the local trafficking ring is nigh dead around here. In fact, I think there's only one or two more original members left. From my understanding, they're barely operating anymore. Masked Justice has done exactly what we wanted him to - crush the inhumane money mongers who would take advantage of children. He has done so splendidly."

"The results are splendid indeed." George looked back

at him. "However, if his method was questionable, like if the girl is involved, it's a whole other story."

"That is true." Dillon leaned to the right and stared out the front window. "He's coming out. Can you tell if he's alone or not?"

George reached over to the top of the dashboard and picked up a pair of binoculars. He raised them to his eyes and looked at the house. "He's getting a hug from his girl, and he's leaving alone."

"I see," Dillon said. "Then take us back to the motel. I want to get an early night's rest. Tomorrow will be make or break for us. Either we get enough evidence to send to the higher ups, or we leave for real this time. A good night's sleep will do the both of us some good."

"Yes, sir. I hear that." George pulled out onto the road after Jim was well gone...

Just earlier, inside Cynthia's house...

Cynthia opened the door and let Jim inside. "That was quick," she said. "You must be desperate to find out what I had to say. You know you could have just watched the news."

"There is that, but I have another reason for being here."

"If that reason begins with Masked Justice, I'm kicking you out right now."

"How rude," Jim feigned offense, taking a step back. "I just want to talk to my ward is all about something personal." He looked around, making sure Ashley wasn't nearby. "Has she been acting alright?"

"As normal as a teenage girl can. Why?" Cynthia asked.

"She had her first kill not too long ago. I've been trying to keep an eye on her."

"Fantastic," Cynthia said. "She's been acting normal as far as I can tell."

"There he is," Ashley said, emerging from a door down a nearby hallway. "Who was that last night? He's calling himself Silent Justice."

"How could you know that?" Jim asked.

"Like I said, dumbass, it was on the news," Cynthia said, pointing at her television. "Apparently this Silent Justice left a note for the authorities. It was cut out of newspaper clippings. There are no fingerprints on them from what they said. Whoever it was, was careful."

"All the note said was, 'Silent Justice comes for the wicked,'" Ashley said. "You didn't see the news? It was plastered all over it. They said the body had an arrow in it. Is that true?"

"I saw it myself," Jim said. "I even saw this Silent Justice with my own eyes."

"You're lucky he didn't kill you," Cynthia said. She crossed her arms with a frown on her face.

"Nah." Ashley moved over and plopped down on the sofa. "If he named himself Silent Justice he wouldn't want to hurt him."

"Is this speaking from experience, Ms. Blind Justice?" Cynthia asked. "In my experience, killers are killers regardless of their intentions."

"She was about your height," Jim looked at Ashley. "I could have sworn I heard her voice before too. I can't put my finger on who it was though. Her identity concealers were very similar to ours, but not identical. She had the pull up mask and she also had those little masks we put over our eyes. They weren't color coordinated, but she legitimately tried to look like me."

"Imitation is the sincerest form of flattery they say,"

Cynthia said. "Congratulations. You have a murderous woman who loves you enough to kill and act like you. Aren't you proud of your life decisions? You've inspired yet another to kill."

"It's not like I want them to go around doing this."

"You were the one who gave them the idea obviously," Cynthia said. "They could be someone you saved, they could just be an edgy teenager who thinks you're cool, or it could just be a normal copycat murderer trying to associate themselves with your good press that you're getting – which, by the way, boggles my mind. That republic must have far reach in the media. I've only heard Masked Justice called a murderer and serial killer a couple of times. Every other personality claims you're cleaning up the streets. It's no god damn wonder that someone wants to imitate it with all the praise Masked Justice is getting."

"I've been trying to figure out who this Silent Justice character is all day. Charlie and I have hit a brick wall. She just appeared last night out of nowhere."

"It'd be impossible to find her without a hint of where she is," Ashley said. "What about your little assassin problem? I heard on the bug I left that he's gone?"

"What is it with you and assassins coming after you?" Cynthia asked. "You've had two after you in nearly as many weeks. You don't see a problem here?"

"He's gone. He stopped by my house earlier today. He told me himself he's leaving, which leads me to believe he's not really gone."

"I see you've turned paranoid now too," Cynthia said. "Not that I can blame you when you lead this shit life of death spiraling out of control. I'd be out of my gourd too."

"It's not crazy if someone's actually out to get you. I thought you'd have learned that lesson before. Must I remind you of the hitman you distracted and helped me dispose of?"

"We both know why you're in this situation. You've made your bed, and now you're laying in it."

"Thanks for that. Can I speak to my ward in private for a few minutes? Where is her room?"

"Just down that hallway. The same one the kids stayed in when you were here."

"Come on." Ashley hopped up from her seat and led him to the room. She threw the door open and rushed inside to fall onto the bed. "What's on your mind?"

Jim closed the door behind him and moved to sit beside her. He kept his voice low. "Do you remember what I promised before? That it was only the one job I couldn't take you on?"

"You'd better not be saying what I think you are." She sent him a dirty look.

"No, I'm not suggesting you sit out another job. This one's slightly less official, if you catch my meaning."

"I don't get it. You only do assignments your Republic sends you on or approves, yes?" Ashley asked, looking up at him, still laying down on the bed.

"Most of the time, but this is my own side job of sorts, and I want you to help. I have a feeling this will be right up your alley."

"I'm listening."

"Look, in the interest of safety, I can't take you home and get you suited up before we leave for tonight."

"What? Are you picking me up tonight then?"

"Not quite." Jim laughed. "I know that Cynthia has a bike out in the garage, and that's good cardio right there." He reached into his pants pocket and handed her a paper. "This place isn't too far away. Be there tonight at two a.m. if you want to be involved. It's not a kill mission. I'm just going there to scare the absolute fuck out of this guy."

"Why are you doing this anyway?" Ashley sat up and took the paper, inspecting the handwriting. "You never leave them alive."

"This isn't a child abuser. This guy sent a friend of mine a death threat. I'm going to show him why that's a bad idea. I just thought Blind Justice and Masked Justice would be a greater show of force than Just Masked Justice alone. I need my partner if she can make it. If you need rest for school, then never mind all of this. You should be focusing on that to be honest. It's a selfish request I realize."

"I'm going," Ashley said, a beaming smile on her face. "You couldn't stop me if you wanted to. You will have my equipment in your car, yes?"

"Obviously I would." Jim got up and moved to the door. He threw the door open. "Alright then. Remember what I said. I'm heading out for now. I'll do the prep work." His voice grew loud enough for Cynthia to hear in the living room. "You just make sure you get your homework done." He finished his statement with a grin and a wink.

She returned the silent gesture. "I got it already," she said.

"Wonderful," Cynthia could be heard. "Does that mean you're leaving then?"

"I'm afraid so," Jim walked back to the living room and moved behind the recliner she was sitting in. He looked down at her. "I know, it breaks your heart to be away from me. You always push me away when I know you don't mean to."

She purposely leaned the chair back into him. "Whatever you've got to tell yourself to get a good night's sleep." She got out of the chair and grabbed his hand. She dragged him over to the front door. "Now get out already. I need to keep studying."

"You're always so pushy," Jim said. "If I didn't know better, I'd think you just wanted to put your hands all over me. Look," he raised their conjoined hands. "You couldn't wait to hold my hand again."

"I see you haven't changed much. You're still insufferable." She yanked her hand free.

"You still react the same way too."

"Get out already." She gripped the door handle only for his hand to cover hers.

"You know," he said in a low husky voice, "they might still be watching me out there."

"You are not serious right now," Cynthia said. "Are you?"

"It's better safe than sorry as they say." Jim smiled and lifted his hand off hers. "You can help a guy out one more time, right?"

"Fine." She threw the door open and pushed him outside. She stepped out and gave him a warm embrace before backing off. "Be careful out there," she said before shutting the door. She turned around to see Ashley standing outside her room's door, just staring at her. "What? It was just in case."

"Uh huh, sure…"

17

Jim reclined in the driver's seat. His seat was reclined so much, it was akin to lying in an uncomfortable bed. He had his eyes closed and was listening to the radio while he waited. "She should be almost here." He cracked open an eye and peeked at the digital clock on the dashboard. "It's almost two." He shut his eyes again, trying desperately to steal some sleep.

He had almost fallen asleep when a knock at his window jolted him upright. "What the fuck?" He looked to his left to see Ashley with a wide grin, knocking on his window. He pushed the nearby button on his left and unlocked the back door.

She threw open the back door and sat down behind him. "I hope I didn't interrupt your beauty sleep. You looked adorable lying there like that."

"Adorable is not a word I've ever been called before now," Jim said, shaking his head and rubbing his eyes. "I don't think you're using that word correctly." He reached over to the passenger seat and grabbed his own masks and vest. He donned those without further words.

"Here they are," Ashley said, picking up the pile in the backseat beside her. "Let me suit up and you can tell me what the hell the plan is for scaring this guy to death." She placed the blade on the seat before separating the apparel and putting them on one by one. She put the vest on first, followed by the eye mask and finally she put on the neck gaiter before pulling it up past her nose. She made sure it was secured. "I'm ready." She picked up the blade and placed it in her lap. "What's the plan?"

"I figure Manny is fast asleep by now," Jim said through the cloth in front of his mouth. "We go in there, find his room, and then we stand over his bed. I ready my blade while you wake his ass up. I'll take it from there. Just watch his hands. As bad of a gang banger as Edmund says he is, he might have a gun under his pillow. We take no chances."

"Agreed," Ashley said. "I'm just happy to be out of the student life for another night. It's suffocating doing nothing but going to class and studying at night."

"Follow my lead and keep calm. Are you ready?" Jim asked.

"You bet your ass," Ashley said.

"Then let's go." Jim got out of the car and headed toward their target's home, running to get between the two houses. He pressed his back to the yellow painted wooden exterior and looked to his right to see Ashley running after him.

She got to his side and looked up and over at him. "I don't think anybody saw us."

"I left the engine running, so let's hurry this up. I'm not made of money."

"I'm pretty sure you're paid better than most CEO's. I saw how many catcoins they sent you per kill."

"Being a smartass is not always what you want to be." Jim gave a light swat to her shoulder. "Now be quiet and follow me." He moved to his side and saw a window head high. He got on his tip toes and peered inside.

"See anything?"

"I can't see shit," Jim said. "He's definitely in bed." He brought his hands up and tried to open it.

Ashley watched him struggle for a moment before reaching up and assisting him. Within a few seconds the window pushed up a few inches before eventually rising steadily.

"There we are. Let's remember this window and make this our exit plan. Our ride's not too far away, and we're out of the line of sight of the street. It's perfect." He crouched down and made a step using his hands. "You're first. Don't go anywhere once you get in. I'll climb in after."

"Alright then. Sweet!" Ashley placed a hand on his shoulder to steady herself and stepped into his hands. He lifted her up as she pulled herself up. She climbed over and into the house. She landed on her feet, barely making a sound inside on the carpeted floor.

Jim jumped up and had a bit more trouble climbing inside but did so without significant issue. His landing was heavier and certainly made more noise. The pair stayed perfectly still, allowing their eyes to adjust to the darkness inside compared to outside. The sound of silence surrounded them other than an otherwise loud ticking of a clock coming from nearby.

"Let's go." Jim grabbed Ashley's hand and dragged her along through the house. He dropped her hand once the pair reached the stairwell leading upward. "Up we go," he said. He led them up the stairs, the sound of creaking with every step.

Jim reached the top and saw doors in the narrow hallway. He looked over his shoulder, spotting Ashley right behind him. He pointed to the left door and saw her nod. He stalked over in the dark and opened the door. Soft snoring met their ears, when suddenly a loud chiming could be heard. It kept repeating every few seconds.

Jim turned around, pushing Ashley backwards. He pushed the door across the hall open and directed her inside. He quickly shut the door behind them and pinned her against the wooden door. He pressed his ear against the door, trying to hear anything beyond the periodic chiming.

"What the fuck?" Manny's loud irate voice asked. Loud stomping accompanied the voice, growing closer until it faded. The sound of a door opening could be made out.

Ashley felt the wood on her back and looked up at Jim's entirely too close body. "Can you move?"

"Quiet," Jim used a hand to cover her mouth. He used the other to cup around his ear and pressed it against the door. "I think he opened the door."

Ashley smelled the scent of his aftershave and tried to ignore it in their close proximity. "Can you hear anything?"

"I can hear them talking if you'd stop talking." He leaned closer to the door, trying to squeeze as much extra clarity in their words as he could.

"Why are you here at this time at night?" the same male voice, still obviously angry, asked. "I told you to come back tomorrow morning and tell me how it went - not wake my ass up in the middle of the night, you stupid ass."

"I'm sorry, Manny, but there was a complication I thought you should know about," a different male voice said. His words were rushed, almost out of breath. "I just didn't know what to do, so I came over here."

"Spit it out then," Manny said. "What happened that was so God damned important?"

"I went to that hole in the wall with the doctor that you

said to. I busted in there and there was some crazy old homeless dude there. He got in my way, and I think I beat him to death. I got out of there right after. I didn't know what to do, man. I didn't do this for you just to go to prison because of some crazy old guy."

"Are you serious?" Manny asked. "What about the doctor? Did you at least take care of him too while you were there, or did you bitch out?"

"I got out of there when it looked like the guy might be dying, dude."

"You're fucking useless. I should have done it myself."

Jim audibly growled listening to the pair. "Those shit stains hurt Ray?" His right hand withdrew his pistol and got it ready. He grabbed Ashley's left hand and pulled her away from the door before opening it slowly. The downstairs light was on, but the upstairs was still as dark as ever.

He pointed the firearm ahead of him as he reached the stairs. He recognized the man from Edmund's photo downstairs along with the new man. He aimed at the new man after seeing that his target was unarmed. He couldn't tell with the second man, so he aimed at him.

"What the fuck? Is that Masked Justice?" one of them asked, pointing at the stairwell as Jim descended while aiming his pistol.

"Do not fucking move, or I blow your ass away," Jim said. His voice was filled with barely restrained rage.

"Don't try running either." Ashley squeezed by him and unsheathed her sword. "I guarantee I'm faster than either of you.

"Blind Justice is a girl?" Manny asked. "I can't say I expected that."

Jim kept his eyes locked on his targets as he reached the bottom of the stairs. "Take their weapons. If I see so much as your arm twitch, I'm shooting first and asking questions later."

"Masked Justice? I thought you only went after perverts. Why are you here?" the newcomer asked.

Ashley frisked the guest and found a pistol. She took it and threw it behind her quite some distance. "You got anything else on you?"

"No,"

"A likely story," Ashley said, sheathing her blade. She continued patting him down until she felt another hard implement near his belt line. "That's either a knife or you're happy to see us." She found the hunting knife hanging on his side and tossed it along with the firearm. "Since you can't be trusted, let's give you one more once over before I'm satisfied."

"I never touched any kids!" Manny yelled. "You got the wrong guy here, I swear."

"I'm not here about any kids," Jim said with barely restrained anger. He reached into his pants pocket and tossed two zip ties to Ashley. "Tie them up to the stairwell handrail columns for now. I don't want them moving while I question them and punish their transgressions." Jim watched Ashley drag them over to the stairs and tie them up."

Ashley fastened the men to the wooden support using the zip ties. "They're not moving unless they rip these columns out."

"Good," Jim said, putting his pistol away.

The two men breathed a sigh of relief only to have their eyes bulge when he unsheathed his wakizashi and walked closer to them. "You are going to tell me everything you two idiots did to this old man you spoke of."

"He wasn't even the target, man," the visibly sweaty one said.

"Shut up, you idiot. Don't tell them anything else," the de facto leader of the two said. "We aren't going to tell you shit."

"Oh, is that how you're going to play this?" Jim asked. He took another step forward and pressed the tip of the sword into his groin. "Are you sure about that? I've never mutilated someone in such a way, but I'm willing to try with you two. You just piss me off so bad."

"Don't think he's bluffing either," Ashley said. "I've seen him go absolutely apeshit before. The aftermath was a thing of horror. I mean there were body parts scattered all over the room. A little neutering isn't out of his reach, trust me."

"What do you want to know, man?" the scared one asked. "I'll tell you, even if this guy's too stupid to realize it's in our best interests."

"You keep your mouth shut if you know what's good for you," Manny snapped at his cohort.

Jim moved the blade up, trailing against Manny's clothes, occasionally ripping a hole. "Do you feel that? That's sharpened steel against your flesh."

Ashley, not one to be left out, unsheathed her weapon. She extended the end toward the other terrified prisoner. "You'd better spill it before your boss's stupidity gets him sliced up."

"He sent me after that saw bones back-alley doctor earlier tonight," he said in a hurry.

"Why did you follow that order?" Ashley asked. "Your piss ant gang isn't known for violence. What are you guys known for anyway?"

"I was just supposed to rough them up is all."

"We're known for dealing grass," the leader said. "This

order was unusual, but the guy disrespected me. We couldn't let that go and still hold any respect on the streets."

"Tough luck," Jim said. "You never did have respect on these streets. Now why would some pain pills be so important to you that you'd try to have the guy roughed up?"

"How do you know that?" Manny asked

"Pain pills?" the other prisoner asked. "You sent me over there because of some god damned pain pills?" His voice escalated. "You got me involved with Masked Justice because you didn't want to pay for medication when we have enough weed to dull any pain you'd have? You're lucky I'm tied up right now, or I'd beat the shit out of you."

"Will you shut up?" Manny asked. He turned back to Jim. "Why do you care so much about some old homeless dude he found at the doctor's place? Or is this about the doctor himself?"

"I don't just go after kiddy touchers," Jim said. "Those are just the cases that get the most publicity. I have eyes and ears everywhere. I am Masked Justice. Do not presume to know my methods. That was your first mistake. I stand up for the weak and powerless against bullies like you. It just so happens that when children are involved, that's the dynamic as well."

Ashley moved behind the men, climbing the stairwell. She rested her blade against Manny's wrists. "Have you ever wandered what it was like to lose a hand?"

"There's no need to be barbarians here," Manny said, a bead of sweat rolling down the side of his face. "It was an honest mistake is all. It won't happen again."

"I know it won't happen again," Jim pressed the blade harder against Manny. "You had better pray that old man isn't dead. If he is, I'm coming back, and I won't be so nice as this visit."

"You're not going to kill us?" Manny asked. "Why?"

"Be quiet, man." The mortified one stomped on Manny's foot.

"Take your subordinate's advice," Jim said. "Now what should we do with you two chuckleheads? Shall we take a finger, a hand, or maybe we should get a different trophy. People like you only learn with force, and I'm an expert at applying just that."

"I don't like this guy. Let me do the honors," Ashley said. "I've already got a finger picked out we can take."

Jim saw the unadulterated look of horror on the two men's faces. "You both know what I do, correct? I am no stranger to taking lives, and I have to admit you..." he pressed the blade a little harder into Manny's chest, drawing a thin line of blood to trail down. "You piss me off. You harm an innocent old man in your quest for power. As for you..." He withdrew the blade and sidestepped. He raised the steel until it was eye level and walked forward. "You were the one who did the deed, weren't you?"

"I'd never have done it if I'd known the old man was there. I swear it."

"Wrong answer," Jim said. He moved the blade to his shoulder and sliced downward. "The correct answer was 'I never should have done it' period. Neither of you two numbskulls or any of your little group is going to step foot in that office ever again. If I find out this happened again, you two won't survive. Do I make myself clear, Manny?"

"I won't do it ever again, Mr. Masked Justice. I swear I won't," Manny's accomplice said.

Manny rolled his eyes at his cohort's antics. "Don't you have any pride, man?"

"Pride goes before the fall," Ashley said. "That's a lesson I highly suggest you take to heart, tough guy. You keep just dealing your weed and stop hurting people, and you never see us again. You try to play above your station like you're some damned mafia mob boss, and we'll be the last things you see. Is that clear?"

"I get it," Manny said.

"I want to hear the words out of your mouth." Jim gave him a look full of hatred. "Say it. Say that you won't hurt anyone else. Do it right now."

"I won't hurt anyone. Are you happy now?"

"Next time make it sound believable." Jim moved his blade over to Manny's face and cut down his cheek. "Let's just mark you. This is so you never forget our visit. Anytime you get a stupid idea, you can look in the mirror and remember there are consequences to being a shitbag." He dragged the blade down the entirety of Manny's cheek, drawing blood as he went. "We can't have you forgetting our kindness, can we?"

Ashley kicked Manny's hands that were behind him, crushing the digits against her shoe and the wooden support beam. "That one's from me."

"You broke my fucking fingers, you bitch," Manny said.

"Watch your mouth." Jim finished his work and pulled the steel away. The gash he left in its wake bled freely. "Come here, Blind. Tell me, what do you think of my handiwork?"

Ashley jumped to the bottom of the stairs and came side to side with Jim. "The line is a little crooked, but overall I like it." She put her weapon away with the comment.

"Are you going to let us go before you leave?" Manny asked.

"Hmm," Jim acted like he was thinking before responding. "Nah. One of your home boys can have that pleasure. You're going to sit there until one of them comes and gets you. I guess you could tear the shit out of your stairwell if you really want out. It's up to you. I hope you boys have a good night." He flicked his blade to the side, causing blood to spatter on the floor before sheathing it with great care and precision. "I don't like dirtying my blade for worthless scumbags like you, but sometimes it's necessary."

"Now you two remember what we said. The next visit won't be so friendly," Ashley said.

"If the old man dies, we're coming back tonight. You'd better pray you didn't kill him. Trust me when I say we will know if you go after them again. Do not test us." He looked to Ashley at his side. "Come on. Let's get out of this shit-hole." He walked over to the nearby light switch and flicked it off, cloaking the room in darkness.

Ashley followed along behind him.

Jim opened the door and dashed out the front toward their waiting car. He heard rapid footsteps behind him. He circled around the car and got into the driver's seat as Ashley climbed into the passenger side.

He lowered the mask covering his nose and took off the eye covering mask before getting the vehicle moving. "Take off your disguise," he said, pulling out onto the street.

She removed the garbs covering her identity and tossed them in the back seat. "Do you think they got the message?"

"For their own good, I hope they did. I went easy on them."

"Are we going to that doctor's place now?" Ashley asked.

"You bet your ass we are," Jim said, a look of determination on his face.

Fifteen minutes later at Edmund's office...

Jim didn't bother knocking, choosing instead to enter

unannounced. He saw Edmund sitting near a cot with someone laying on it.

Edmund perked up and turned around at the sound of the door closing. "You scared the hell out of me."

"I heard about what happened when we were at Manny's house. How is he?" Jim and Ashley rushed across the room and looked down at the unconscious Ray on the bed. "The guy's partner said he thought he was dead."

"He did look it when it all went down," Edmund said. "It all happened so fast. The guy busted in while Ray and I were talking, and he stormed over. I tried talking to the guy, but he was having none of it." He reached up and pointed to a growing black eye. "He punched me in the face for my trouble."

"The guy just went off?" Ashley asked. "We might have been too nice back there."

"That caused Ray to jump up and try his best. He'd never been in a fight before, you could tell. He just put himself between us. The guy delivered a hook to Ray's jaw. He fell down, caught his arm at a bad angle and bonked his head pretty good. Then he kept kicking him while he was down, causing multiple lacerations. Eventually he lost his bloodlust and looked down at what he had done."

"So that's why he has that cast on," Ashley said.

"He looked dead at first. The guy freaked out when he realized Ray was out cold. He ran out of here quicker than a flash. I guess he was scared he'd killed him. Truth be told," Edmund paused, "I thought he did at first. His arm was bent at an odd angle, he was out cold, and he was barely breathing. I think I got him stabilized though."

"You're a good man doing so much for him when you know he can't pay," Jim said.

"He threw himself between us, trying to protect me. He

had to know he didn't stand a chance to calm the guy down, but he did it anyway," Edmund said. "I owe him at least this much. It's not a matter of money this time."

"How long do you think it'll take for him to get better?" Ashley asked.

"There's no way of telling," Edmund said. "He probably has a concussion. Hell, he could be in a coma and I'd have no way of telling. I don't have the necessary machines to make an accurate diagnosis in here."

"Would the hospital?" Jim asked.

"Of course, but good luck with that," Edmund said with a sad smile. "We both know he wouldn't have medical insurance. As much as I love the capitalistic state of medicine in this country, this is the one time I wish he could go there and get the care he really needs. I can't pay for his hospital fees even if I wanted to. It'd be in the tens of thousands with all the procedures he'd need."

"There's no way I could cash out that much money in time without drawing attention," Jim said. He looked down at Ray's peaceful face. "Dammit to hell. I should have gone earlier."

"You had no way of knowing he'd do this," Edmund said. "I was even the one who told you he probably wouldn't do anything. This is my fault, not yours."

"I think you both should fuck off with this pity party of sorts," Ashley said in a firm voice. "The man is older than the both of you combined. He knew exactly what he was doing. He did this for you." She pointed at Edmund. "It's disrespectful to talk like you are right now. He's a good man. We can all agree on that, right?"

"Damned right," Jim said.

"Obviously, girl," Edmund said. "You are right. It was his

decision to jump in front of him. It doesn't stop me from feeling guilty though."

"I get that, but instead of focusing on how you feel, you should put all your attention on his treatment. You used to be a doctor, right?"

"I did."

"You did everything you could, yes?"

"I splinted his arm, treated the cuts, and kept him warm. As you can see," he pointed up at the IV bag, "I've pulled out all the stops that I have access to. Normally this much care would cost someone thousands."

"You're not going to charge him though," Jim said.

"No, I'm not." Edmund sighed.

"You're still going to charge me the next time I come in, aren't you?" Jim asked, a faint smile on his face.

"Of course I am."

"It was worth a try."

Ashley looked down at the old man laying on the cot. "Is this the guy who helped you out before that you told me about?"

"He's the one alright," Jim said. "He's the one who led me to Kensington as well. I'm sure your friend would like to thank him if she knew."

"What?" Edmund asked. "What did he do?"

"Gave me intel that led to the guy abusing her friend dying mysteriously."

"He was behind that? Well, I knew you did it, but you got the intel from Ray?"

"I sure did." Jim's downcast eyes trailed over Ray's frail body laying below. "Because of him, a lot of kids were saved from evil people. Defending you was just the latest good act he'd done."

"I'm going to stay here tonight," Edmund said. "I'll keep

watch over him and see if he wakes up. You two should head back home yourselves.

"That's a good idea. Oh shit," Jim said. "Cynthia's bike is still near that house, isn't it?"

"Yep," Ashley said.

"That's fine. I'll drive you back there and you can get it back to Cynthia's. She'd kill you if you left it there." Jim took one last long look at Ray on the cot. "I'll see you later, buddy. Come on, Ashley. Let's get going so we can get some sleep tonight."

"You're sure they won't come back?" Edmund called out after the retreating pair.

Jim stopped in his tracks and looked over his shoulder. "I made it clear that if they did they wouldn't survive next time. They know that I know where they live. They're chuckle fucks, but they're not suicidal. Just tell me if they do, and I'll end them permanently."

"I need your number if I'm to do that," Edmund said. "Only Ray has it on his phone."

Jim relayed his number to Edmund and continued moving toward the door with Ashley. "Don't hesitate to call if something else happens. Let Ray know we stopped by if he wakes up, yeah?"

"I'll tell him everything you two did," Edmund called out to the pair now opening the door.

18

"It's good to be back home." Ashley took a deep breath and looked around the living room. "Where's Charlie?" Ashley asked, coming through the front door with Skye.

"He hasn't been here all day. I've no idea. Welcome home by the way," Jim said, working on his laptop in the kitchen. He looked up from his work and looked over at the two girls. "Oh, sorry. Hello there, Skye."

"Hey," was the only response he received from Skye.

"Sorry, girls. I've just fallen behind on work lately. I'm going to keep working. Don't let me interrupt you two." He stopped talking and got back to work. "You go get your homework done or whatever you came to do. Don't let me stop you."

"Come on." Ashley let her caretaker be and climbed the nearby stairs. "We can go to my room. We don't want to interrupt him."

"Okay," Skye said, following her upstairs and into her room.

"Make yourself at home. We'll get started on homework and be done so we can play some games after." She threw her backpack down beside her bed and sat near the table in the middle of her room. She put her legs under the table and dug around in her backpack.

Skye sat across the small table and unzipped her backpack. "There's something I've been meaning to ask you."

"Go ahead." Ashley placed the math textbook on the table in front of her.

"You didn't really get in a fight with Vick, did you?" Skye asked.

"Why would you think that?" Ashley asked.

"I talked to him today. He said he never gave you that black eye."

"He just doesn't want everybody to know a girl got the better of him." Ashley saw the look Skye was giving her. "Alright, fine. You caught me. What about it? It wasn't Jim down there, I swear to you. He's the nicest guy you ever met."

"I know it wasn't him," Skye said.

"You do?"

"Yeah. I know how you got that black eye alright. I just haven't really known how to broach the subject for reasons that will be obvious soon."

"What are you saying?" Ashley asked. She felt her stomach doing backflips with every word she spoke.

"I know who you two are," Skye said. "I saw you get hit that night with the book. We both know the night I'm talking about."

"Oh, shit fuck," Ashley said. She looked down at the table before looking up at Skye. "You really have a wild imagination." She forced a laugh. She saw Skye's serious demeanor and stopped. "Wait, you're serious?"

"As I have ever been about anything. I heard your voice that night you know. You tried to disguise it, but it didn't work as well as you think it did. I heard you cursing to yourself. I heard you tell that piece of shit to die already. I heard everything. I was just petrified and didn't move for fear."

Ashley's normally jovial tone and smiling face was now straight and even. "That's quite the accusation to throw at your friend."

"Am I wrong?" Skye asked, pushing the long forgotten homework to the side. "Tell me I'm wrong while looking me in the eye."

Ashley brought her gaze up to Skye's and sat there for a long moment, trying to disagree with her. She shook her head and looked away.

"I knew it," Skye said. "I never knew who to thank for that." She reached across the table and touched Ashley's arm. "Thank you for what you did that night. I assume Jim down there is the big man himself?"

Ashley remained silent at the question.

"Look, I'm not here to turn you guys in. It's just that we both know what happened that night. I'd rather you'd not found that out about me. It's embarrassing. I tried to hide what he was doing to me for so long. To be found out while he was dying was mortifying to me."

"Trust and believe I know exactly how you feel," Ashley said. "Let's just say Jim down there is not officially my foster parent."

"You don't mean?"

"I do. My parents had sold me to Oswald Planter for rent money essentially."

"I know that name from somewhere. Who was that?" Skye asked. "Wasn't he in the news recently?"

"He was," Ashley said. "The memory of what he did to me was scorched into my memory for the rest of my life."

"Oswald Planter, wasn't he the head of that local grocery chain?"

"The very same. He had me tied to a bed twenty hours a day. He let me get up and walk around only under his supervision. He kept me on a leash even then. He would pay me nightly visits for over six months. I thought I'd go crazy. My whole life revolved around whatever I could find on television and him violating me at night. He'd give me morning after pills every single morning. He was a disgusting piece of filth."

"I'm sorry," Skye said. "You don't have to tell me everything if it hurts."

"Jim's the only one who knows. Hell, you already know my biggest secret, what's one more. I just need to know one thing."

"Go ahead."

"You can never, and I mean never, tell anyone this shit."

"I don't intend to out my rescuers," Skye said. "I'd rather die than get you two in trouble."

"Good," Ashley said. "Anyway, one day I saw on the news that a Masked Justice had rescued a bunch of kids trapped in a storage container down at one of Oswald's warehouses."

"He was the one behind that? The media said it was that one guard who died."

"They lied. It was his doing. My point is, once I'd seen that report fantasies flooded my mind. Maybe Masked Justice might come and save me. I'd dream of him busting through the door and getting me out of there like a knight carrying his princess."

"I take it he did?" Skye asked.

"Less knight in shining armor, more surprised to find me. He did get me out of there though. He also let me watch as he brutally ended Oswald's life. I relished every fucking moment, watching him struggle as Masked Justice stabbed him over and over until the whole bed was red. I watched with glee as the life faded from his eyes. I didn't know I could still feel. I've been helping him ever since. It's only recently I put the masks on and took a more direct approach. In fact, Kensington was my first kill."

"I have a confession to make myself regarding all of this," Skye said, biting her lip.

"You know you can tell me. What is it?" Ashley asked.

"Before I do, I need to ask you a question." Skye's bottom lip quivered. "How do you deal with taking someone's life?"

"By realizing the world is a better place without people like him. I felt odd after it happened. I felt kind of empty if that makes sense?"

"More than you know.

"I didn't feel bad for what I did, I just felt off. Why are you asking me this?" Ashley asked.

Skye tapped the table below and fidgeted before answering. "I was the one you and Jim ran into the other night."

"You're Silent Justice?" Ashley asked, eyes widening. "I mean that wasn't me there, but that's a whole other story. You're the one Jim's looking for then. He's not hunting you or anything, but he's running around like a chicken with its head cut off trying to find out who Silent Justice is. Why did you go there that night?"

"The same reason I suspect that you have been doing this," Skye said. She shifted her position so she was sitting with her legs under her. "I don't want people to go through what I did. I wanted to end the threat. It's just been tearing me up inside. I don't know if I can keep doing it."

"You don't have to you know." Ashley got up and moved to beside her. "It's not for everyone. Did it help at all when you did it?"

"At first I was scared shitless." Skye delivered a nervous laugh. "Shooting a deer is a completely different thing than a man. He woke up before I got him, you know. He even managed to get up before I instinctively let the arrow loose. You know what the most jarring thing about the whole experience was for me?"

"The sound," Ashley said.

"It was a rush. Sure, he fell back after the first, but he wasn't dead yet. I didn't have time to think, my body rushed forward. I grabbed another arrow and buried another into him. Then I did it again and again until I heard a noise downstairs. By then my elation had moved to sheer horror, and nervous didn't begin to describe it. You said sound," Skye said. "Why?"

"Well, you were there. Don't you remember the noises Mr. Kensington made as he died on that bed? He was gurgling, wheezing, and trying to scream. It was the stuff of nightmares. I almost couldn't do it. I froze up when I had the blade perched above him."

"What made you go through with it?" Skye asked.

"I remembered the things Jim said he did to his victim, who we didn't know was you at the time. I imagined you in that position, and I lost it. The blade was in him before I realized it. That's when I remember you being awake."

"I'd been awake a few minutes earlier, but that's when I moved, yes."

"I got in a lot of trouble because of that night actually," Ashley said with a small chuckle. "I snuck off while Jim snuck upstairs. It was my first time going along with him inside. If I'd followed the plan, he'd have been the one who got him."

"I never did get the chance to say it, but thank you - for killing him I mean."

"Look, I'm not trying to be all weird or anything," Ashley said, "but are you alright? You look like a kicked puppy right now."

"I was just realizing we have to tell Masked Justice himself now," Skye said. "He's going to be pissed off I bet."

"You may be surprised."

"Can I ask you something?" Skye asked.

"Go ahead."

"Is he single?"

"What?" Ashley leaned back away from Skye. She sputtered out her next response. "Why are you even asking me for?"

"It was to lighten the mood is all. You always get so worked up whenever someone's love life is mentioned. Not to mention I've seen how you look at him."

Ashley turned and delivered a swift kick to Skye's leg. "Maybe we do need to check your mental stability if you're able to come up with such absurd ideas."

"It could have been my imagination I guess. I'll file that away for two years in the future then."

"You'd have your work cut out for you. He has someone he's interested in, apparently. It's a childhood best friend kind of deal." Ashley looked away.

"You're not interested in him at all, not at all." Skye's relatively serious voice was betrayed by her trying to hold a laugh back.

The pair was interrupted with a sudden knock at the door. "Would you two girls like some refreshments? I brought up some water and snacks." Jim's muffled voice came through the door. The door opened to reveal Jim holding two water bottles in one hand and a white plastic bag filled with snacks in the other. "Hopefully I'm not interrupting."

"It's fine," Ashley said. She caught the bottle of water tossed at her.

Jim placed the other bottle down in front of Skye and placed the bag in the middle of the table. "Alright then, I'll get out of your hair."

"Skye's going to stay for a while today."

"Then I'll prepare a little more than I was planning. Do you like steak, Skye?"

"I'm not a vegan if that's what you're asking," Skye said. "Steak is perfect as far as I'm concerned."

"Perfect," Jim said. He backed up to the door. "You two can get back to your homework. I'll leave you alone." He exited the room and closed the door.

The remaining pair of girls waited a minute before they looked back at each other.

"That was close," Ashley said.

"Do you think he heard any of that?" Skye asked.

"If he did, he would have mentioned it," Ashley said, twisting the cap off the bottle and taking a drink. "He's not known for his subtlety. We now have a few hours for planning how we're going to tell him."

"I still think he'll be furious."

"I think you may be wrong. Charlie would be a different story, but Jim's easygoing."

"Let's hope you're right..."

After dark...

"That was delicious, Mr. Benning," Skye said. She placed the knife and fork onto the plate.

"Thank you. You can just leave it there. I'll get the dishes done after we all finish," Jim said, still finishing his meal.

"I don't mind," Skye got up and moved over to the sink.

"I'm used to cleaning up after myself." She washed the dish and assorted implements.

"You're quite responsible," Jim said. He turned to Ashley. "That's something you should work on."

"I'm plenty responsible as it is," Ashley said. "I get my homework done every day. What else do you want from me?"

Jim got up from his seat, picking up his plate. He circled around the table and picked up hers as well. "You two can go. I'll handle clean-up from here."

Skye spoke, still focusing on her cleaning. "I'm almost done."

"We need to talk after dinner's cleaned up anyway," Ashley said, pushing her seat out from the table.

"You two can go talk now, that's what I'm saying."

"Well," Ashley said, "that's not what we're saying. We need to talk to you specifically."

"Me?" Jim replaced Skye's position in front of the sink. "Why would you two need to talk to me?"

"You'll see," Ashley said. "We'll be waiting in the living room."

"I don't mind helping with those, Mr. Benning," Skye said, still standing beside him near the sink.

"You're a good kid," Jim said with a momentary look over before returning his attention to the task at hand. "Your parents raised you well. You don't have to, but if you insist, here you are." He moved to the side a few feet and handed her one of the two dishes.

The two stood side by side in the kitchen cleaning the dishes from dinner in relative silence other than the sound of running water and scrubbing.

Skye looked to the living room as they worked to see

Ashley sneaking glances at the pair still in the kitchen. "I'm just going to say sorry now."

"Pardon?" Jim asked, finishing his dish and setting it aside. "You have nothing to be sorry about."

"You'll see soon enough," Skye said, finishing her plate.

"Come over here," Ashley said. "We can get this show on the road."

"She's certainly antsy," Jim said. "Come on, we don't want to keep her waiting. She'll never let us hear the end of it."

"Yeah," Skye didn't sound excited. She moved into the living room and sat down on the nearby couch.

Jim sat in his favorite recliner and put the leg rest up. "Now then, what was it you wanted to talk to me about?"

The trio fell into silence.

Skye scratched her arm and looked to the ground, fidgeting all the while.

"Well?" Jim asked.

"I guess I'll do it then," Ashley said. "It's a good thing you're sitting down because you might faint when you hear this."

"I'm sure it's not that bad," Jim said. "What is it? You want advice about dating? I'm not qualified to give advice in such areas." He laughed. "As you can see, I'm single."

"What? No," Ashley said. "Promise to not get mad?"

"How can I promise that if I don't know what it is?" Jim asked. "I'll try not to get mad, alright? Now what is it? I'd like to get more work done tonight. I've fallen a little behind lately."

Skye finally spoke up. "I know who Silent Justice is."

Jim gave her a puzzled look. "Sorry?"

"It's just what I said. I know who Silent Justice is."

"You should probably tell the news about that," Jim said

with a chuckle. "They'd give you a bunch of money if you told them."

"Jim, just listen. She's trying to tell you something important," Ashley said.

Jim quieted down and stopped laughing. "Alright, you seriously know who Silent Justice is?"

"Well of course I know her." She used her right hand to point to herself. "She's me."

Jim's mouth dropped temporarily, his eyes widened, and his voice raised. "Wait, what now?" He kicked down the leg rest and leaned forward, looking across the room. His eyes locked with Skye's. "Run that by me one more time."

"I am Silent Justice."

"Assuming that's even true, why are you telling me this? For all you know, I'd turn you in for murder."

"I don't think Masked Justice and Blind Justice are in a position to turn me in." Skye didn't back down from the impromptu staring contest with Jim. "I know who you two are as well."

Jim's tone turned from even to no nonsense. "You don't know half as much as you think you know. It's dangerous to air such rumors. You should be careful who you sling that at."

"I know you're playing dumb right now, but I already have proof," Skye said. "There's no need to worry. I have no plans of turning anyone in. In fact, I should thank the both of you."

Jim looked over at the quiet Ashley. "You knew about this. I bet you two were talking about this all day, weren't you? What did you tell her?"

"I didn't tell her anything," Ashley said. "Don't snap at me. She figured this out all by herself. She ambushed me with this earlier today."

"Why exactly do you think we're Masked and Blind Justice?" Jim asked, narrowing his eyes in Skye's direction.

"Well," Skye raised a finger and counted. "One is because I heard Ashley's voice the night of Kensington's murder. Two," she raised a second finger, "I saw her get hit with a book that night and the next day she had a bruise there. Three," she raised a third digit, "I debunked her story about a fight at school. Four," she raised the penultimate digit on the hand, "that wakizashi I saw was nigh identical to the one I saw in your room. Five," she raised the last finger on the hand. "You two are identical in height to the Masked and Blind Justice that I saw that night. I figure a few of those may be coincidence, but that many is too much to dismiss."

Jim seethed in his seat, digesting all that he'd just heard before responding. He grit his teeth. "What do you plan on doing with this information. Are you planning on going to the police?"

"What?" Skye asked. "Never! You two freed me from that fucker's influence. Ever since I watched him die, I've felt liberated."

"Liberated enough to put multiple arrows through a guy I saw," Jim said. "How do you even know how to use a bow, anyway?"

"My father taught me. He'd take me hunting almost every weekend growing up. With enough practice, you become proficient."

Jim shook his head, a stern look on his face. "Even if you were right, and I'm not saying you are, that would take a lot of guts to say that to Masked Justice's face."

"Jim," Ashley said before Jim cut her off with a lone finger raised, shushing her.

"Be quiet," Jim said. "Skye, why did you kill who you did

that night? Why did you start this life of death? Surely it wasn't for fun?"

"I don't find killing much fun, Mr. Benning. Sure, the act was a rush, but the feelings afterward are nothing like it. As for why I did it, let me think on how to phrase it." She paused for a good twenty seconds before continuing. "I guess I just wanted to keep some other kid from having to go through what I did with Kensington."

Jim brought a hand up to his face and covered his eyes. "Oh Lord, why me? You said it was a rush, was it?"

"It was until I heard a noise downstairs. Honestly, I thought you were the police, and I just knew I was going to spend life in prison at that moment. As mortifying as it was looking back, I'd be lying if I didn't say the struggle was invigorating."

"I'd call killing a great many things. I'm not sure invigorating would be one of them," Jim said. He pursed his lips together before speaking further. "I know the feeling of which you speak, but it takes a special kind of person to do it repeatedly and not go crazy.

"I didn't do it for a rush or anything along those lines. It was just a byproduct."

"What are you saying? Are you going to continue doing this? I ask because this could be trouble for me."

"How would me going around affect you?" Skye asked.

"Have you heard of the Pedophile Hunting Republic?" Ashley asked from her side.

"I thought they were just a conspiracy theory," Skye said. "It's just a bunch of people live action role playing as hunters, right?"

"You couldn't be further from the truth," Jim said. He turned the television off with the nearby remote controller. "I'm an agent of theirs. They pay very well, but here's the thing. They don't take kindly to surprises. The local sect of the republic, meaning me and a few others, are scrambling to find out who Silent Justice is. Christ, what am I supposed to do now that I know? I can't turn your name over. You're just a kid, no older than her." He pointed over to Ashley. He fell back in the chair and stared at the ceiling. "Why is my life never simple lately?"

"I'm sorry," Skye said. "I don't mean to cause trouble for you - if anything it's the opposite. That night you both saved me was liberating. I just wanted to help others the way you did me."

Jim reached up and rubbed the sides of his head. "I get it. I heard that enough from your friend over there."

"Because it's true," Ashley said. She raised her foot and placed it on the coffee table between them. "We just want to help others that were in our position."

Jim got up and paced in the middle of the room. "This should go without saying, but you never tell anyone any of this."

"Like I said, I just wanted to help."

"You can help by following what I say. When people go rogue," he glared at Ashley, "then people get hurt. I don't want either one of you getting hurt. Being Masked Justice isn't all fun and games. Jobs don't always go smoothly like yours did. I've been shot, stabbed, and punched in the face. That is why I'm going to act like a hard ass. It's for your own good." His lecture was interrupted by his cell phone ringing in his pocket. He pulled it out and looked at the number calling. "Oh shit."

"Who is it?"

He didn't answer, choosing instead to answer the call. "Hello?"

"You need to get over here," Edmund's out of breath

voice said. "Manny's back, and he's brought a couple of friends with him. I locked the door, but I don't know how long it'll last. Please, Ray's still in here."

"God damn it," Jim said. "I'll be right there. Barricade the door with anything you've got."

"I'm on it. Just hurry!" Edmund's frantic voice said over the line.

Jim hung up and pocketed the phone. "I need to take care of something."

"What was that about?" Ashley stood up. "You can say it. We're all in on this now."

"That was Edmund. We need to go suit up. Manny paid them a visit and he's outside his door trying to get in. Ray's in there still unconscious." He looked over at Skye. "It's a bunch of piss ant wannabe gangsters trying to kill a doctor and an old man essentially that's helped me a lot. I'm going to go suit up. Ashley if you want, you can come along."

"What about me?" Skye asked.

"I have a bow you can use if you really want. Are you sure you want to?"

"If I can help a friend of yours, I'm in. Do you have any spare masks?"

"Of course. Follow me and we'll get you suited up. Just hurry." He ran up the stairs, causing the girls to follow...

19

"How much does this vest cost?" Skye looked down at the unfamiliar garment she was wearing. She had a bow sitting on her lap, taking up most of the back seat. She also had a quiver of wooden arrows on her back.

"You don't want to know," Jim said. "We're almost there. When we get there, we're getting out immediately. They'll know we're here regardless unless we walk the streets which isn't an option. You two have your masks on, right?"

"We do," Ashley said from the passenger seat. "Are we using force when we get there?"

"It depends if they have weapons. I suspect they do, so yes, probably. The first salvo will be Silent's. We'll take over from there. Be careful out there. If they get close, can you defend yourself?"

"I don't have experience with deer trying to punch or stab me if that's what you're asking. I'd be making it up as I go. I'd rather they stay at a distance.

Jim turned the wheel. The rain coming down battered against the windshield as the wipers droned left and right.

"Then we'll make sure they're preoccupied. Be careful out there. These guys are out for blood."

"I'd be lying if I said I wasn't nervous though," Skye said. "You said these guys were gangsters?"

"In the loosest meaning of the word, sure." Ashley opened the glove compartment. "They're stupid, incompetent, and incredibly aggressive. That doesn't mean they're not dangerous."

"Here we are. Get ready." Jim pulled the car into the alley he'd traversed so many times before and shut the engine off once it was out of the street's view. He quickly put on the mask covering his eyes and pulled the other up over his nose. "Around that corner is our target. Let's get out and see what we're dealing with."

The group got out of the vehicle and immediately heard a loud crashing noise along with a grunt. This was accompanied by raucous cheering from noticeably intoxicated voices.

"You got this shit, dude," one yelled, slurring his words. "I got next turn."

Jim led the girls to the corner and peeked around. He saw two men standing on either side of a third. Manny stood to one of the sides with his back to the group. The one in the middle backed up from the door before dashing forward again and slamming his shoulder into the metal door.

Jim hid back behind the corner and looked to the two girls at his side. His voice was near silent as he leaned toward them and whispered. "Skye, you're up. As soon as you release the arrow, I'm charging in. Ashley, you're behind me. Make sure one of them doesn't flank me. Are you ready?"

Skye reached up into her quiver. "I guess there's a time and place to try this out for real." Her hand emerged from the container holding not one, but three arrows. "There's nobody else in the alley, right?"

"None, are you sure you can manage that? One's more than enough."

"I've done it before with some accuracy." Skye stepped forward and turned toward the corner. She gripped the bow in her left hand, her right hand clutching the wooden arrows. She saw Jim give her a silent nod as he pushed his blade's handle out of the sheathe. She nodded back and sidestepped after another loud crash met their ears.

She cleared the obstruction and found her three targets. She adjusted her aim and drew the string back. She took a deep breath and exhaled. She let loose the shot.

Three arrows shot out into the confined alleyway. One struck the farthest from them in the eye. He died on the spot as the arrow pierced into his brain matter. His body flopped down to the ground unceremoniously. The second clipped Manny in the leg, causing him to stumble to a knee. The third missed completely, leaving the one in the middle unscratched.

Jim raced around the corner, his hand hovered above his weapon's handle, ready to attack. He pulled the blade out and thrust it forward into Manny's chest. He twisted the blade and yanked, popping the blade free from his person.

Ashley had her blade out at her side as she ran at the unharmed man.

Her prey's hands reached for his belt line, fumbling for his weapon. His eyes were wide, and his hands shook. He finally gripped the pistol and pulled it out. Unfortunately for him, it was only once she was within reach.

Before he could raise the weapon, she slashed her blade into his abdomen before it got caught, still inside his side.

Ashley heard a woosh and squelching noise. She saw an

arrow sticking out of her target's chest, only mere inches away from her arm. The man crumbled to the ground.

The trio inspected their work.

Jim delivered a kick to Manny who was still on his knees. The blow forced him to fall to the ground on all fours. "I told you I'd be back, you moron. You just had to have your revenge, huh? Does this prove you're more of a man now?" He stomped on the arrow sticking out of his leg, driving it deeper before it snapped. He thrust the blade through his neck as Manny started screaming, muffling the noise while transforming it into a strained gurgle.

He pulled the blade free and watched Manny slump to the ground. He and Ashley sheathed their blades. He beckoned Skye over and pulled out his phone once his blade was firmly secured at his side. "Open up. We took care of them."

Ashley placed her hands on her knees and inspected the corpses. "They came packing heat alright. Look," she pointed down at a spare pistol that had slid across the asphalt below in all the chaos.

"Oh God," Skye held a hand over her mouth as she approached. "The smell is awful. She took care not to step in any of the blood nearby.

The door finally opened. Edmund looked down. "Oh, horse shit. Help me get these bodies inside now. The rain will wash away the blood. I can dispose of these." He reached down and grabbed the nearest body before dragging it inside onto the tiled floor.

Jim shrugged and did as he was told. He grabbed another and looked over at the two girls. "You two get Manny. He's the smallest. You'll be fine. Close the door once you're inside." He dragged the body off into the office.

Both girls got near the body, their shoes sloshing into

the blood. "Oh my God!" Skye reached down and grabbed Manny by the feet. "You get the arms."

"Fine. Let's hurry." Ashley hooked her arms under Manny's. "On three, one, two, three!"

The pair lifted in unison and carried his corpse into the office. Ashley let an arm dangle as she slammed the door shut behind them.

"Put him over here," Edmund called out from across the room. He opened a nearby door and pointed inside. "Get them in here."

"What is that room, bones?" Jim asked, struggling to haul the carcass into the directed room.

"People die occasionally in this business, Mr. Masked Justice. I cannot simply call the police."

The girls eventually reached the doorway.

Skye looked over her shoulder, guiding the pair into the room. "That is a lot of bottles."

The walls of the room had counters with untold amounts of different liquids. All of them were labeled clearly. There was a large plastic tub in the middle of the room along with a table large enough to have two bodies on it simultaneously. Jim's and Edmund's bodies were already laying atop it.

"Just put that one down beside the table," Edmund said.

"This is gnarly." Skye dumped Manny's carcass on the tiled floor. She looked down at a row of grates surrounding the table. "Is this for the blood?"

"It sure is. I'm usually forced to wait for a rainy day, but we're in luck tonight. The blood just goes outside. It'll wash it away. Nothing like seizing the opportunity. Am I right?"

Jim forced a loud cough and gestured toward the girls. "Girls, why don't you head in the other room and check on Ray? You're not going to want to see this."

"That goes for you too, Mr. Masked Justice. This is not for the squeamish. I recommend you go see how he's doing. I'll have these bodies disposed of by tonight. They'll never appear on the news until they're declared missing. Just knock on that door hard when you leave so I can go and lock the door again behind you."

"I understand," Jim said. "I'll collect their weapons on the way out. We don't want some kids wandering in the alley to find loaded pistols after all." He turned and headed toward the still open door. He could see the girls standing near Ray's bed. He whistled, drawing their attention. "We're picking up the weapons. We don't want anyone finding them. We can visit Ray after we secure everything." He beckoned them over and marched toward the back-alley exit.

The girls jogged over.

"I guess we did leave the guns out there," Ashley said. "We can't leave that unattended."

The trio got outside and picked up all the different weapons that came free in the scuffle from earlier. They packed them all in Jim's trunk. "Thank God there are no cameras in this part of the neighborhood."

"No need to worry even if you forgot," Ashley said.

"Why?" Jim closed the trunk. "If we get caught on camera and any of us have a mask on, they can run my license number. I'm fucked then."

"Do you remember when Charlie introduced you to swapping the plates?"

"I do. He mentioned it was illegal to go around with false plates too as I recall."

"Yes, but you underestimated your own laziness." Ashley opened the door, leading the three back into the underground clinic. "Those plates that are on the car, those are fake. You forgot to put the real ones back on after you last changed them."

"You've been driving around with false plates?" Skye stifled a giggle into her hands. "Aren't you a regular criminal mastermind? Imagine if Masked Justice was caught because of such a stupid reason." She devolved into full on laughter that spread to Ashley.

"Yeah, laugh it up," Jim walked faster toward Ray's bed. He was the first to reach it, leaving both girls in his dust. He towered over the bed and looked down at Ray. "Hey, old man," he said. "Are you going to wake up anytime soon? You're starting to worry us out here."

The two girls caught up, finally containing their laughter at their joke. Ashley stood at Jim's side while Skye was at the foot of the bed. "I heard you can wake someone up by tickling them," Ashley said.

"If you want to reach down and touch him, be my guest," Jim said.

"Can you kids keep it down?" Ray rolled over with a grumble.

"Holy shit," Jim said. "You're awake?"

"You all keep yammering on - how am I supposed to sleep?" Ray opened his eyes. He scanned left to right, seeing the three masked people standing by his bed. "Who in damnation are you people? For that matter, what happened? How did I end up in bed? For that matter, why does my arm and head hurt?"

"Easy, old man." Jim reached down and rested a hand on Ray's shoulder. "You're safe here."

"Who are you? Get your hand off me."

"Relax," Jim removed his hand. "I don't see the harm seeing as you already know, but if it'd make you feel better –

here." He reached up and pulled his neck gaiter down, revealing his nose and mouth. "Recognize me?"

"Jim?"

"That's me alright. As for Blind and Silent here," he gestured to the other two girls, "they'll be remaining anonymous for their own sakes. The point is, you saved Edmund from getting whacked you know."

"I did?" Ray asked.

"That's according to him too," Jim said. "If he admitted it, it must be true. He said you got in front of him when that asshole busted in here. He thought he'd killed you and ran out. We paid him a visit and scared them, but he doesn't learn lessons apparently. You lot don't have to worry about it now. They're gone."

"Thank you, young man. I knew I was right in telling you to talk to him. I just knew something was going to happen." Ray looked at the other two. "So, these are the Blind and Silent justice everyone's heard about, huh? You both should follow this man's instructions. He's a force for good in this world. I may not know much, but I'd bet my life on it."

"You did bet your life on it," Jim said. "Look at where you are now. You're lying on a cot with broken bones."

"I'm alive, aren't I?" Ray asked with a smile. "That's what matters. You're fighting for what's right. In a time when everybody wants to pretend good and evil don't exist, where everything is morally grey, there needs to be someone proving them wrong. You may be ambiguous in your methods, but your results are irrefutably good in this old man's opinion."

"We're just glad you're awake. We were worried you might never wake up." Jim showed a genuine smile.

"I'm not that fragile. I graduated life's school of hard

knocks. A little shove isn't going to kill me." Ray placed his good hand on his chest. "Even if I am getting up there in the years."

"We'll let you rest some more. We'll tell Edmund on the way out so he can get you some food or something. Just uh," Jim looked back at the door Edmund was behind, "make sure he washes his hands thoroughly. Trust me."

"Will do," Ray said. He extended his good arm up at Jim. "Thank you, Jim. I owe you all my life."

Jim reached down and took the extended hand and gently shook it. "You don't owe me anything, old man. I did it because it was the right thing to do, and that's all." He looked over at the girls. "Come on. Let's get home and let him rest. You two get out to the car, take the gear off, and stow it away while I get everything settled in here."

"Got it," both girls answered at the same time.

He watched them turn and walk off toward the door, quietly talking along the way.

"Get some rest, old man," Jim said backstepping. He turned and walked toward the door Edmund was still behind. He banged on the door with all his strength three times with a few seconds between strikes. He backed up and waited. He looked away from the door, not wanting to see the carnage inside when Edmund opened the door.

The door did indeed swing open not even a minute later. Edmund quickly squeezed into the room and shut it behind him. "Why are you still here?"

"I thought you'd want to know that Ray's awake over there." He pointed over at the cot. He looked Edmund over to see the apron he was wearing over his front completely covered in blood. The gloves he wore went up to his elbows. They too were slathered in blood. "On second thought, you might want to clean yourself up first before you scare the shit out of him."

"This is great news," Edmund said. "That means he either wasn't in a coma or he came out of it by God's grace. It means eventually he'll make a full recovery if he eats well. I'll make sure he comes over every day for breakfast and dinner. I'm tired of the status quo. He's a better friend than I ever deserved. I'm going to treat him as such."

"I'm happy to hear that." Jim took a few steps back. "I'll leave you to your business then. We're heading home. Remember to make sure those bodies are never found."

"There will be no bodies by the time I'm done. You can't find what doesn't exist."

"Good." Jim now turned around and got to the door. "I'll see you two around. Goodbye." He exited the building and slammed the door shut. He looked down to see the once blood-stained asphalt, now back to its normal shade. He looked over toward the main street. "The gutter," he said with a smirk. "It washes away the evidence of our sins." He walked over to the car. "There's something almost poetic about it."

He threw open the driver's door and popped the trunk. He stowed away his sword in the trunk and shut it before getting into the driver's seat. He took off both masks and looked over at Ashley. "Let's go home already."

20

J im looked at the time in the corner of his laptop's screen to see it was just after ten in the morning. "I should check my email and see if anything's new." He opened the private browsing software and navigated to his secret email only the republic knew of. He logged in and saw there was a lone new message waiting to be read. Instead of the usual address, this one was from Charlie's address. "That guy better not be nursing his bruises after giving me so much shit with mine."

He clicked the message and read it to himself. "We have another job. This one is time sensitive. The target is leaving tomorrow morning by five am. It is imperative he's eliminated by then. We cannot let him get away and fade into the masses. I left the address and his name at the bottom of this message."

Jim looked at the bottom of the page and confirmed the details were in fact where Charlie promised before jumping back up to where he left off. "It's back to business as usual," Jim read out loud. "Feel free to look up and corroborate the Republic's findings as usual. I've already done so, but I know how much you love doing it yourself as well just in case. You should let Ashley go to bed early tonight. You won't need her on a job as easy as this."

Jim furrowed his brow, rereading the last sentence again. "Odd," he said. "Why does he care if she goes or not? He was the one who got her the gear in the first place. Oh well, he's always been an enigma. It's no use trying to make sense of him sometimes." He placed the laptop on the coffee table in front of him. "That means I have until tonight to get ready."

He hefted himself out of the comfortable sofa and moved into the kitchen to get himself a glass from the nearby cabinet. He stood in front of the refrigerator and pressed the glass against the lever, causing water to fall into the container. "I have an idea. I can invite Cynthia, Charlie, and even Skye over for dinner tonight. We can have a cookout. It'd be just like old times, with the addition of a couple teenagers." He took the glass and moved into the living room and back to his seat.

He pulled out his cell phone once he was seated and dialed.

An annoyed Cynthia answered. "Yeah? This isn't a good time. Class is about to start."

"I'm just calling to invite you to a cookout I'm hosting tonight. I know you don't want to cook while you study so hard. I'm hosting it around six tonight"

"I'll think about it. I have to go. The teacher just walked in." She hung up without warning.

"Fair enough," Jim said to himself, ending the call. He dialed another familiar number he'd memorized long ago.

"Jim," Charlie answered. "What's going on?"

"I've been wondering where you've been, you lazy bum." Jim smiled. "You haven't been around in a minute."

"I can't be hanging around at your place all day every day you know. I've been taking care of things on my end."

"I just thought I'd call and invite you to a cookout I'm hosting tonight. Cynthia and Skye are coming. It'll be like old times."

"Why are you inviting the kid?"

Jim rolled his eyes. "I think Ashley would appreciate having someone her age there. I don't want her to feel like a figurative fifth wheel."

"Ahh," Charlie said. "I see. Sure. What time's the little shindig going to kick off? I have work until five tonight."

"I told Cyn it was at six. Just come over whenever you're ready. I'll get Ashley to invite Skye. I think this will be a nice little break from our busy work schedules."

"Speaking of which, you did check your email, yes?"

"I saw it alright. Don't worry, there won't be any booze imbibed. I'll be good and ready."

"Then we're good," Charlie said. "Well, if I want to make it by six I need to get back to work, buddy. Take care."

"Have a good one." Jim hung up and pocketed the phone. "Then that's done. I should go make sure I have enough steaks for everybody." He got up and made his way to the refrigerator. "I guess I'm going shopping..."

That evening...

"I'm surprised you showed up." He stepped to the side allowing Cynthia entry.

"Is it really so hard to believe I wanted a free meal?"

"Ouch," Jim said, feigning hurt. "Here I thought you were coming for my charming personality, and that you wanted more of my flirting."

"You two haven't changed a bit I see." Charlie walked

over to the pair. "Hey, Cynthia," he said. "Don't tell me you're still leading this loser on. You've been playing hard to get since high school. Aren't you afraid he'll give up and move on?"

The two teenagers were in the kitchen at the table watching the trio in front of the front door.

Skye leaned to her left toward Ashley and whispered. "Did they used to be together or something?"

"She left him as far as I understand it," Ashley said.

"He's stubborn as a mule and as dense to match," Cynthia shared a laugh with Charlie and Jim.

"That'll teach me for bringing the gang back together." Jim got between the pair and threw his arms over their shoulders, bringing them together. "Then again, I always was the punching bag, wasn't I? I should have known this would happen."

"They look happy," Skye said, watching the group in the other room.

"Good for them," Ashley looked away from the display.

"Don't be jealous he has his arm around her. That will be you one day I bet."

"You think so?"

"After you're eighteen, possibly," Skye said. "It's just a matter of if you're willing to wait and pass by other boys in the meantime.

"What are you two whispering about?" Charlie pulled a seat up to the table. "I bet it's about boys at school, right?"

Cynthia came up behind him and slapped him in the back of the head.

"What was that for?" Charlie looked to his side where she sat down. He rubbed the back of his head as he waited for an answer.

"It's rude to invade someone's conversation, and slightly sexist to assume they're talking about boys."

"Not really," Charlie said. "If they were boys, I'd assume they were talking about girls. Don't be so sensitive. It's what high schoolers do after all."

"He's got a point." Jim cut through the kitchen and moved to the back door.

"No he doesn't," Cynthia said. "It's a stereotype is what it is."

"Whatever you say, your royal highness. Stereotypes are usually rooted in some truth." Jim opened the back door and disappeared outside.

"That's my cue," Charlie said, pushing the seat out and standing up.

"You're cue for what?"

"To stand around the grill and commentate on how the cooking's going. Haven't you ever noticed that? There's always a guy doing that at cookouts." Charlie followed Jim outside.

Cynthia watched the door close before turning back to the girls. "Sorry about him. He's as insensitive as Jim is. Arguably he's even worse."

"It's not a big deal," Skye said.

"Yeah, I don't pay him a lot of attention," Ashley said. "He's more of a jester to me. Entertaining, but not someone I take seriously."

"Besides," Skye snickered, "he was right."

"Skye!" Ashley elbowed the girl in the ribs. She narrowed her eyes at her friend and huffed.

"Ow," Skye held a hand to where the elbow connected. "There's no need for that now. I'm just telling the truth."

"One of you has a crush on a boy in school, huh?"

Cynthia looked off into the distance. "I remember what that was like. Relish that feeling. It's all too fleeting."

"That's -" Skye was cut off by Ashley's hand flying to her mouth.

"Embarrassing. It's just embarrassing is what she was saying."

"I guess it is," Cynthia said. "Come on, girls, let's go see how the boys are doing outside. I don't know about you, but I don't want mine well done. If you don't watch him, he'll overcook it." She got up from the table. "Besides, we may as well all hang out together. It's the first time we've had the chance in a while. It'd be a shame to waste it."

The girls watched Cynthia exit and looked at each other with a shrug. "We may as well, right?" Ashley asked. She got up and followed the rest of the group along with Skye. They emerged into the backyard.

Jim was nearby with a barbecue fork. Below him was the sizzling steaks on the grill. "It's nice to get a little rest every now and then." He stabbed one of the slabs of meat and flipped it. "It's for times like this that I splurged on a bigger grill, because these smell delicious."

"You have no idea," Cynthia said. She stood near the men a dozen feet away in the backyard. "I haven't even taken the time to cook for myself lately. It's all been instant food."

"You'd better be careful," Charlie said. He reached over and pinched her stomach before she batted his hand away. "That's a surefire way to gain weight."

The two girls approached the group as the men shared a laugh. Ashley yawned as she came to a stop a few feet away from the grill.

"You look tired," Charlie said. He reached up and tapped below his right eye. "I think I see bags starting to form there. You should work on that. Guys don't tend to like that look."

"Aw, who cares?" Ashley asked. "I just stayed up late studying is all."

"Right." Jim flipped another steak. "Speaking of which," he looked over at the two high schoolers, "who's you guys hated teacher this year? I know that old crone Ms. Bagwell still works there."

"She's retiring next year I heard," Cynthia said. She looked at Jim. "Remember how she'd always single you out? Why did you try to piss her off so often anyway? You were always talking with your partner in crime there."

"My favorite was the time we rigged that bucket of water above the door," Charlie said.

"That was you?" Cynthia asked.

"Nobody was ever punished for that," Charlie said. "It was us though."

"What a caretaker," Ashley said in her sarcasm laden voice. "You all were juvenile delinquents?"

"I'll have you know I never once got a detention or any disciplinary action in my entire schooling," Cynthia said. "I also was the valedictorian."

"I don't find that difficult to believe." Ashley turned to Skye. "She must not have had a fun childhood."

"You'd be surprised," Jim said, taking off one of the steaks and putting it on a nearby platter. "She got into way more mischief than she'd ever admit." He winked at Cynthia. "Isn't that right?"

"You may as well admit it, Cyn," Charlie said. "If you don't, I'll tell them. You fooled all the teachers, but we know you better than that. Now fess up."

"Fine," Cynthia brushed a strand of hair out of her face. "I may have done a few things that my parents disliked."

"Disliked?" Charlie laughed for five seconds straight. "Your parents forbade you from leaving your room for an entire three months after you snuck out to hang with Jim. What was it you two did again?"

Jim finished placing the last steak on the platter. "We went -"

Cynthia stomped on his foot, effectively stopping him from continuing. "It's in the past. Let's leave it there."

"They went to the local park and sat on a bench to star watch together." Charlie, to his credit, managed to dodge the immediate stomp attempt. "Isn't that romantic?"

"Fine," Cynthia said. "It turns out someone called the police when they saw two kids without an adult alone in the park at night. A police car came by and dragged us back to our houses. There, are you happy now?"

"You really need to express your emotions in a nicer way." Jim hopped on one foot away from the group before circling back around, still hobbling. "Now let's go eat before they get cold."

After dinner in the living room.

"I think we'll go upstairs and leave you three to reminisce or whatever." Ashley and Skye walked up the stairs.

Have fun." Jim watched the pair disappear upstairs before looking back at the television. "How're those bruises feeling?" Jim asked once he heard the door close upstairs.

"I'll survive," Charlie said. "The guy didn't want to kill me. He just wanted it to hurt."

"What on earth happened? I didn't want to bring attention to it with the kids around, but Jesus, this looks painful." Cynthia leaned closer and inspected the bruises visible all over Charlie's arms and face. "Did you rip off some drug dealer? Have you been to a doctor?"

"Cut it out," Charlie leaned back. His normally playful tone was replaced by an annoyed one.

"Then tell me what happened."

"It was a simple misunderstanding," Charlie said, successfully swatting away one of her palms from a bruise on his arm. "It's not my fault he gave me a little extra in the bag, now is it?"

"You will never change," Cynthia said. "It'll be the death of you if you're not careful."

"How wonderfully morbid," Charlie said, a tinge of sarcasm to his words. "I'm fine. The guy was just proving a point is all."

"He certainly made it." Cynthia cringed and backed off.

"Ignoring Charlie's poor life decisions," Jim said, "how long has it been since we were together? A few weeks now? It's been too long."

"Things change," Cynthia said. "Why should we be any exception? We're not in high school anymore, even if some of us still act like it." She gave Jim a dirty look. "I'm just glad for a night off. I figure I can't study every single day. I'll burn out like when I did for finals in high school."

"At least you still got straight A's," Charlie said. "My parents were pissed."

"That's not the point."

"Whatever you say," Jim said. "I hope your exam goes well, Cyn. I'm sorry about bothering you about that whole babysitting thing right before your big exam."

"She is annoying but not a bad person. Just don't make a habit of it."

"Speaking of bad people," Charlie said, "I'm thinking of going into politics soon. I bet neither of you expected that."

"Politics? What? Do you want to be the mayor or something?" Cynthia asked.

"It wasn't mayorship I was dreaming of. My first step would be to be a representative in our state house. I think I could manage it."

"With your work ethic?" Cynthia scoffed. "You'd never get elected. Not to mention you don't have a wife. Voters love to vote for a married person. It makes it look like you have your life figured out."

"Nah," Jim said. "You'd want to go into the race single if anything. That way you don't have anything holding you back. Think of all the fun flings you could have as a single politician."

"He'd just look like an irresponsible playboy. Women wouldn't vote for him."

"Why not?" Jim asked.

"Yeah, why not? Charlie echoed the question. "I clean up well. I bet I could have the single ladies out there voting for me. They'd just dream about one day being my Mrs. Didn't you guys ever notice young attractive single women get elected regularly. There's no reason to think it wouldn't work the same way."

"What are you going to say when they ask what your previous job was?" Cynthia asked. "I don't think stoner would go over well."

"Being a stoner isn't my job, genius." Charlie said. "I do make a living you know. Just because that's not the stories I tell you, doesn't mean they don't exist."

"Fine, just don't blame me when they don't vote for you," Cynthia said.

"I'd vote for you, buddy," Jim said, "for what it's worth."

"Now we just need to get you two straightened out, and we'd all have our lives relatively figured out. Jim works from home, Cyn's going to become a lawyer, and I'd be a politician. You two just need to get your heads out of your asses and see what's right in front of you."

"Maybe one day, but I don't think that's in the cards yet." Jim looked over at Cynthia.

"One day?" Cynthia asked. "I doubt it with how you act. You need to change a little before I'd ever give you a chance."

"Be wary of tossing aside something beautiful in pursuit of Mr. Perfect," Charlie said. "That's my advice to you, Cyn. I'm tired of seeing you two bicker and fight over stupid shit when you should be happy together."

"Forget about it. I dictate my love life." Cynthia looked away from both men.

"Sorry, buddy," Charlie said. "I tried my best..."

Upstairs in Ashley's room.

The girls sat side by side on the floor with a game controller in their hands. The sounds of clicks and various sound effects filled the illuminated room.

"Did you know that old guy from before?" Skye asked, her voice soft.

"Ray?" Ashley asked. "I know of him, yes. Jim's told me stories. Why?"

"I was just replaying the scene in the alley over and over in my head. The dead bodies just laying out in the rain, because of me." She pressed the start button that paused the game. She raised a hand to her face, wiping away a stray tear.

"Look," Ashley said, putting the controller down in front of her on the wooden floor. She turned and looked at her friend. "I'm sorry things went down like this." Her voice grew quieter. "We should have never taken you along, especially when you were already having problems dealing with your first kill."

"Tell me it was worth it. Tell me he was worth killing those three men. That feeling of emptiness is bigger now than before. I need to know he was worth it."

"I don't know him personally, but he's helped Masked Justice on plenty of jobs. He's saved Jim and Cynthia down there according to the stories they've told about him. He's a peaceful soul. He said Ray had never put his hands on anyone. He was just a quick talker that helped Jim get out of a few jams. Like that one time he managed to distract an elite assassin sent to kill Jim and Cynthia. There's good reason Jim was so adamant we go and keep him safe."

Skye was still wiping away tears and sniffling. "I guess that helps."

Ashley looked at the door and back to Skye. "Look, uh I'm not usually one to do this kind of thing, but uh..." She looked around the room. "Did you need a uh hug or some- thing? It'd be strictly plat-"

Before she could finish her conditions, she felt Skye crying into her shoulder. She felt arms wrapped around her and a growing wetness on her shoulder.

"Platonic," Ashley said. She awkwardly wrapped an arm around Skye and patted her on the back. "Just let it all out I guess." She kept talking as she comforted her friend. "It'll be alright, probably. Sorry I'm not good at this kind of thing."

The only answer she received was a muffled noise.

"You helped save an innocent life today by taking three guilty. That's what I tell myself on jobs like this. There's no sense feeling bad for trash bag human lives when they went there to kill anyway. You just stopped them is all."

Skye pulled away and looked down at the ground, her voice brittle. "I'm sorry. I've never done that before. I just couldn't stop myself." She wiped her nose with her sleeve and looked up at Ashley, her normally neat black eyeliner was trailing down her face, and her eyes were red and puffy.

"Hey, don't worry about it," Ashley said in a soft voice. "Just remember what I said. He was an innocent harmless old man that multiple people wanted dead. You did a good thing tonight. If you've ever trusted anything I've ever said, then trust me on this one." Ashley gave her a genuine smile. "You did good."

"I appreciate that even if you are just trying to console my mess of a self. It's just a whirlwind of emotions that I'm feeling now. Excitement, worry, guilt, and anger are all swirling around in me right now."

"It'll settle in time. Just remember what I said. We're removing evil by defending the good in the world. That's all there is to it as far as I'm concerned. It's like excising a tumor. The tumor dies for the individual to live. It's an apt comparison too since tumors are just cells that are deformed like the people we go after."

Skye got up and walked over to Ashley's nightstand, retrieved a few tissues, and took her seat beside Ashley. She blew her nose and threw away the tissue. "I think I just need a break from that whole activity for a little while to get my head straight. You know what I mean? I'm not quitting. I just need a break while I wrap my head around it."

"I get it," Ashley said.

"Sorry to interrupt our game." Skye wiped her face with the last remaining fresh tissue before tossing the balled-up tissue in the trash can near Ashley's bed. She picked up the controller again. "I'm fine now. Let's keep going."

"If you're sure..."

21

"Charlie's not coming along?" Ashley asked as they walked to the car.

"He left and went home. He's probably still in pain from his questioning at Dillon's hands." Jim loaded the masks, weapons, and everything else into the back of the car. "You don't have to come along either, come to think of it, if you don't want to. He said it would be a routine job so long as we caught him before he flees tomorrow morning."

"Nothing is ever routine with us. Someone needs to make sure you don't get yourself killed, right?"

"I think that's my job regarding you actually." Jim got into the driver's seat as Ashley slammed the passenger door shut. He started the engine and pulled out onto the road. "The guy lives in a nearby suburb. Charlie said he's planning on catching a flight about five."

"He must know he's being hunted," Ashley said. "Masked Justice has been getting quite the treatment on the news lately after all. If any of his ilk are paying attention, I bet they're scared shitless at seeing it."

"They deserve to feel nothing less," Jim said. "If he's petrified he'll lose a hand or get ran through, then that means he's not looking for his next victim."

"This is a simple go in and kill the guy in bed job, right?" Ashley asked. "Then let me take point for once. I promise I can do it."

"I know you can, but I still insist on going first. You never know what's going to happen, and if anyone catches a bullet, I'd rather it be me. Just know if I ever die on a job, I want you to run. Get out and never look back. Do you understand me?"

"Way to kill the mood. Jesus," Ashley said. "You're not going to die. Don't try and raise that death flag."

"Death flag? What is that?"

"It's not important. Let's focus on how to not die rather than preparing for it."

"Fine. We're finding a way in, then we find his room, and we do the deed. It's a simple plan, but things can always go wrong. Stay on your toes in there."

"I got it." Ashley looked out the window to her right at the overcast night sky. "I think we shouldn't include Skye in our operations for a while."

"I wasn't planning on it," Jim said. "Why do you say that though?"

"She wants a break from the killing she said. She used the word break for a reason I think. She's good to go but needs to wrap her head around it is what she said."

"That better be what she means, or we're in deep shit," Jim said. "She knows who we are. She can't go feeling too guilty, or she'll turn us in."

"She wouldn't do that."

"You have no way of knowing that. Everyone reacts

differently. It doesn't matter right this minute anyway. I have no plans of involving her further than she already is. She can take the time she needs. In fact, it'd be better if she took a break or quit permanently. It'd draw less attention."

"I just thought I should let you know," Ashley said. "She's fine, by the way. Thanks for asking."

"I'm more concerned with you." Jim turned and slowed down. "I know it's not the place, but I haven't asked yet. How's your classes going?"

"Seriously?" Ashley asked. "The two tests I've had I scored an A and a B. I'm doing fine."

"How are you dealing with this life? You're free to stop any time you wish too you know," Jim said. He had a sad smile on his face. "It'll happen sometime. I hope you do anyway."

"What the hell does that mean?" Ashley asked. "You don't want me around?"

"No, not in the slightest." Jim hit the gas. "I mean I hope you lead a normal life at some point, get settled down, and be happy. Look at me." He used one hand to point at himself. "Does it look like I'll ever be able to have a normal life? No, it doesn't. I was dumped because of this as a matter of fact. I don't want the same for you."

"I make my own decisions if you haven't noticed."

"Now, we're only a few minutes out. You have been maintaining your blade, haven't you?"

"You never showed me how to do that," Ashley said, reaching over and slapping his arm. "All I did was wipe the blood clean. I don't know how to sharpen it or whatever."

"I guess that's something I'll need to teach you then. It should be fine for tonight. I'll be doing the finishing blow after all."

"Why am I here then?"

Jim pulled over to the side of the road and put it in park before turning the engine off. He looked at Ashley and spoke. "You're backup. Just in case something goes wrong. Maybe I get knocked on my ass. You can help. It's a big responsibility."

"Don't patronize me, even if you are right," Ashley said. "I'll keep your sorry ass alive. I owe you anyway. You did get me out of that hell of a life."

"Don't stay because you feel some debt to me. It is forgiven officially now and forever," Jim said. "Understand me? I only want you here if you truly wish to be here. Are you sure what you're doing here is worth the risk?"

"Don't ask stupid questions. Now where are we? This isn't the place."

"I didn't want to pull up until we were ready to go," Jim said. He started the car again and pulled out. "Look in the glove compartment."

Ashley didn't answer but did open the storage space only to audibly gasp when she saw a pistol. "Whoa,"

"I want you to carry that from now on."

"Won't they be able to trace this to us?"

"No, but it is punishable by like ten years in prison if you get caught with it. It seems like small potatoes when compared to other charges like say, manslaughter." Jim pulled off onto a smaller dead-end street. "Here we are. When I stop this car, we put on our masks and go. This guy is going to be on edge, so stay behind me."

"I heard you earlier." Ashley blew a stray hair out of her face. "It's your show, Masked Justice. I'm just the sidekick, right? That's what they call me on the news. Skye and me are your sidekicks. It's a little insulting when you think about it."

"Be glad that's your biggest problem right now. That could soon change."

"You said it's an easy job."

"Never get complacent. That's how people get hurt," Jim's voice was stone cold. "If you do, you get benched. I won't have you get yourself killed because of my poor mentoring. I did say it should be easy. I don't know that it will be. Be prepared for the worst and bring backup. You are my lifeline. I want you at your best."

"I like the sound of bodyguard a lot better than accomplice to Masked Justice. I'll be serious." She cleared her throat. "I promise."

"I sure hope so." He pulled to the side of the road in front of their target. He pulled the cover up over his nose and donned the mask covering his eyes. He looked over and saw Ashley already ready. "Let's go."

The pair exited their vehicle and dashed as they had so many times before. Jim reached the front door and waited until Ashley caught up a moment later. "We clear the bottom floor first, and then we move upstairs. Stay on me," Jim said before he wrapped his right hand around the doorknob and twisted. The mechanism offered no resistance, opening easily.

Jim slipped inside and surveyed the darkened interior. They were inside what could be called the home's living room. A couch and a recliner faced a large flatscreen television in the corner of the room. The television wasn't off however, illuminating the room faintly as static filled the screen, along with a terrible noise accompanying it.

"Something's not right," Jim said in a low voice. He heard the door close behind him. He felt a hand on his shoulder.

"Why's the tv on?" Ashley whispered. "Is he on the couch?"

"I'll check. Cover me." Jim stalked forward in the relative darkness away from the screen. He got close enough to see over the furniture only to see nobody laying on the cushions below. "Nobody here."

"Maybe the guy is just lazy and forgot to turn it off?" Ashley asked.

"Or something's off here," Jim said. He looked left and right, scanning for any possible threat or abnormality. "Get down now." He got to a knee behind the sofa. He heard a loud thump behind him.

"Jesus, that almost hit me." Ashley looked back at the wall near the door to see an arrow sticking into the drywall.

The lights flipped on amidst the sound of applause. Jim's left hand grabbed the pistol he always kept on his belt line. He brought the weapon up, ready to bare.

"Easy now, Masked Justice." Dillon's voice said with a laugh. Two masked men stepped out from different exits of the room. His voice was coming from behind them toward the stairwell. He stepped into view; his left hand held a giant riot shield. "We don't want this to come to shooting, surely. That's not good for anybody's business. We came to fight like real men. In our organization, we eliminate traitors with duels with our blades. Not that you'd understand anything like that, what with you shacking up with a sixteen-year-old girl and forcing her to kill with you."

"We call that corrupting a minor," An electronic but altogether familiar voice came from one of the two masked men. "It's almost as bad as ruining their innocence."

The other masked one spoke up, their voice scrambled as well. "You just couldn't wait to get back to ruining someone else's life, could you? You ruined your little wannabe girlfriend's life a few weeks back. Did burying that body help her prepare for her bar exam?"

Dillon reached the bottom of the stairs with a heavy grunt. "Now put the firearm away. It's not like it can get through this anyway." He slapped the front of the clear material. "This baby's special made. It can withstand blade attacks and small caliber gunshots, and I don't feel a damned thing." He held it in front of him. It dwarfed even large tower shields. It went from the floor all the way up to his chin.

"I'll tell you what. Since I'm feeling generous tonight, I'll let you two have the honors. You get first crack at Masked Justice."

"You're just wanting us to tire him out," one of the masked assailants said. "Fine, I got him. You get the girl."

"Why do I get the girl?" the other asked before unsheathing the blade hanging at his side. "I don't want to hurt a kid."

Everyone got their respective melee weapons out. The front door opened, drawing attention from everyone inside to reveal George entering the house, effectively making it a four versus two.

"I take it that this means I'm fired," Jim said. He reached his left hand behind him to make sure Ashley was still behind him. "Then I guess I can finally say something I've been holding back."

"What are your final words, Masked Justice?" Dillon asked, holding up a hand, ready to snap his fingers and signal the attack.

"If you're not going to fight fair, then why should we?"

Dillon snapped his fingers, causing the two assassins on the ground floor to rush forward.

Jim raised the blade and deflected the incoming overhead swing. He tried to take advantage of his attacker's blade losing all momentum by swinging in a wide horizontal arc in front of him. His assailant jumped back, avoiding the blade.

"Hold, George." Dillon's voice said in a commanding tone. "We never interfere in a man's duel to the death."

"But, sir," George said.

"I said hold." Dillon's voice brooked no room for disagreement.

"Yes, sir."

Jim dodged to the side as another swing came down, aiming at his head. He kept his sword between him and his opponent, keeping a close eye on their weapon at all times.

Meanwhile Ashley saw the other attacker walking toward her at a slow pace. Her attacker spoke in that electronic voice they'd heard earlier. "Let's just make this easy, kid. Throw down the weapons, and we let you go. We don't want to hurt you."

Ashley maneuvered her way to the only part of the room not occupied, giving her a little room to fight. "If you're trying to kill him, I'm going to kill you," she said holding the blade in front of her. Her hands were shaking but her voice held firm. "Don't underestimate me if you know what's good for you."

"You stubborn brat." The voice turned angry. "Don't blame me if I scar that pretty little face then." He wasted no more time and raised his blade. "Let's go."

"It's your funeral." Ashley readied her weapon and waited.

"You're giving me first strike? That's bold and stupid." Her attacker swiped at her in a wide arc.

She parried the blow as best as she could but could not

launch a counterattack due to the force of the blow. She had no time to rest or reassess as the bladed weapon was headed toward her head this time from the side. She ducked down and thrust the sword forward, landing squarely between the man's thighs, scraping against the inside of his right leg.

"Christ!" the masked person yelled. "I'm going to kill you for that."

Meanwhile Jim had his hands full. He and his opponent were matching each other blow for blow, steel clanged against steel as sparks flew from the force and speed they were colliding. He backed up as the exchange continued. His attacker pressed the advantage and chased after him while continuing the onslaught. Jim had no opportunity for counterattacks. He was fully focused on keeping himself alive.

"Just fucking die," Jim's assailant yelled. "How are you still alive? You're not trained." He accentuated the words with a heavy downward smash.

Jim managed to deflect the blow and knock his opponent's blade to the side. He kicked him in the gut, causing him to back up a few feet until he regained his balance. "I'm just that good, or you're just shit with the blade. Take your pick."

"Beginner's luck doesn't last forever," he said. Their eyes narrowed in hatred. "You're not leaving here alive tonight. Not after what you've done."

Meanwhile Ashley twirled the blade in her hand and tilted her head. "Don't tell me that's all you've got."

"I'm trying to keep your dumbass alive, kid. You're making me regret that decision." Her attacker had one hand on his leg.

"You're dismissed," Dillon said.

"Sir?" Ashley's attacker asked.

"You're injured. George here will take over. Get out. I will make sure you are trained so well that next time an amateur won't graze you. You've embarrassed yourself tonight. Get out of my sight."

"You'd best do what the boss man says, or he'll kill you next." Ashley's mask hid her grin. "You did just get beat by a girl after all."

"As you command." The man bowed and sheathed his blade. "You're going to wish I'd stayed, girl. George doesn't give a fuck who he faces." He turned and noticed the still ongoing fight before circling around Ashley, giving her distance before exiting via the front door.

"Don't you ever get tired?" Jim asked. His back touched the back door. Without missing a beat, he dashed to the right into the next room. He kept retreating, keeping his blade between himself and his would-be assassin.

"Your fear is showing." The attacker's voice was no longer as confident and interrupted by heaving breaths. "You'll never win by retreating and defending."

"Whatever you say." Jim held the blade with both hands, his eyes were locked onto the blade across the room. "Come at me if I'm scared then. I dare you."

"Big talk, but it's worthless if you can't back it up." He dashed toward Jim, causing him to backpedal nearly as quickly. He unleashed a flurry of blows, each one meeting nothing but steel as their weapons intermingled into a clanging song of death.

Jim redirected the last blow away from him and saw his opportunity. His opponent was overextended, he was off balance, and he was out of breath. He didn't have time to really wind up the swing, but he mustered what force he could and swung for his opponent's face.

His mask fell off along with a yell of pain.

Jim looked at his handiwork, his eyes widened. "Charlie?"

Charlie reached up and held his hand to his wounded cheek. "You're already a dead man anyway. I'm out of here." He turned and sprinted away and out the back door.

Before Jim could even make sense of the revelation, he turned and saw Ashley struggling to fend off George.

George had a knife in both hands and was swinging them with wild abandon in her direction. His hands, and by extension knives, were almost blurs with the speed of the swings.

She stayed light on her toes and jumped over various furniture, evading the death by a thousand cuts. She tried blocking one blow, only to have her balance thrown off ending with her falling on her butt.

Jim ran back into the main room, blade at the ready, rushing George.

"Everyone halt!" Dillon's deep voice boomed.

George halted his swing just shy of Ashley's throat and paused. He backed up away from her and kept Jim in his line of sight all the while.

Ashley however did not deign to obey the command and instead used the opportunity to pull out the pistol in her belt line. She lined up the shot center mass and squeezed the trigger. A deafening gunshot rang out and George stumbled to a knee.

"You little bitch," George said, dropping a blade and holding his stomach. "I'll kill you for that."

"Foul play will not be tolerated in duels, little girl." Dillon had a foul look about him as he stomped forward toward her.

"You'd best back off, or you'll get some lead too, old man." Ashley's voice betrayed her breathlessness.

"We all need to get out of here or we're all busted," Jim said in a calm voice. "Somebody's going to call that shot in." He got to Ashley's side and guided her to the front door. "Besides, he's dead anyway." He reached for his firearm and took the final shot at George. His head had a new hole as he fell to the floor, dead for all to see.

"You'll regret this breach of conduct. This isn't over by a long shot!"

Jim holstered his firearm and quickly flung the door open and pushed Ashley out first. "We'll see about that, big boy." He slammed the door shut and sprinted back toward the car they'd come in. Once they were both inside, he wasted no time in pulling out and getting away.

They both tore their masks off and regained their beath.

"Did I hear you say Charlie?" Ashley asked.

"It was him alright. I gave him a good scar to remember me by. It cut his mask right off. I got a good look. He set us up."

"He betrayed us is what he did." Ashley finally caught her breath. "Why though?"

"Power," Jim said.

"How does that get him power exactly?"

"He's going into politics," Jim said. "They have political pull. If he gets elected, he's another Republic member in a position of power. He probably had to turn on me to prove his loyalty if I had to wager. I should have killed him when I had the chance." He paused. "I just couldn't do it. I let him get away."

"That's not even the worst part here," Ashley said. She kicked back in her chair and placed her foot against the glove compartment. "You're blacklisted. That means you're radioactive now. The good press will stop, and people will start hating you. We can't stay here. Do you realize this?"

"I'm more concerned with where we're staying tonight. If Charlie's turned on me, then he knows where we live. They're liable to try and kill me while I'm asleep."

"What do you suggest?" She looked out the front window as small spatters of rain started falling. "There's always a motel I guess."

"Christ, I really would fit their accusations if I did that."

"I don't think that's the problem. You're already marked for death. It'd be best to go somewhere unexpected."

"Unexpected? I have a few ideas then."

"You don't mean Cynthia?"

"No, I'd rather not involve her when we're being hunted. It's not going to be fun though. Have you ever been camping?"

"I think I did once when I was little." Ashley crinkled her nose. "I don't remember liking it."

"It may come to it," Jim said. He took a hand off the wheel and reached into his pocket before tossing his cell to her. "Call Edmund."

"I doubt he's up at this hour."

"Then he'll wake up, or we go to plan B. Trust me, you'd rather not go to plan B if you hate camping so much."

"At least tell me your phone's password. You don't expect me to know it, do you?"

"I already unlocked it, now stop lollygagging and get on with it. I need to know where to go. They're already trying to find us I imagine."

"Fine." Ashley found the appropriate button to push under the contacts list and selected Edmunds before raising it to her ear.

Edmund's voice met her ear. "Yeah? What is it?"

"I don't guess you have a place we can stay for a night?"

"What? No, I'm not a motel service."

"Really? We did save your and Ray's ass, remember?"

"Fine," Edmund said. "I'll do you this favor. Go to my office. Call Ray and have him let you in. Don't touch anything, and I better not find anything missing."

"We understand. We'll head there."

22

"We're going to sleep where exactly?" Ashley asked. "I only remember one cot in there."

"We're lucky to have a roof over our head at all," Jim said. "We should be thankful for that at least. Not to mention I never did unload the trunk from before on the camping trip with Cyn. We have two sleeping bags in that. Besides, we'll have good company. I know Ray doesn't look it, but he's got quite a head on his shoulders"

"You said he saved your life before, didn't you?"

Jim scratched his ear, keeping the vehicle steady. "He did. He could have blackmailed me for cash using my identity for leverage, but he doesn't have a mean bone in his body that I've seen." He brought the car to a stop and looked over at Ashley. "Just be nice. I know you can be."

"I'm always nice." She looked away from him. "What do you know?"

"Here we are." Jim backed into the alley and put the car in park. "I suppose we'll also have to tell the school you're moving since we will have to get out of town as soon as we can." He got out of the car and slammed the door shut. He looked over the car at Ashley as she got out and stretched. "You'll also need to tell Skye. You can't just leave without telling her what's going on."

"That would have been easier if you hadn't destroyed our phones earlier." Ashley followed him to the familiar door.

Jim opened the trunk and pulled out the two sleeping bags, handing one over to Ashley. "They would be able to follow us. Don't worry, you called Ray before I destroyed them. He should be waiting on us." He banged on the door and took a step back.

The door flew open after a few moments of waiting. Ray took a step backward, flinching with every move. He used his good arm to gesture inside. "Hurry and get in. You'll catch your death out there with how cold it is." He rushed the pair inside with a shiver before shutting it behind them and locking it. "What brings you two over here at this time of night?"

"It's a long story, but to shorten it," Jim said, "we were betrayed, and we needed a safe place to bed down for the night. It wouldn't be safe at my place since the rat knows where I live."

"What are you going to do now?" Ray was helped back over to the bed and sat down. He looked up at Jim. "If they're hunting you down then you need to get out while you still can."

"That is the plan," Jim said. "We just needed a good night's sleep before we did."

"What about that girl you like?" Ray asked. "Aren't you going to tell her about all this? You two were thick as thieves last time I saw you. Maybe she could help? She did help you with that assassin fella after all."

"I also nearly ruined her life, Pops." Jim unfolded the

sleeping bag on the tiled floor. "She's lucky to almost be a lawyer now, no thanks to me. I don't want that for her again just because of me. Don't you get it?"

"I understand."

Ashley tossed hers to the ground near Jim and got it ready. "I'm the only help he needs anyway. I kept you alive earlier. You're welcome by the way."

"It also pissed the big man off," Jim said. "That could come back to bite us."

"It's better than being dead. A thank you wouldn't kill you, would it?"

Jim locked eyes with her and didn't waver. "Thank you sincerely for your part in that battle. It helped us both get out of there."

"You just can't swallow your pride and give her this?" Ray laughed before he groaned. "Oh, that hurt. Don't make me laugh." He laid down on the cot and slipped under the sheets. "Sometimes you have to swallow your pride, buddy. If you learn anything from me, learn that."

"It's as good as I'm going to get." Ashley unzipped the bag and climbed inside.

"We're going to have to call you in as absent tomorrow," Jim said. "I'll also probably have to go there tomorrow and finalize your withdrawal from that school, you know, since you're moving and all if you're staying with me."

"You two are leaving town?" Ray asked. "For how long?"

"Possibly for good," Jim said. "I doubt the republic's going to give up on taking me out. Anywhere I stay here, they're liable to find and take me out. We're just here long enough to pack and get out."

"Is going back to your house even on the table?" Ashley got into the sleeping bag. "Wouldn't they be watching your place?"

"They wouldn't be able to do much during the day, and Charlie would know it. You know that one guy who always mows his lawn at the same time every day? We could go when he's out. They're not going to try and kill us while he's out and about. They may follow us, but we can lose them. It'd be worth getting our things out."

"Won't they just blast your identity out to the police, sonny?" Ray asked. "If they're out to get you, it's what I'd do. It'd cut down on their work and send the police after you."

"That is an option," Jim said. "I can't rule that out. They seem to have an honor code though, and it says they kill me. I assume it's so I don't get arrested and squeal about their little organization, drawing attention to it."

"At least we still have your laptop in the car," Ashley said. "Hopefully you brought the charging cable."

"I always keep it with me just in case. It's not much good if it runs out of batteries." Jim rolled over in his sleeping bag to face toward Ashley. "Why? Do you think Charlie will send me another email explaining his grand betrayal? I already have an inkling as to why he did it."

"Why do you think he did it?" Ashley asked. "He seemed to be your best friend except maybe Cynthia."

"He's going into politics. What better way to get money, power, and clout than allying with an organization that can get things done? He sold us out for power and to stay in the good graces of the Republic. I'm a wildcard that threw a wrench into his plans. He used me while he could and then he threw me away."

"He sounds like a sociopath," Ray said. "You're better off without him if you ask me. Then again, I don't know the man."

"He damned near killed me tonight," Jim said while closing his eyes. "I only survived because I ran the whole time. He was better trained with the blade than I am. Hell he was the one who taught me what I know. I'm just lucky I'm in better shape than he is. He gassed out, and I took advantage."

"His partner nearly took my head off. I'm just lucky I'm naturally short anyway, and I'm flexible."

"Where were you two planning on moving anyway?" Ray asked. "Hopefully it's not too far away."

"This has all happened so fast," Jim said. "I hadn't had much chance to think about it yet honestly."

"I was just hoping I could visit you occasionally is all," Ray said, his voice audibly sad. "I don't have many people I can talk to besides Edmund here."

"Come on, old man," Jim sat up and looked over at Ray. "You have a phone - you're always welcome to call. I'll even pay for the renewals to the plan on that phone, so it'll always work. As far as visits, that's another thing entirely."

"I guess so," Ray said.

"Don't be so down," Jim said. "It's not like I want to leave my hometown. This place is all I know. I don't have the luxury of choice in this life I've chosen. We can either go to Kansas, Texas, New Mexico, or Arkansas if we want to stay close. Those places should be far enough away to evade our pursuers."

"Why not Colorado?" Ashley asked, her voice whiny. "I'd like to live there."

"I know why you want Colorado, and while yes, it'd be very fun to have legal weed, it's not our biggest concern."

"I'm just saying Denver is a big town that's far enough away that headlines wouldn't appear here. We'd be a nameless duo in a giant new town. I think it'd work well."

"She has a point," Ray said. "You want something big, and probably close enough so your folks can visit."

"I'll think about it. For now, let's all get some shut eye. God knows we need it..."

23

"You're officially no longer a student at that school," Jim said. He shut the driver's side door and looked over at Ashley in the passenger seat. "I have your records now so we can enroll you wherever we end up if you want."

"What does if I want mean?"

"I mean you're sixteen, so technically you can decide to quit high school if you want, I think. You don't have to go."

"Now that's an idea," Ashley said.

"Give it some thought. It's your life after all, but an education could prove handy when you want to find a job."

"A job?" Ashley asked as the car pulled out of the parking space.

"I assume you will want your own place at some point. Every teenager does. I'm not going to kick you out or anything, I just figured every teenager wants their independence. I doubted you'd be the exception."

"Where are we going now?"

"Colorado apparently," Jim said. "We may have to stay in a motel for a week or two while I get us a place, but it'll be fine. We'll just say we're parent and daughter. No one will bat an eye. Before you know it, all this shit will be behind us. We won't have to worry about being hunted."

"What about our hunting?"

"We can hunt, just not right off the bat. We need to get settled in first and get everything settled. We don't want to be wanted without even a house to call home."

"So, I should settle in," Ashley said. She reached into the back seat and retrieved the laptop. She opened it. She typed a few characters before the tell-tale login sound effect played out the speakers.

"How did you know my password?"

"That's a secret. Oh," Ashley said, "you just got an email like ten minutes ago."

"Get out of my personal email."

"It's not your personal email account though. This is your other account, and it's from the same email address as your last one."

"What?" Jim's attention snapped over to her. "What does it say?"

"Hold your horses, I'm checking. I'm lucky to get a network that stays long enough for it to hold with how fast we're going. Pull over into that parking lot so I can get a stable connection for long enough."

"Just make it quick. I want to get out of this town quickly," Jim said. He pulled over and into one of the nearby parking spaces.

"Alright. It's loading now. It's slow since this connection sucks, but here we are." She cleared her throat and read the text out loud. "If you thought this was over regarding last night, you are sorely mistaken. We're taking Cynthia out camping tonight. We picked her up just now. If you want to ever see her alive again, you're going to show up. He put the location next. It's in the middle of the woods from what I can tell. He wants us there at seven tonight." She turned to Jim. "Do you think he's serious?"

"With Charlie? Any message he sends should be considered truth. He knows where she lives. He can probably sweet talk her into getting in the car with him, and she wouldn't have a clue until it's too late. It's the best way to kidnap someone."

"We're going there, aren't we?"

"You're damned straight we are," Jim said. "If he has Cynthia, it's my duty to get her out. I'm the reason she's in this shit."

"You know it's a trap though," Ashley said. "It's obvious. They're going to have way more than four people there this time. I don't like those odds."

"Then we'll just have to even them."

"You don't mean Skye? She said she was taking a break from this," Ashley said. "We can't just drag her into a hide and go seek in the woods with trained killers."

"She can decide for herself when she hears the situation. I'm going to want every advantage we can get. If she's willing, we need her. What's a better weapon when going hunting in the forest than a bow and arrow? Besides, she'd be in her element. She learned how to use it while hunting in the forest."

"Fine. I'll ask her."

"Then let's find a pay phone - if any still exist nowadays. You can call her on her cell even if she's in school. I have a feeling she'll say yes when she hears an innocent is in danger."

"You're basing that on all your time speaking to her, are you?" Ashley asked.

"I'm basing that on what I can tell about her personality, limited as our interactions have been. She was willing to go with us when Ray was in danger, and she'd never even met the guy previously. She's met Cynthia before. I'm betting she'll go. Or we can just buy a phone from this place here." He pulled into a nearby electronic shop's parking lot. "Wait here. I'll be right back."

"Make sure you get one you can text with."

"Right." Jim slammed the door shut and disappeared inside.

"Of course. She's gotten herself caught up in this shit, and he has to run off and play hero." She slammed her closed fist into the door at her side. "Maybe I am stupid. What am I even doing with my life, running around with him?" Flashes of her old life, chained to the bed appeared in her mind's eye. "No, this has to be done so no one else goes through what I did. I made a promise to myself, and I'm going to keep it. If I end up in prison, at least I'll know it was worth it."

The driver's door opened. "Having fun looking like a crazy person? I saw you talking to yourself in here." Jim climbed into the driver's seat. He passed a small box over to Ashley. "If it needs to be charged, we can charge it in here," he pointed to the appropriate plug-in spot near the radio.

She tore open the box and pulled out the phone. "Just let me set it up first. It'll be a few minutes."

He started the engine. "Did you have any interesting conversation while I was gone? You seemed pretty into it."

"Nothing you need to concern yourself with. I was just reevaluating my life choices and came to the same conclusion I did the first time around. That I need to stop the evil people who go after kids."

"If you say so." Jim looked over to Ashley as he pulled the vehicle into traffic. "I don't think I ever told you, but you handled yourself well last night in that brawl. You even drew first blood, which I did not expect."

"Are you saying you didn't believe in me?"

"I'm saying I expected the relative novice to take a little longer against the veteran. You proved me wrong though."

"Is this your way of saying I saved your ass?"

Jim paused and looked ahead at the store he was just in before answering. "Maybe it is."

"Then I'm happy. As long as Masked Justice operates, he'll need a bodyguard. I'll be there."

"If you're my bodyguard, then when this all settles down we need to enroll you in martial arts. I'm sure in a big city like Denver they have some sword fighting styles we could both learn from."

"You're going to join the class too?" Ashley asked.

"Yes. There's nothing wrong with improving ourselves."

"The phone's nearly set up." Ashley rotated the phone, showing Jim. "I am not looking forward to this call."

"Call her as soon as it's ready," Jim said.

"What am I going to ask? Hey, do you want to come with us to kill a dude?"

"I'd probably play up the hostage angle. She wants to do good in the world, right? It's the best chance to get her to help us." Jim exhaled a deep breath. "Do your best."

"I can't believe I'm about to ask her to do this." Ashley shook her head as she heard the ringing in her ear.

"Who is this?" Skye asked.

"It's Ashley on a new phone."

"Where are you?" Skye's voice was hushed. "Why aren't you here?"

"Something's happened. Do you remember Cynthia?"

"The woman from the cookout? Yeah, I remember her. Why? What happened to her?" Skye asked.

"We need your help to get her back safe and unharmed."

"What the hell are you asking me right now?"

"Well, it's complicated." Ashley fidgeted in her chair. Her right hand tapped on the arm rest all the while. "Can we at least pick you up today and talk face to face?"

"Fine, whatever. I can't talk right now." She accentuated her statement with ending the call.

"How did she answer?" Jim asked. "It sounded like she was hesitant."

"More like she was surprised in the middle of algebra class. She couldn't really talk freely so I did the only thing I thought of, improvise. We'll see what she says. If she says no, we can always drop her off before heading off ourselves to get Cynthia back."

"That's true. I just don't like the idea of hanging around while we wait. What should we do to be productive? I got it - we can buy new gear from the nearby hunting store. Night vision goggles would be helpful in the woods after dark."

"You have money for all that and an apartment?" Ashley asked.

"It's rude to ask about finances you know," Jim said. "I have enough in reserves, but this will totally drain my wallet until I can get more out. Which would be in another two weeks. We'll be living on noodles for a little while, but it's worth it." He turned on the turn signal and slowed down the car. He turned the wheel. "Unless you manage to get us some money, that is."

"What are you suggesting?"

"Nothing, it's not like I had a job at your age or anything."

"Go pound sand."

After School in front of the building.

"There she is." Ashley looked over at the front door to the school.

There were crowds of students filing out of it and splitting off into smaller cliques of friends. Skye had just managed to escape being caught in a mass of humanity and was now visible. She seemed to recognize the car and made her way over.

"Let me do the talking," Ashley said as her friend got closer.

"Whatever you say, but I'll say my piece if I need to."

The back door opened, and a backpack flew into the back seat. Skye got in, slammed the door shut, and buckled her seat belt. "What the ever-loving shit was that phone call? Some woman was kidnapped, was that what you said?"

"Cynthia is her name, yes." Ashley said. "She's been taken by the PHR this morning. They're holding her hostage."

Jim started the engine and got them moving. "They're in the nearby woods. Ashley can show you the specifics on my laptop there. It should be back there under your backpack."

"Oh shit, I'm sorry." Skye picked up the backpack and threw it on the floor. She picked up the laptop and passed it forward to Ashley. "I didn't see it there."

"Here. I found it." Ashley already had it open and on. She held the screen to the side so Skye could see. She clicked on the touch pad, causing the map to zoom in until it was of the local area. She pointed to a patch of green on the map. "My best guess from the location he gave was right about here."

"Why there of all places?" Skye asked. She closed her eyes and took in a deep breath before exhaling. "That's where I made my first elk kill with a bow and arrow. I wish I'd never made that shot."

"That's not the kind of reaction I'd have expected from a successful hunt," Jim said.

"The kill itself was perfect. I got him through the heart, and he went down instantly. My father said it was the best shot he'd ever seen. There was just one problem, and it was a big one."

"Were you two not licensed?" Jim asked. "That's the only thing I can think of."

"No, it was because that," she pointed at the monitor where Ashley was referencing but a moment ago "is private land technically, and we didn't get written permission to hunt on his land. He called the police, and of course we were still there trying to get it home."

"I see where this is going," Jim said.

"The point is, yeah, I know that area. I wish I didn't, but I do. I imagine I know the clearing he wants to meet you at. It is perfect for an ambush. There's tree cover all around. You'd be a sitting duck out there for any good marksman," Skye said.

"I don't think guns are off the table thanks to a certain thing we did before," Jim said. He gave a silent look over to Ashley before looking back to the road. "You're saying we need to clear the tree line first?"

"If not first then I'd suggest simultaneously. If you get him talking for a bit, that could be all the time another team would need to put them down," Skye said. "So now we come to the question you had for me when I got in the car. Am I going? Is that right?"

"You are quick," Jim said. "I'm going to tell you straight up. She was my best friend growing up. I'm going regardless, but I'd appreciate any help getting her back safe and sound. I know you're going through a lot no doubt with the kills you've recently had, but can I ask for one last favor?"

"Last? Are you expecting to die or something?"

"Not quite. We're going to have to move after this. We're not moving all that far away but this is the last thing to do before we head out."

"We're going to stay in touch regardless," Ashley peeked around the seat. "I assume you're going to stay in school, or your parents would have a bitch fit."

"It's not a matter of if I want to or not," Skye said. "You need me to go, or you'll get lost in the woods after dark. Not to mention a bow is nice and quiet. If it's to save your friend, I'll go. I just need to go back to my house and get my gear. I don't keep it on my person during school."

"That's where we're headed regardless," Jim said. "Our gear's already in the car. It probably needs a wash, but we'll deal with it for now. I would like to stop by the house after all this and get all the spares and such. It's risky though."

"After we take out Dillon and Charlie, we could chance it. They're going to be reeling from that blow," Ashley said. "It'd be the perfect time."

"Here we are," Jim stopped the car in front of Skye's house. "I assume you're going to tell your parents you're coming over to do schoolwork or something? You'll need that backpack to fit your kit in I'd imagine."

"That's the plan," Skye hefted the bag up from the floor and gripped the door handle. "I'll be back in a few minutes." She opened the door and got out before running to the front door and entering inside.

"We have a fighting chance with her aboard." Jim stared at the house as he spoke. "I feel better knowing you two are watching each other's backs while I deal with Charlie."

"How many people do you think Charlie has out there with him?"

"There's no way of knowing but if I had to ballpark it, I'd

guess eight to ten. They want results this time, you could tell from the language they used in that message. They've also stooped to kidnapping a relative innocent. That's not their normal MO, which tells me they're desperate for this to end."

"I don't know if we can deal with seven to nine people in the woods, even with Skye," Ashley said.

"If you follow her lead and let the arrows do the work, it'd be a snap with night vision goggles. You have a blade, she has a bow. You watch her back, she watches yours. You're just being a bodyguard to a different person is all. She'll clear the way forward, and you keep anyone from sneaking up on her. The PHR men are going to be by themselves I bet. They're not going to expect a strike force to sneak up on them. They think I'm in a panic and rushing around."

"You have a point, but it doesn't make it any less intimidating. Four versus two was bad enough, never mind nine versus three."

"It will be more like nine different two versus ones if you do it right."

"There she is," Ashley looked out the window at Skye standing in the open doorway. She was looking back inside the house, seemingly speaking to someone before shutting the door and jogging back to the pair in the car. She climbed inside again and hefted her backpack back to the floor. "I couldn't fit my bow in there, so I'm not sure what I can do. Dad would never let me leave the house with it."

"You can sneak out, yes?" Ashley asked. "You told me you perfected it."

"So?"

"So go back in there under the pretense you forgot something," Jim said. "Is it in your room?"

"Always," Skye said.

"Then you get it and sneak out the window or whatever your method is. Come to think of it, I am a terrible influence, aren't I?"

"You just figured that out?" Ashley chuckled. "Can you do that? We can't go back to our place for the time being."

"I've done it before," Skye said. "I can do it again. Wait here." She exited the car again and went back to the house.

"Bad influence doesn't even start to describe you," Ashley said.

"I know..."

In the woods, inside Charlie's car.

Cynthia moaned as she regained consciousness. She opened her eyes and tried to bring a hand up to her face only to find her hand's movement impaired. She looked down to see them zip tied together. "What?" She looked to her side and saw Charlie driving the car down a gravel path. "What happened?"

"You fell asleep."

Cynthia's eyes looked down at the plastic bag hanging between the front seats. Among the various trash she saw a used needle. "You drugged me is what happened. I thought we were just going out to lunch."

"You believed me too."

"Why are you doing this?" she asked.

"Jim old boy has made some new enemies, myself included at this point. You are caught in the crossfire here, and let's both be honest. You're not innocent anymore, are you?" He flashed a smile at her before returning his focus to driving.

"Ah shit," Cynthia said.

"Is it dawning on you now?"

"Yeah. Damn it. I'm never going to live this down. Jim was right about you after all."

"That's what you're worried about?" Charlie asked. "You may not live through the night depending on how Dillon feels. Jim and that girl really pissed him off last night."

"I imagine that's where you got that scar by your right eye too." Cynthia said, referring to the injury. "Is it personal for you too, now?"

"I was careless is all. It wouldn't happen again, not that I'll have the chance tonight. I've been ordered to prepare for something else entirely. I'm just dropping you off. My advice for you? Don't piss the big man off. He's already in a bad mood after he lost his right-hand man and had the dueling etiquette broken by that brat."

"Why have you turned on Jim? Why aren't you helping him?" Cynthia asked.

"Jim's a sinking wildcard. Haven't you noticed? Put yourself in my position and tell me what you'd do," Charlie said. "I'm in an organization that's cutthroat. They hunt child touchers, and their newest acquisition has a sixteen-year-old unrelated minor living with him. Would you want to stand by him? They'd kill me if I didn't prove my loyalty."

"So, it comes down to you being too much of a coward to stand by your friend who is doing the right thing? That's what you're saying?" Cynthia asked.

"The right thing is it now?" Charlie asked. "Is that why you dumped his ass? Or was it because you couldn't be associated with him with your preferred profession? Be honest with yourself. You're no better than me. We're both dropping him when it suits us. Don't give me this holier than thou bullshit, sweetie. I know you and him as well as anybody."

"I'm not kidnapping old friends and using them against

the other, you idiot." Cynthia struggled against her bonds. "I'm not the one trying to get him killed to save my own ass. We are nothing alike. I couldn't believe it when he told me you were his partner. Maybe I didn't want to. That will teach me."

"Jim will get what's coming to him tonight. As for you? I wouldn't get my hopes up. Dillon has men in the tree line just waiting for Jim to show up. You'll have a first-row seat to his death right before you meet yours. It's kind of romantic when you think about it. The unrequited love of the vigilante for the damsel in distress is snuffed out right in front of her before she meets him in the afterlife."

"You've changed," Cynthia said. "Don't you see that? This group has turned you into a monster. All for what? A little power and money? Does friendship mean nothing to you?"

"Not with you two," Charlie said. "You're old news. I have more powerful friends now. Ones that can actually change the world via politics. Meaningful change is on the horizon. Jim's little crusade won't change much in the grand scheme of things. Stricter laws that enable police to act on kid touchers will though. I'm not the bad guy here when you think about it - just the one with realistic expectations."

"If you have to tell someone you're not the bad guy, you're the bad guy, you idiot." Cynthia looked to her right at the passing trees...

24

"Pull to the side of the road here," Skye said. "Ashley and I will walk from this point. Give us twenty minutes, and then attend the meeting."

"We will?" Ashley asked. "Isn't this a long way from the clearing?"

"That's why," Skye said. "We don't want them hearing an engine. We're going to sneak up on them, right?" She tried to get the night vision goggles strapped to her head but gave up after a few minutes. "Can I get a little help here?"

"Turn around," Jim turned in his seat and helped her secure the device to her head. "It's not too bulky?"

"It'll take some getting used to, but since it's dark out now, it'll be well worth it. They could have similar tech, and we can't be at a disadvantage even if we are ambushing them." Skye reached up and grabbed them, making sure they were secure. Her right hand gripped the bow laying across her lap, and she checked the quiver on her back making sure it was secured. "Right, let's go."

The pair got out of the car and made their way into the tree line.

"Stay behind me," Skye said. "Watch our backs. I have a good idea where they'd be if they're ambushing that clearing. Just make sure they don't get us from behind. Stay low to the ground as we move too, and try to avoid any twigs on the ground. One snap could give away our position."

"You think they'd hear one twig snapping?" Ashley asked in a quiet voice.

"Deer would, and they're going to be waiting for anything unusual. Treat this like a hunting expedition, because it basically is. We're just hunting kidnappers instead of deer this time." Skye didn't say anything more and led the pair deeper into the woodland.

The chorus of insects replaced the silence of the pair along with the sound of crunching grass with every step. The moon above was covered by assorted branches, but the moonlight that did filter through enabled the goggles to paint a picture clear as day.

Skye raised one arm and stopped. "He's back further than I imagined," she said barely above a whisper. "He's definitely one of them we're looking for though. I can see the rifle beside him." She got her bow ready and pulled out an arrow. She nocked the arrow and pulled back. She released the shot and saw it penetrate his chest cavity. She quickly readied another arrow and put him down before he could even cry out. He crumbled to the ground with nary a whimper.

"Nice shots," Ashley said from behind her.

Skye looked behind her to see Ashley watching behind them. "Let's keep moving. Who knows how many more are in here? We're not even to where they should be yet,"

The pair crept through the dark woods, delving deeper and deeper.

"Another ten minutes and we should be near the clearing," Skye said, keeping her voice low. "I'm not seeing anymore. Let's keep moving."

"I wonder why that one was so far behind their front lines."

"He was watching their flank I imagine. Too bad for him, he couldn't see us in this dark," Skye said. "Which means they're exposed, thinking they're safe. Let's focus up and keep quiet from here on."

"Got it," Ashley said, sticking close behind her friend.

They both stopped when a twig underfoot snapped. They stood perfectly still as they waited for the inevitable. Once a full minute passed Skye looked behind her with a frown. "Watch your feet," she said.

"Sorry," Ashley said.

They kept moving until the clearing was in view.

"Now comes the hard part, we have to sweep this entire tree line without getting caught. I have plenty of targets here it looks like." Skye readied her bow and took aim at the closest target. She saw him leaning against a nearby tree, looking in their direction. He didn't notice as the bow pulled back and fired.

Bullseye, the arrow found its mark. The arrow penetrated his chest, slightly off center. He fell forward, wriggling on the ground amid the grunts of pain.

"Shit, he's drawing attention." Skye whispered.

"We've got company," Ashley said, drawing her short sword out of its sheathe. The sound of metal sliding accompanied the action.

"That's all yours. I'm going to thin out his reinforcements before they get close."

"I swear I think it came from around here," a male voice said, approaching them from the side.

Ashley pressed up against a nearby tree on the other

side from the interloper. She waited until he passed her cover before thrusting the blade forward into his chest cavity. She saw Skye a dozen or so feet ahead of her let loose another arrow. The distant sound of another body hitting the ground met her ears. She saw Skye backing up and firing yet more shots as fast as she could. Ashley saw that not all of the shots hit their mark as their targets got closer and ducked behind nearby trees.

"I got this part. You keep them busy," Ashley said.

Skye kept nocking arrows and letting them loose, hitting the trees they were hiding behind, keeping them from moving.

Ashley used the opportunity to creep closer to their positions until she heard a voice nearby.

"Who the fuck is out here? I'm pinned down over here. Someone get them already!" The voice was panicked.

She got the blade ready as she circled around the tree.

"Get over here, you idiot. There's an archer out here killing us," the voice said. He looked over to see Ashley. "Wait, who are -"

His question was interrupted by cold steel puncturing through his lungs. His question died on his lips as he coughed up blood before falling forward. She stepped over his writhing body and saw more men from there. She saw arrows now colliding with their cover. One especially brave man turned and sprinted in Skye's direction only to catch an arrow in the leg and tumble to the ground with a scream.

Ashley darted out and dragged her blade along his throat on the ground, ending his life.

Rapid footsteps came from her side only to end with an abrupt thud. She turned and saw another enemy laying on the ground. "Nice save," Ashley said. She looked back at Skye and saw one more man charging her.

Her arrow missed the target. Skye's eyes widened, her heartbeat spiked. She could see the glint of a knife at his side.

He never reached his target as Ashley charged at him. She sliced him in the legs as she got closer, causing him to tumble to the ground, mere feet in front of Skye.

Ashley stopped her forward momentum and turned to deliver the fatal blow only to find an arrow already in him.

"I thought I was going to die there," Skye said.

"Not with me around, you're not," Ashley said. "Now let's do another sweep and make sure we got them all."

Skye's eyes caught movement behind Ashley. She immediately nocked an arrow. "Get down,"

Ashley hit the ground just in time for the arrow to release. A man fell on his back just a few feet behind Ashley.

"Jesus," Ashley got back to her feet. She stabbed the assailant in the chest with her sword before placing her shoe on him and yanking it out. "Now as I was saying, let's keep this moving. I don't want any more surprises..."

In the clearing around the same time...

"God, I hope I didn't just send them on a suicide mission," Jim said. He drove along the gravel road. He had waited the time that Skye advised and was now on his way toward the meeting. He saw the clearing ahead with a lone car parked with its lights on. He could see someone sitting on the front of it and the very tall Dillon standing nearby with his riot shield in one hand.

"Nothing for it now. I just have to trust they got the job done, or we're dead." He pulled up a few dozen feet away. He got out of the car and walked over.

"Do you really need the mask still, Mr. Benning?" Dillon

asked. "Does it make you feel better to hide your face? I would too if I fucked kids."

"I see you're as dumb as you look," Jim said, striding forward. He stopped ten feet or so away from the giant of a man. "I never touched her that way once in my life."

"You can't expect me to believe that. You hid her away when we came by and immediately brought her back when you thought we were gone. Those are not the actions of an innocent man. Those are the deeds of a man who knows he's done wrong."

"You obviously don't know who you're talking to," Cynthia spoke up from the front of the car. "The man may be insufferable, but he hates those types as much as you do."

"Assuming you're correct, then he's still corrupted a minor to kill. It's the same punishment either way. We do not use kids in our work, Mr. Benning." Dillon readied the shield in front of him. "You have lost your way, and I'm here to put you out of your misery." His right hand went behind him and pulled out a small device.

"You're finally ready to fight like a man and not use your pawns, huh?" Jim asked. His right hand reached over toward his wakizashi and hovered over it. He unsheathed the weapon and held it in front of him.

"There is only one thing to this duel, Mr. Benning." Dillon smirked. "You didn't fight fair in your last duel, so why should I? I believe those were your words. I took your advice." He raised his right hand before lowering it.

Everybody waited to see what would happen.

"What?" Dillon looked over to the tree line. He gave the signal again.

"Waiting for your men to shoot me?" Jim gave a devilish grin. "They're too busy right now to do much else than pull arrows out of themselves. It's just you and me, big boy," Jim said. "Show me what you got."

"Have you ever been tasered, Mr. Benning? He held his right hand out, fully revealing the long stick. "This is more powerful than any cattle prod. Most would just incapacitate you, but this one has much higher amperage. Just one touch from this and your heart is liable to stop. I don't need tricks to beat you. I just need one good hit." He flipped the device on, and it buzzed to life. Occasional arcs of electricity were visible as the hum grew louder.

Jim didn't wait for anymore dialogue between the pair and charged ahead toward Dillon.

"Come claim your death, fool." Dillon planted the shield in front of him, bracing for the inevitable impact. His right hand was primed and ready to spring forward.

Jim swung with all his might in a downward strike. His blade bounced. He regained his balance and jumped back as Dillon's right hand jabbed forward. The electric prod was within a hair's breadth from his person as he gained more distance.

"It's useless," Dillon charged forward holding the shield in front of him as a pseudo battering ram. It collided with Jim knocking him back and onto the grass.

He scrambled to his feet as the hum of the prod struck the grass where he'd previously occupied. He backpedaled as fast as he could and regained his balance.

"Be careful, you idiot!" Cynthia screamed, tears falling down her cheeks.

"You made the poor girl worry. Isn't that sweet?" Dillon asked. He roared as he charged ahead again.

Jim chose to sidestep to his right, away from the electric prod. He tried to do a quick slice, trying to catch Dillon's leg.

Dillon was quicker than he appeared as the blade caught nothing but a few blades of grass.

"A good idea, but you're not quick enough. What will you do now? You can't hit me in the front, and you can't even hit me in the back. You'll get tired long before I will," Dillon had a maniacal smile plastered over his face as the battle high claimed him. "It's just a matter of time."

"I still have a few tricks up my sleeve, don't you worry," Jim said, flashing a smile.

"Then show them. I dare you." Dillon's voice was one of pure anger.

"Run at me again and I will, you bloated monstrosity."

"Sticks and stones, dear boy," Dillon said. "They don't break bones, but I do." He took off into an even quicker sprint directly at Jim.

Jim's right hand sneaked behind him and grabbed the pistol in his belt line. He dove to the right just before Dillon would have collided with him. He laid in the grass as Dillon had his back to him. He quickly fired off multiple rounds into his back and Dillon grunted.

"I expected as much," Dillon turned around. He grit his teeth. "That's not good enough." He marched toward Jim.

Jim got to his feet and backed up, holding his pistol in one hand and his short blade in the other. "Alright, now I got nothing."

"Shoot him in the head next time," Cynthia said.

"Easier said than done, sweetheart," Jim dove out of the way of another charge and got back to his feet. This time Dillon didn't give him time to fire as he immediately turned around and ducked behind his shield.

"You had that opportunity," Dillon said. "You won't get it again." He took heavy step after heavy step toward Jim. Each movement was slow and deliberate.

Jim watched the approaching behemoth, his mind going a mile a minute through different scenarios. He took a step back with Dillon's every step.

"Are you scared, Mr. Benning?" Dillon asked with a derisive laugh. "Good, you should be."

Jim circled to the side, bringing himself near the car. "You're right. I probably can't beat you, but that isn't going to stop me from trying." He stepped back, leading Dillon closer to Cynthia on the hood of the car.

"It's a fool's errand, but you're welcome to try." Dillon passed Cynthia, drawing ever closer to Jim.

Jim stood his ground and looked up at the giant of a man. "This is my last stand, so let's make it a good one."

"Maybe you do have a sliver of honor left in you. Very well," he hunched down behind the shield and his right hand was at his side.

Cynthia's hands were behind her. After Dillon passed, while the men were talking, she managed to bring them under her legs and pulled her legs back, allowing her to slip the handcuffs under them. This gave her access to her arms in front of her. She waited until Dillon hunched behind his shield before standing up on the front of the car.

Jim saw what she was doing behind Dillon and smirked. "Come on then, show you walk the walk and not just talk the talk."

"You sniveling little runt," Dillon snarled.

Cynthia jumped from her perch and landed on Dillon's back.

"What?" Dillon asked.

Cynthia landed with her cuffed hands wrapped around the front of Dillon's neck. She pulled back as hard as she could, choking the man.

"You can't use that prod," Jim smiled. "If you do, you'll shock the piss out of both of you. It's your choice though."

"You fucking little shit," Dillon managed to get out. He swung the prod up, making contact with Cynthia.

The electric coursed through Cynthia's body and into Dillon's. He fell to a knee as the prod fell from his grasp.

Cynthia's chokehold hadn't abated. She kept pulling back with all her might. The gasping man beneath her reached up and grabbed her by the hair. "You cunt," he gasped. "I'll kill you both."

"Not with me here." Jim towered over the pair. "Hold his head steady, dear," He raised his sword up, preparing to deliver the finishing blow. His hands flew forward only to halt as Dillon leaned even further forward, placing Cynthia directly in the blade's path.

Dillon hurled Cynthia forward with another roar.

Jim used the opportunity to kick the prod behind him as Dillon stood up again, coughing all the while. He helped Cynthia get to her feet. "Get the prod. We can beat him together. Just do as I say." He caressed the side of her face as he spoke. "Can you handle that?"

"I don't have a choice." She retrieved the weapon and held it in her still tied hands. "Just help me out of these zip ties."

"No problem," He delivered a vertical cut, severing the ties.

Dillon finally caught his breath and had his right hand resting on his throat. "You little filthy whore." He coughed again. "You deserve to die alongside him."

"There are worse places to die," Cynthia fired back with an air of defiance. "You wanted me? You fucking got me! You're going to regret pissing me off."

Jim circled around Dillon. "Now don't forget me. I'm

your main target here, yes? I wonder if your vest stops blades as well. You're surrounded now. No one's coming to help you. You're going to die out here in the middle of nowhere all alone and cold." He had a sadistic smile as he paced around Dillon. "Do you feel the adrenaline rushing through your veins? That cold pit in your stomach is your brain telling you to run away. You're too stubborn for that though, yes? Honor has killed millions. It's never saved one life."

"Enough," Dillon charged forward toward Jim.

He barely managed to get out of the way of the juggernaut. He backed up to near Cynthia as Dillon turned around.

"He's going to charge me again, stick that prod in him and this is as good as over. You don't even need a flush hit. Just get him to the ground and keep it on him once he falls."

"I got it," Cynthia said.

"Stop mumbling to each other and let's finish this." Dillon took off even faster than before. As a result, he managed to clip Jim, knocking him to the ground.

Cynthia didn't hesitate and managed to hold the prod out, barely grazing Dillon with it.

The glancing blow was enough as electricity immobilized Dillon. It cramped his muscles, causing him to fall forward onto the ground. She dashed forward and stuck it into the small of his back. "Stay down, you fucking asshole," she said through her teeth.

Jim sat up and shook his head. He saw Dillon on the ground convulsing under Cynthia's onslaught of electricity. He dashed over as fast his battered body allowed. He held the blade with both hands and angled the blade down. "Turn it off now,"

Cynthia took her finger off the button. "Do it now,"

Without waiting he plunged the blade into the neck of Dillon. He yanked the blade left and right before twisting and yanking it out. He looked down at the man, still moving in the grass. "You're a stubborn one," Jim said. He raised the blade high above his head and brought it down in one swift motion, severing Dillon's head from his body.

"I think I'm going to be sick." Cynthia held a hand over her mouth. She tossed the cattle prod to the grass below. Her now free hand moved to her stomach as she watched the head roll away.

Jim tried to get as much blood off his blade with a quick flick before sheathing the weapon at his side. He moved over to Cynthia and placed both hands on the sides of her face. His voice was soft and full of concern. "Are you okay? I was worried sick when I heard they had you."

She didn't answer verbally, choosing instead to shove her face into his chest. She looked up at him. "I'm not okay right now." She wrapped her arms around him and pulled him tight against her.

"I know." Jim returned the embrace. He raised a hand to the back of her head and held it against him. "I'm lucky I made it in time. I'm going to kill Charlie the next time I see him. He was the one who took you, wasn't he?"

She nodded into his chest as muffled crying met his ears alongside a growing wetness on his chest.

"It's over," he cooed into her ear. "I'm right here." He looked over to the tree line as she bawled into his chest to see two figures waving at him, emerging from the tree line. He reached a hand up and motioned them over.

"We're about to have company, but you stay there as long as you need," Jim said.

Cynthia pulled away and wiped her eyes and nose. "Who are they?"

"That's Blind Justice and Silent Justice. They took care of the ambush Dillon had planned for me. I owe them my life for that."

"I suppose I should thank them too. I know who one of them is." Cynthia tried to make herself presentable as the pair approached them.

"I see the big man's dead." Ashley looked down at the decapitated head. "Nice job."

"Oh Lord." Skye covered her mouth. "Was that necessary?"

"I wanted to be safe," Jim said. "Are either of you two hurt?" He stepped forward toward them, trying to inspect for injuries.

"A few scrapes, but I'm fine," Ashley said. "Do you want to know how many men he had out in those damned woods? There were eight of them. We had a few problems with the first few, but the ones up near you guys were too transfixed on the field to be a threat."

"Let's get out of here," Jim said. "Everyone in the car so this night can finally end." Jim walked side by side with Cynthia as the teenagers raced ahead toward the car. "I have something I need to tell you regarding all this. Now don't worry. Your part in this is probably over."

Cynthia looked at him. "Tell me when I get home. I can't take anything more right now."

"You got it," Jim said. He forced a smile for her benefit and opened the passenger door for her. He walked around the car and got into the driver's seat. "Does everybody have all their gear? Ah hell, who am I kidding? You're not going back in that forest if you forgot anything." He started the engine and turned the car around.

"I can't believe it," Cynthia said. "Just this morning

Charlie invited me out to a brunch and next thing I know I woke up in his car."

"That sounds creepy," Skye said. "He used your friend-ship to bait you? What a creep."

"If you'd said that this morning, I'd have called you nuts." Cynthia looked over at Jim and reached over. She laid a hand on his right shoulder and spoke in a soft voice. "You told me before, and I didn't believe you. I'm sorry."

"Apology accepted," Jim said. "Just next time trust your best friend, eh?"

"You didn't listen when he warned you?" Ashley leaned forward between the front seat, removing Cynthia's hand from his shoulder. "I know he was your friend, but..." She paused and looked out the front window, "I don't know. Come on." She fell back into her seat and crossed her arms.

"I realize now that while I hate what you do, you are genuinely trying to do good in this world. I knew you weren't a liar, but part of me didn't want to believe that Charlie was capable of what you were saying. I was hoping my one other friend hadn't gotten caught up in this. I wanted to believe he was still just the hopeless stoner that we knew growing up. My own willing ignorance caused this."

"I'm just glad you're safe," Jim said. "We'll get you home, and you can get back to your life."

"What life?" Cynthia asked. "Yeah, so I passed the finals last week, and I'm preparing for my bar exam. So what? If you're ever caught, any of you," she turned around in her seat and pointed at both girls. "If any of you are ever caught, my professional life is over. You all know my face and my secrets. If the media ever got wind of my connection, I'm serving a life sentence alongside you. Do you call that a life? To add on to that, you've saved my life. That means I can't turn you in, and I'll feel that blood on my hands for every life you take."

Silence filled the cabin after the rant.

"Talk about a mood killer," Skye said. "Look, lady, I don't know your damned secret. Alright? Even if I did, I don't give a fuck. I've chosen to do morally questionable things, and I'm aware of the consequences. I'm not trying to rat."

"You say that now," Cynthia scoffed. "Do you want to know the statistics? Do you know how often a suspect charged for murder turns state's evidence? For the non-law students here, that means rats on their friends for a lighter sentence."

"Thanks for the lesson, lady." Ashley kicked Cynthia's seat. "Make your point already."

"Of the few cases that go to trial, most of them are from criminals turning state's evidence. Another fun fact - almost all of them are found guilty. It's only natural someone will turn and expose everyone to save themselves prison time or at least lessen their term."

"Aren't you a ray of sunshine?" Ashley asked, now turning to look out the window. "With that attitude, your life's going to suck. You need to look at the better side. Namely the being away from that monster of a man."

"That meathead was intimidating, sure. True fear comes when you look your best friend in the eyes," Cynthia was staring at Jim as tears welled up in her eyes. "Then you realize you don't really know them as well as you thought you did. When you realize they've done terrible things in the name of good or wealth and power - that's when you know true fear."

"She's looking at me, isn't she?" Jim turned out onto paved road. "We'll have you home soon. Try to relax."

25

"What was it you wanted to tell me back there now that we got your sidekick to go to bed?" Cynthia fell onto her couch. She leaned forward and took her shoes off. She laid down on the couch and closed her eyes.

"We're wanted now by the PHR," Jim said. "I have to get out of town."

"You mean for good?" Cynthia asked. "What about me?"

"I can't stay here. Now I'd love for you to move up with us, but I don't expect you will. If I stayed in town, I think they'd kill me in my sleep. At this point that could extend to Ashley too. I can't allow that to continue. We're packing up and moving to Denver." He reached into his pocket to pull out a folded-up slip of paper. He walked over to the bar and placed the paper down. "Here's the number you can reach me at. Please don't hesitate to call."

"You're just going to pack up and leave when those maniacs could come to my house again?" She got up from the couch and marched up to Jim. She poked his chest with her finger as she spoke. "They know this address as is apparent from the kidnapping. I'm not safe here. I don't have a choice. I either go to the police and end up in prison with you and the other girls, or I go with you and have you keep me safe."

"What do you want me to do right now?" Jim asked. "I'm trying my best here."

"Stay with me the night at least and help me pack in the morning. You said you were moving to Denver?" Cynthia asked.

"That's the plan right now," Jim said. "You're moving with us tomorrow?"

"I am not moving in with you," Cynthia said. "You wish I would I'm sure. I can afford my own apartment with the inheritance my parents left me. Which is a damned good thing considering I need to study for a brand new Colorado bar exam. I only threw away a couple weeks of studying, and truthfully, I probably wouldn't have passed anyway."

"I doubt that," Jim said. "You always were the smartest of us."

"That is not a high bar to compare myself with."

"Ouch," Jim winced. "That was uncalled for."

"After the day I've had, you're lucky it was that mild of an insult." Cynthia brought a hand up and rubbed her eye. "You are staying the night here, yes? In fact, that's not a question. You're staying here and making sure no one else kidnaps me tonight. That's an order."

"Then who am I to argue? I'll have to swing by my house in the morning to grab my spare sets of gear and some clothes, but then I'll be back and help you pack up the bare necessities. I assume you're going to hire a moving crew for everything else."

"I'll also have to hire a realtor to sell this place. Oh God," she whined, "why me?"

"I'll make sure to wake up Ashley when I leave so you have one of us up to keep you safe."

"You're going to trust my life to a kid? Jim, I know she's competent and all, but she's still only a kid."

"It'll be for like maybe an hour max. It probably won't even be that long. I'll be back before you're even up. She's trained in combat. You'll be fine." He rubbed his hands together in front of him. "Now I assume I'm going on the couch?"

"Not quite," Cynthia said. She turned around and moved toward the hallway leading to the bedrooms. "Follow me." She brought her finger up and waved him over with it.

Jim walked behind her a few feet. He saw Ashley through a crack in the nearest door. She was under the covers in the bed and already fast asleep as evidenced by the soft snores.

"Get in here," Cynthia drew his attention back to her as she stood in front of her bedroom's open door.

"Seriously?"

"Just do it, asshole." Cynthia reached forward and grabbed his hand, yanking him toward her. "You better not try anything."

"I'll be a perfect gentleman."

"You'd better be." She walked into her room first and sat on the bed. She slipped her legs under the covers. "You're on this side," she patted the other side of the bed.

Jim entered the room and shut the door behind him. "If you say so," Jim moved around the bed and sat down. He took off his shirt, leaving his chest bare. He got under the covers and laid down on his back.

Cynthia reached over to her night table and turned off the light before laying her head down on the pillow.

"Why do you want me in here anyway? I got the impression you wanted nothing to do with me the past few weeks," Jim said.

"We don't always get what we want, now do we?" Cynthia asked. She rolled to her side to face Jim. "I'm stuck with you if I want protection, unless I want to turn myself in."

"Stuck with me now, are you?" Jim asked.

"Shall I go tell the police about my kidnapping then? They'll ask all kinds of questions, and the truth will inevitably come out in the ensuing investigation. You tell me. Is that an option if we all want to stay out of prison?"

"No, I suppose not."

"So, if you're in charge of keeping me safe, your job number one is calming me down. That's one thing you've always been good at despite your poor decisions in life." She draped her right arm across his bare chest and lifted her right leg to rest on his leg. "Don't get any ideas. I'm still pissed. I just need help getting to sleep is all. I need to feel safe, even if I'm laying next to a lunatic."

"Lunatic is a bit much," Jim said. His right arm cradled Cynthia against him as it rested along her back. "I prefer vigilante to lunatic."

"Those are the same things, jackass." Cynthia didn't let Jim see the smile she had as she buried her face in his chest. "Though I guess even vigilantes have their uses from time to time, even if I disagree with their methods. Come to think of it, have you told your parents you're moving?"

"Ah shit," Jim said. "No, I hadn't yet."

"You need to, or they'll worry themselves sick. Hopefully you have a good excuse as to why. It's not like you can just tell the truth," Cynthia said. "Tell me you have some idea."

"The only believable thing I can think of is if I tell them Ashley's father wants me to take her to him."

"The guy who sold her?"

"What? No. My parents think her father is an old high school friend."

"That could work. You could just tell them you fell in love with the new place. You're young, impetuous, and don't think things through. It's perfectly believable."

"You know, for a soon to be lawyer, you have no tact whatsoever. Not many juries will like that attitude," Jim said.

"Speaking of, I do not relish trying to learn a new state's laws. At least Colorado has more potential clients than a small ass town like this one. That also means more competition I'm sure."

"You'll do fine. Isn't this every young person's dream? You know, moving to a new city and starting fresh."

"Until they realize bills exist, and then that dream crumbles to dust," Cynthia said. "Still, a fresh start does sound nice. Does that include a new start for you, or are you going to keep this foolishness up once you get there?"

"I figured we'd lay low for a while till things cool down. In maybe a year or two when everybody's forgotten about Masked Justice we'd start back."

"Of course, you're going to start back. I shouldn't have expected anything different. It's who you are. I don't guess my pleading with you would change anything?"

"Afraid not," Jim said. "There are still kids out there that need help, and there always will be."

"So, you're just going to keep doing this until you die then?" Cynthia asked. "Surely you don't want to do this kind of shit forever. Look at the past few weeks. You want that for the rest of your life?"

"When I get old and get to be a hindrance in the field, I'll hang up my mask. I don't want to get in the way out there." Jim pulled her closer.

"I guess that's as good as I'm getting, isn't it?" Cynthia asked. "It's not like I have any control left over my life at this point. It's all revolving around you and your little crusade. I just pray none of you ever get caught, or it's all over."

"I'm hoping you'll get an apartment near ours. I'd love to live nearby in a big city."

"I take it Ashley is living with you then?" Cynthia asked.

"The offer of us getting a three-bedroom apartment is still on the table if you want to live with us."

"I'm not looking to play house quite yet. Maybe someday that'll happen."

"You're saying there's a chance then?"

"Shut up and let me get some sleep."

"Yes, ma'am." Jim used his other hand and laid it atop her hand draped over her chest. "Whatever you say..."

26

"I'm back," Jim said, walking through Cynthia's front door. "My gear and clothes are already packed.

"Be quiet," Cynthia and Ashley's eyes were glued to the television.

Jim sat down in the remaining spot on the sofa between the pair and watched the screen.

Charlie was dressed in a formal suit, tie included, and he was being interviewed in a studio. He had his legs crossed as he sat across from the host. He had a congenial smile on his face and a large bandage covering the side of his face, hiding the scar Jim gave him.

The female reporter spoke from a nearby chair. "Welcome back. We're here with Charles Baskin who has recently announced he's running for Oklahoma's state legislature. Mr. Baskins, I understand that this is your first foray into politics. Is that correct?"

"You are correct," Charlie gave a charming smile. "I just couldn't sit back any longer when I know I can make a difference."

"Can you elaborate what you mean by that?" she asked.

"I'm sure you've noticed the same as I have this rise of vigilante justice that's been going around. Heck, the national media is even picking it up now. We cannot allow such maniacs to go around doing as they please. We need to bring order back to society. If this continues it's just going to get worse, much worse."

"There are some who say Masked Justice is doing the right thing. What do you say to his supporters?"

"I'd recommend they take a good look at themselves in a mirror if they endorse a person who doesn't care for rule of law. They go around chopping off body parts based on hearsay and their gut feeling. That is not the bedrock of a functional society. It's the beginning of the end of one. Surely you agree?"

"I do, but there are still others who deny the severity. Masked Justice has lost a lot of public support lately, but they still have their loyal fanbase it seems, as scary as that is."

"I aim to cut down on violent crime, not by taking away people's right to defend themselves, but by allowing law enforcement to do their job more efficiently. That's the proper way to make real change. That is something no vigilante, no matter who they are, can understand."

"I apologize for the personal question, Mr. Baskins, but everybody's dying to know."

"It's about this," Charlie pointed up to his bandage covered cheek, "isn't it?"

"I don't mean to be rude, but our viewers are no doubt curious."

"I was the victim of a violent crime a few days ago as a matter of fact. He had a knife, and he didn't like it when I stood up for myself. That's what I'm going to do if I get elected too. I'm going to never stop fighting to improve our great country."

Cynthia turned off the television. "I've had enough of this bull shit. I can only take so many lies before it pisses me off. She pointed to a pile of boxes near the door. "Those are my essentials. Help me pack those in my car, and we can go."

"Get up, Ashley." Jim reached over and slapped her knee. "You're helping with this if I am."

"Oh man," Ashley whined.

"Think of it as strength training, and don't complain. It's unsightly." Jim chuckled.

The trio got up from their seats and each walked over to pick up a box. Cynthia had the smallest and used it to her advantage to unlock the doors. "Just put those in the back seat. The trunk's already full."

"Yes, ma'am." Ashley rolled her eyes. "I feel like the hired help here."

"Then I've done my job." Cynthia placed her box on the seat before heading past the two, back into the house to grab another.

"At least the hired help gets paid," Ashley said.

"Look on the bright side," Jim said, placing the larger box down in the back seat. "At least after this we're off to our new life in the big city."

"I guess so. I'm a little worried about Skye though. She doesn't have many friends at school." Ashley plopped the package down on the floor between seats before following Jim back inside.

"She'll be fine. If anything, I bet she'll be relieved to have things go back to normal," Jim said.

"Less chatting, more working, ladies." Cynthia passed them with another box in her hands. "There aren't that many to begin with. Let's get out of here as soon as we can."

Jim was the first to enter to see three more boxes. "I'll just take these two," he pointed to the larger boxes. "You get the smaller one, and we're done."

"Are you sure you can handle that much weight, old man?" Ashley bent down and picked up the smaller container.

"I'm only twenty-two I'll have you know." Jim stacked the two boxes on top of each other before lifting them off the ground. He followed Ashley out of the house. Cynthia waited for him near the back door of her car and took the top box off and placed it inside.

"Get that loaded up, and we're good."

"You did remember to pack my clothes when you went back to the house, yes?" Ashley asked.

"It was awkward to do so, but yes I did."

"Don't tell me you got excited handling my underwear? Was it too stimulating for you?" Ashley had a devious smirk on her face as she asked the question.

"Ladies," Cynthia interrupted the banter. "Let's just get on the road. The longer we're here, the more likely the PHR finds us."

"Agreed. We'll take my car, you take yours."

"Can you even afford an apartment in the big city?" Cynthia asked. "It'll be like four thousand dollars on the initial down payment."

"We'll have to stop by some smaller towns that have crypto currency withdrawal machines, but I'll be good. I have my paper wallet right here," he patted his pants pocket.

"If you say so," Cynthia said. "You're sure they can't track that?"

"The only thing they can track is if someone else sends

funds to it. A manual cash out machine would have nothing to trace."

"Alright then." Ashley leaned back against Jim's car. "Last check, is there anything we missed?"

"I got our gear, our clothes, and my paper wallet. We're good. Cyn? What about you?"

"I'll get a moving company to get my furniture and crap. I'll have to make due with a spartan interior for a week or so. I'm good. I have my clothes, books, and money."

"You want to follow us there?" Jim said.

"Why not? Sure."

"Alright then." Ashley threw open the passenger door of Jim's car. "Let's kick the tires and be on our way."

Cynthia got within a few feet of Jim and got to her tip toes. She whispered in his ear. "If you tell anybody including her, you know what will happen, yes?"

"Perfectly."

Ashley got in the car and looked over at the pair. "What are you two whispering about?"

"Nothing important." Jim stepped back from Cynthia and got inside his car's driver's seat. He looked past Ashley and saw Cynthia getting in her car.

Jim started the engine. "I can't believe it," he said. "I'm moving out of my hometown finally. I never really thought I would to be honest."

"A new scene would be a nice change of pace. I'm going to be keeping in touch with Skye. I'll call her when we get there so she knows the number, and we can still play games online and chat."

"How nice," Jim said. "Just remember, for the next two years we're training heavily. You'll have to fit that in somewhere on your own time."

"Training? Is this for our inevitable return to hunting?"

Jim pulled out and looked up into his rear-view mirror to see Cynthia pulling out after them. "I figure a couple years of laying low will suffice. By then the media will have forgotten about Masked Justice. Not to mention we'll be training with bows, working out, and practicing our sword play. We'll be ready when it comes time."

"Aw man, a couple years? Why so long?"

Jim spared a momentary glance over at Ashley before returning it to the road. "I made a promise to Cynthia we'd lay low for a while."

"I never did," Ashley said.

"Ashley,"

"Hey, I didn't."

"We both need that training. We got lucky with that last rescue mission. We need to be beyond ready. We need to be in peak physical condition. I don't know about you, but I'm not there."

Ashley pinched the small amount of fat on her stomach. "I guess you have a point."

"You're damned right I do."

"We are going to hunt again? You promised me that."

"Of course we will…"

The End.

THANK YOU FOR READING!

The adventures of Jim, Ashley, and everyone will continue in Blind Justice coming soon in April. If you'd like to show support for this work, please consider leaving an honest rating or review on Amazon. Have a great day!

ABOUT THE AUTHOR

Alex J Fischer has been writing for close to a decade and has won six National Novel Writing Month challenges in a row.

Alex grew up in a small town in Ohio and still resides there. Hobbies include writing, video games, and watching crime shows.

ALSO BY ALEX J FISCHER

Morris Crime Family:

Welcome to the Family

The Silver Lining

Any Means Necessary

The Fourth Bullet

A New Generation

Full Circle

Order of Vengeance Motorcycle Club:

The Order of Vengeance

Vengeance Above All

The Collector:

The Debt Collector

Masked Justice:

The End of Innocence

Masked Justice